MW00583465

MURDER ON GRANGE ROAD

MURDER ON GRANGE ROAD

GEORGE ENCIZO

Columbus, Ohio

This book is a work of fiction. The names, characters and events in this book are the products of the author's imagination or are used fictitiously. Any similarity to real persons living or dead is coincidental and not intended by the author.

Murder on Grange Road

Published by Gatekeeper Press
2167 Stringtown Rd, Suite 109
Columbus, OH 43123-2989
www.GatekeeperPress.com

Copyright © 2019 by George Encizo

All rights reserved. Neither this book, nor any parts within it may be sold or reproduced in any form or by any electronic or mechanical means, including information storage and retrieval systems without permission in writing from the author. The only exception is by a reviewer, who may quote short excerpts in a review.

ISBN (paperback): 9781642376203
eISBN: 9781642376210

Printed in the United States of America

"For nothing is hidden, except to be revealed; nor has anything been secret, but that it would come to light."

Mark 4:22

PROLOGUE

November 1995

Friday night when most of the county was at the big football game, a dark blue pickup turned onto a beaten path and meandered through a field of wiregrass. A doe and its fawn crossed in front of the truck and paused. The whites of their eyes sparkled in the truck's high beams. They scampered away and disappeared into the darkness.

The truck came to a halt with its high beams on. The driver sat looking through the windshield as if expecting someone to appear. After a while, the driver stepped out, grabbed two shovels, and handed one to another person standing beside the truck. They then dug a two-foot trench about fifteen feet ahead. When they finished, they lowered the tailgate and pulled a bundle off the truck bed and carried it to the trench. They dropped it into the hole and covered it with dirt. Next, they tossed the shovels onto the bed, raised the tailgate, and climbed into the cab. The driver made a U-turn and followed the tire marks back to the path, turned right, and sped off.

Two hours later, three pickups with locals coming from the Bucket & Boots Country and Western Bar rambled down the path and past the spot where the dark blue pickup came from and stopped near the shoreline of Lake Azur where they dropped their tailgates and spread blankets on the truck beds.

With a small fire crackling and a bottle of Wild Turkey among them, they shed their clothes and ran hooting and hollering into the lake. After their fun and games, they climbed back into their pickups, turned and drove back onto the path.

One of the drivers was a young JD Pickens, home for the weekend to attend the game.

CHAPTER 1

November, 2017

JD PICKENS WAS at home watching football with his father, Russel Pickens, a burly man in his mid-seventies at six-foot-two with hands the size of ham hocks. His precocious nine-year-old daughter, Sarah, was on the floor reading a book. Next to her was the family dog, Bailey, sound asleep. It was an annual ritual for the Pickens men.

JD stood for Joshua Daniel, but Pickins insisted there be no periods in the initials. The nickname was given to him by Leroy Jones, his friend in high school, and Pickens had stuck with it ever since.

Pickens was the sheriff of a small rural county in Central Florida that had two cities and several small towns. Creek City was the largest and Warfield, the other city, was thirty-five miles to the south. The primary industries were agriculture and horse and cattle ranching. Although both cities had mayors, the County Commission was the governing body and handled business affairs for the entire county. Although Pickens reported to the commission, he kept his independence—which occasionally angered a few commissioners.

Pickens' wife, Dr. Marge Davids, was in the kitchen with Pickens' mother, Jeanette, fixing Thanksgiving dinner. Jeanette Pickens was in her early seventies with graying hair and still dressed in loose-fitting jeans. She could still put a fright in JD, same as she had when he was a boy.

Dr. Davids was the county medical examiner. She kept her maiden name because it was the name she was known as in the forensics field. Dr. Davids was often a guest lecturer at medical schools and forensic conferences. She used the initials MDP—and included them in her license plate number— MDPME.

She had auburn shoulder-length hair and was something to admire at forty-seven—a year younger than Pickens. She always lit up the room when she entered and caused sparks to fly whenever Pickens saw her.

Marge had already stuffed the turkey and put it in the oven. Mrs. Pickens was preparing the vegetables while Marge prepared the salad.

Marge noticed that her mother-in-law was exceptionally quiet, unlike her usual jovial self.

"Jeanette, are the onions making you cry? They always do that to me."

Mrs. Pickens didn't look up. "I was thinking about this woman I met last Sunday at the church social after Mass. She and her husband sat at our table. They were much older than Russell and me. The woman asked if we had children. I thought it odd since we'd never met before."

"What did you say?" asked Marge.

Mrs. Pickens continued slicing. "Naturally, I told them about JD and Sarah."

"And what did she say?"

"I'm not sure. She said she had a daughter and two grandchildren, but she hadn't seen her daughter in over twenty years."

Marge's curiosity piqued. "Why, what happened?"

"She said her daughter disappeared in 1995 and hadn't been heard from since. Her husband filed a missing person's report, but it was never resolved." Mrs. Pickens sniffled. "So sad, two children had to grow up without their mother."

Marge thought about her daughter in the living room with JD and what it would be like if she hadn't been there for Sarah and Sarah had had to grow up without a mother. Those poor children. Marge couldn't imagine.

"So it's still a missing person's case?" Marge asked.

Mrs. Pickens shook her head. "The woman said her daughter was declared legally dead in 2000. The daughter would have been fifty-six next month."

"Did she say what happened to the children?"

"They're both adults, but she hasn't had contact with them for several years. Apparently, they wanted to get on with their lives, and remembering their mother was a distraction." Mrs. Pickens sniffled again. "Anyway, after the social ended we said goodbye, and I watched her leave with her husband's arm around her."

"You must have been heartbroken. It would have made my heart ache."

"I was."

"Do you think you'll ever see them again?"

Mrs. Pickens hunched her shoulders. "Maybe, but I never saw them before and don't know if they're members of the congregation." Mrs. Pickens rubbed the back of her hand across her brow. "No more talk about it. Today's supposed to be a day of thanksgiving, and I'm thankful I have you, JD, and Sarah."

"And we're thankful we have you and Russell." Marge wrapped her mother-in-law in her arms and hugged her.

Mrs. Pickens smiled. "Thank you, sweetheart."

Suddenly there was shouting from the den.

"Their team must have scored a touchdown," said Mrs. Pickens. "Guess it's about time for dinner." Mrs. Pickens shook her head. "It's a shame that couple won't be celebrating with their family."

After JD's parents left and Sarah was tucked in bed, JD and Marge lay in bed. Marge was stroking his arm.

"While you and your dad were watching football," said Marge, "your mom and I had a strange conversation."

"What about?"

Marge stopped stroking his arm. "She and your dad were at last Sunday's church social . . ."

"So, they always go to the church social."

"Let me continue, please."

He pinched his lips.

Marge told him about his mother's conversation with the woman.

She sat up straight. "She said her daughter supposedly up and disappeared without leaving a note or saying goodbye to her children. A missing person's report was filed, but nothing ever came of it. She was declared legally dead five years later."

Pickens sat up straight. "That's awful."

"I know. The woman doesn't think her daughter just up and disappeared."

"Let me guess—she wants to know for certain. If her daughter is dead, she wants to bury her and have closure."

Marge wiped a tear. "Wouldn't you if it were me?"

"If it was you, I'd never give up searching, and I'd never declare you legally dead."

"I know you wouldn't, and I'd do the same if it were you." She leaned in and kissed him softly on the lips.

"If there were something I could do, I would. But if it happened in this county twenty years ago, the case file would be paper only, and most of those files have disappeared due to remodeling and moving offices around. I wasn't here then, and neither were any of my deputies, so we wouldn't know where to start looking."

"I know, JD, but could you anyway? For me?" She smiled then leaned in again and kissed him. "You're a good man, JD Pickens, and I love you."

He kissed her. "I love you, too."

"Want to play football, quarterback?"

He smiled. "Anytime with you." Pickens wrapped his arms around Marge and lowered her onto the pillows.

CHAPTER 2

TWO DAYS BEFORE Christmas, Bo Tatum, a crusty sixty-seven-year old sportsman, left his house well before sunrise, the temperature was in the low fifties. Tatum had a full thermos of coffee and four cinnamon rings—two for him and one each for his springer spaniel, Rocker and his three-year-old female beagle, Coco. Tatum and his dogs were heading to his hunting lodge to meet a hunting party, and hunt for Bob White Quail.

Tatum loved the thrill of the hunt. His dog would flush the bird, and it would fly out of the wiregrass like a clay target. Bo would sight and pull the trigger. *Bam.* Wings flapped as the bird went down. Rocker then chased after the quarry and brought it back to Bo in his mouth.

Tatum owned a 125-acre parcel of fields overflowing with native Florida wiregrass and broom sage and dotted with scrub pines in Central Florida. Tatum's parcel was in the northeast corridor of the county. He'd purchased it from part of the estate of a dairy farmer. The parcel came with fishing rights to Lake Azur, which got its name from the color of its water. Tatum had built a roughed-in cabin near the lakeshore that he advertised as a hunting lodge. To get to the cabin, he had to take Grange Road, a dirt road that meandered along the edge of his property. And from the lodge, the only access to the lake was by taking Grange Road, or trucking across Tatum's property, or the remainder of the estate owned property.

The money Tatum earned from hunting parties, he used to make repairs to the lodge and to support his pastimes—hunting, fishing, and drinking. The last one he enjoyed the most, but his wife, Anna May, hated it. He loved spending time on his bass boat trolling the lake before dawn or perched in his deer stand waiting for a buck to come within crosshairs of his bow.

Most days found him unshaven and dressed in jeans and cowboy boots with a John Deere ball cap over his thinning hair. He shaved and wore a suit on Sunday mornings when his wife dragged him to church. He'd spent the entire service fidgeting with his tie while Anna May pleaded with him not to sing along with the congregation because his voice sounded like a donkey braying.

Tatum rambled down the road in his custom-made quail-hunting rig kicking up dust behind him. It was one of two he owned, both of which sat four people. He was looking for a particular spot that was half a mile on Grange Road from the lake. He had to set out a marker so he'd know where to turn off the road with his hunting party.

When he reached the spot, the brush was matted. Tatum parked and stepped out of the truck. The ground crunched under his boots. Rocker and Coco leaped out after him. Tatum breathed in the fresh morning air.

"Feel that chill, Rocker and Coco? If it keeps up like this, it's gonna be a good season. Since I'm here, I might as well relieve myself."

The dogs barked.

As Tatum stood near the underbrush, Rocker came up beside him. "Damn dog, find your own spot to pee."

Rocker barked.

"Dammit. I said find your own spot. Now get." Bo shook his foot at the dog. "Damn dog, you made me pee on myself."

Rocker and Coco wagged their tails.

Tatum zipped his fly. "Okay, let's get going before that hunting party gets here and sees us."

Tatum tied a piece of ribbon to a bush then he and his dogs got back in the truck and Tatum headed for the cabin. A few minutes more and the hunting party would have caught up with Tatum. Tatum had just opened the lodge when the hunting party arrived.

There were two couples. One was Mitch Hubbard and his wife, Donna. The other Wiley Baxter and his wife, Harley. The couples parked their trucks.

"Let's go, Bo," said Baxter. "Get the show on the road."

Tatum shook his head.

"Ignore him, Bo," said Hubbard. "We're ready when you are."

"I'm ready. Anybody need to use the facilities or coffee?"

No. We're good," said Baxter.

"Then hop aboard."

They climbed aboard Tatum's hunting rig. He drove to the marked spot, then turned into the fields of wiregrass while they sat on the custom-made seats for comfort.

When the hunt began, the temperature was in the high forties, but after two hours of hunting, it had risen to the high fifties. It was a good hunt. Each shooter bagged several quail.

One of the women got a bead on a bird and shot it. Rocker bolted to retrieve it, Coco hot on his heels, but the Beagle got distracted and wandered off. She paused at a spot fifty-feet away and scratched the ground. Coco stopped, barked, and pointed. No quail came up out of the grass.

"Bo, what's she pointing at?" asked Wiley Baxter. The other three hunters turned their attention to Coco.

Tatum called out. "Coco, what you got?"

Coco barked. Rocker dropped the quail he'd held in his mouth, wandered over to Coco, and the two dogs started digging.

"Damn dogs." Tatum stomped toward them.

Concerned, the hunters climbed down from the rig and followed Tatum to the spot where Coco had dug a six-inch hole.

Tatum paused and peered down. "What the hell was that?" he said. Tatum bent, squinted his old eyes, and focused on the bottom of the hole. Something white shined against the red dirt. "Was that . . . a finger?" He pulled a rag from his back pocket and brushed away the dirt. "Damn." It was a human bone finger. He brushed away more dirt and revealed three more boney fingers.

Behind him, one of the women gasped. He didn't bother to see which one and didn't care. He stood and stepped back.

What Tatum saw looked like a hand. "Son-of-a-bitch," he said.

The women stepped back and cupped their mouths. The men, staring at the hole, put their arms around their wives.

"Damn, Bo," said Mitch Hubbard, "it looks like a hand. Or part of one, anyway."

Tatum imagined what would happen. He'd call the sheriff, who'd investigate. The area would become a crime scene, and he'd have to cancel next week's hunting trips. He didn't want that to happen.

Tatum scratched his head. "I gotta call the sheriff." He swallowed hard. "Sorry, folks. 'Fraid the hunt's over. I'll reimburse ya for the unused time." Tatum shook his head. "You gotta stay until the sheriff gets here and says you can go."

"Can't you just ignore it and take us to our trucks?" asked Harley Baxter, the woman who shot the last bird. "We bagged enough, and you can keep the money."

Tatum considered doing it. Who'd know? He could cover the hand with dirt and forget the incident. But he had no way of knowing if it would happen again on the next hunt. He could avoid the area. But his hunting dogs were too good, and they'd probably find the spot again.

"Sorry, Harley, I can't."

Harley looked at her husband. Eyes pleaded. Wiley scratched the back of his head.

"Come on, Bo, please," begged Wiley. "We can't afford any trouble."

What did that mean? Tatum had always thought that Wiley's character was like his name.

"I gotta do what's right."

"Shit," replied Wiley. "Maybe we should walk back to the lodge, get in our trucks and get the hell outta here." He cocked his head toward the other guy. "Whattaya say, Mitch?"

Mitch Hubbard was a former homicide detective. "Sorry," he replied. "Bo's right. We gotta stay."

"Son of a bitch," shouted Wiley. "Call the damn sheriff. But this is the last time I hunt with you, Tatum."

Tatum's face reddened. "That's fine with me."

Tatum only took Wiley on hunts if Hubbard brought him along. Hubbard and Tatum knew each other from when Hubbard first moved to Warfield. Hubbard owned two acres of land on the outskirts of Warfield and had built a house on it after he retired. Soon after, he and his wife started taking hunting trips with Tatum.

Hubbard shook his head. His wife ignored Wiley's caustic remark, and shook her head, too. They had often told Tatum that the only reason they brought the Baxters with them, was because Harley was Hubbard's wife's friend and she loved to hunt. Harley had started with her now deceased father but hadn't been hunting since a teenager with her father.

Tatum reached into the pocket of his camo jacket and took out his phone. He dialed the sheriff's office.

At the sheriff's office, Pickens and his deputies were merrymaking. Pickens had brought doughnuts and cookies for the deputies that morning and had arranged for pizza delivery for the evening shift.

When the office phone rang, Stacey Morgan, the daytime emergency operator, answered it.

"Is JD there?" said Tatum.

"Yes, sir," said Stacey. "Can I ask what your call is about?"

Tatum took a deep breath. "It's Bo Tatum. Now put Pickens on, dammit."

"Sorry, Mr. Tatum, but I need to know what your emergency is."

"Goddammit," Tatum shouted. "I said put JD on."

When Stacey said Tatum, Pickens heard her and knew she had a difficult situation.

Pickens leaned against Stacey's desk. "What's he want?"

Stacey sighed. "He won't say. Just that he wants to talk to you."

Pickens clenched his jaw and pointed to a phone on a nearby desk.

"Transfer the call here. He better not ruin our Christmas celebration."

Stacey spoke into the phone. "Mr. Tatum, I'm transferring your call to the sheriff."

"It's about damn time," Tatum snapped.

Stacey transferred the call to Pickens.

"This had better not be another one of your body calls, Bo," said Pickens.

"I'm not bull-shittin' you. There really is a body. We found a human hand, and I got witnesses."

Pickens waved Sergeant Amy Tucker over, put a finger to his lips, and hushed the deputies.

Tucker was Pickens' senior deputy and the county's first female deputy. She was considered the mama bear by the other deputies because of her age and the fact that she was old enough to be their mother. Her streaked, dirty-blonde hair was always tied in a ponytail and tucked under a sheriff's ballcap, and her nice figure made quite an impression in a uniform. She was also a licensed family counselor. Pickens addressed her as Amy, as did the other deputies—which she preferred.

Pickens pressed the speaker button.

"Listen carefully, Bo. You and your hunt party turn around and walk back to your rigs."

"There's only one rig."

"Whatever," snapped Pickens. "Just turn around and carefully retrace your steps and wait by your rig."

Amy listened, eyes intense.

"And, Bo, if anyone wants to bolt, tell them I'll send deputies after them."

"Nobody's goin anywhere," said Tatum. "You're ruinin my business again."

"You're ruining my Christmas."

Amy grabbed a pencil and pad.

"Witnesses' names?" Pickens asked.

"The Baxters and the Hubbards."

Pickens mouthed Hubbard and Baxter to Amy. She wrote the names on the pad.

"Put Mitch on."

A moment later, a new voice came on.

"I'd say Merry Christmas, JD," said Hubbard. "but I suspect you're not gonna have one."

"Goes with the job."

"How can I help?"

"I told Bo to have y'all turn around and backtrack to his rig and stay there. Can you make sure you do? Amy and I will be there shortly."

"Consider me deputized, JD. How will you know where to find us?"

Pickens scratched the back of his head. Amy wrote *flag* on the pad. Pickens nodded.

"Have Bo make a flag and hold it up. We'll look for it. And ask him where he turned off Grange Road."

"Will do." Hubbard consulted with Tatum and relayed what Pickens wanted.

"Tell JD I marked the spot where I turned off the road," said Tatum. "He'll see the tire tracks."

"I heard him," said Pickens. "Damn loudmouth."

Pickens heard Hubbard's snicker.

"I'll call him when I get there. I'll call the ME. They may get there before us. I'll have them wait for me." Pickens had a thought. "Mitch, after I call Bo, have him fire a shot, so I'll know which direction to look for the flag. And have him stay on the line."

"Got it, JD," said Hubbard.

"Thanks, Mitch. Guess I'm ruining your Christmas, too."

"Goes with the territory," replied Hubbard, and he ended the conversation.

The hunting party followed Hubbard to Tatum's rig. He had the women climb into the cab. Hubbard, the men, and the dogs stood beside the rig. Hubbard climbed up onto the rig. Tatum grabbed a six-foot long pole from under the seats that he used to chase snakes, and an old rag he used to wipe the guns after the hunt was over. Tatum gave them to Hubbard who fashioned a flag out of the pole and rag and laid it on the seats. If Hubbard stood up and lifted it over his head, Pickens would surely see it.

While Hubbard had worked on the flag, Tatum and Baxter engaged in a pissing contest over why Tatum couldn't just take him and his wife back to their car and leave Hubbard to deal with the sheriff. If they kept it up long enough, Tatum wouldn't have to fire a shot. Pickens was sure to hear them arguing. Hubbard sat on the rig and waited and laughed.

*   *   *

After hanging up with Tatum, Pickens slammed the receiver in the cradle. "*Shit*," he mumbled. "Merry damn Christmas. Just what we need. Tatum and a body. Saddle up, Amy. You're with me." He pointed to Deputy Ritchie Ortiz. "Ritchie, party's over. Follow us."

Ortiz set his cup of eggnog down. "Where to?"

"Bo Tatum's property," Pickens replied. Pickens didn't consider Tatum's place a resort as Tatum advertised. "Were taking my SUV." Pickens took a deep breath. "We'll mount up after I call the ME."

Amy rolled her eyes. "She's not gonna be hap-pee," Amy said, drawing out the last syllable.

Pickens took another deep breath. "You want to call her?"

"Hell no. You're the sheriff."

Ortiz covered his mouth to shield his laugh. The other deputies did the same.

"How about as a Christmas present?" Pickens said.

Amy shook her head.

"What the hell. Might as well get it over with." He dialed the ME's number.

"This better be a Christmas greeting, JD," answered Marge, her voice sharp and sarcastic. In the background, he heard the off-key singing of *Jingle Bells*. "We're having a party here."

"Got bad news," Pickens said warily. "Bo Tatum called."

"*Shit*," Marge replied. "Animal or human?"

"He said a human hand."

"Where this time?"

"In the field off Grange Road. They're waiting by Bo's rig." Pickens coughed. "Yes, they trampled the ground around it." Pickens imagined the fury in her eyes. "We're heading out there now. Who are you sending?"

"I'm not sending anyone," she snapped. "I'll take Tom and the criminalists. Lucky you, my parents are with Sarah. I'll call and tell Mom she may have to make dinner."

After he hung up, Amy said, "How'd it go?"

"She'll meet us there. Mount up. We're goin for a sleigh ride."

At the ME's office, the staff was having a Christmas party. Marge had ordered in a lunch of cold cuts, cheeses, dips, whole wheat rolls, cookies, and eggnog. The plan was to close the office early. Besides her and Morgan, the staff consisted of two criminalists and an office assistant. Marge and Tom would be on call.

Dr. Tom Morgan was the assistant medical examiner and had worked for Dr. Davids since she became the chief medical examiner.

Marge's stomach quivered. The thought that she had to ruin Tom Morgan and her staffs' Christmas made her as nervous as she felt the first time she cut into a cadaver in medical school. She joined in the last line of *Santa Claus is Comin' to Town*.

"I hate to break up the party," Marge said.

Voices stopped. Eyes stared at her.

"We have a situation."

"It's not Tatum, is it?" asked Morgan. "It would be just like him to ruin Christmas."

Marge's lips formed a bitter smile. "Afraid so," she replied and looked at the two criminalists. "You two, we're going out to

Grange Road. Tatum told JD he found a human hand and has witnesses. JD will meet us there."

Betty-Jean Carr and Andy Doring, the criminalists, slumped their shoulders and sighed. They both had plans for the afternoon.

Carr and Doring recently were designated as criminalists because of their knowledge and experience working crime scenes.

"Sorry, guys," Marge said. She was disappointed, too. "I'll make it up to you."

Marge and her team loaded up the crime scene van and headed out to Grange Road.

CHAPTER 3

A T THE CRIME scene, Marge parked behind Pickens' SUV. She stepped out of the van. Pickens and Amy got out of his SUV. Clouds had rolled in, the sky was gunmetal gray, and the wind was blustery. Pickens and Amy pressed their hats tight onto their heads. Marge did, too. A pair of binoculars hung from Amy's neck.

"Okay, where's the body?" asked Marge, with her arms folded across her chest.

Pickens cocked his head at the field. "Out there somewhere. Now that you're here I'll call Bo." He took his cell phone from his sheriff's jacket and dialed Tatum.

"Bout time you called, JD," said Tatum. "What took you so long?"

"We're here. Now, fire a shot, so we know which direction to go. Raise the flag and keep the line open."

"Why fire a shot? Can't you follow the tracks we left this morning?"

"Which one? There's several of them."

"The set that goes straight in. It's the one that's matted down the most."

"I see it. How far are you in?"

"Not far. We were working our way out when we discovered the hand."

"Okay, have Mitch raise the flag. Then you fire a shot."

Pickens heard Tatum tell Hubbard to raise the flag.

The subsequent shot from Tatum's gun spooked some quail. The birds flew up from the brush.

Pickens noticed Marge flinch when she heard the *whack* of the shotgun blast.

Amy raised the binoculars and searched the horizon. She saw the birds before she saw the flag. She pointed in the direction of the flag.

Pickens looked at Deputy Ortiz. "Ritchie, you stay here and don't let anybody use this road unless I say so."

"Should I tape it off?" asked Ritchie.

"No, not until we know for sure what we have. Let's roll, Marge."

As Pickens' SUV approached the hunting party, Hubbard leaped off the rig and stood next to his wife and the rest of the hunting party. They looked like the high school basketball team posing for a team picture dressed in Camo outfits. Tatum stood out as the team captain as his outfit had seen more wear, and he wore a John Deere ball cap.

Pickens immediately recognized Tatum and Hubbard but not the others. Two were females. He couldn't discern their hair color as their heads were covered with hats. Pickens didn't recognize the third man.

"You recognize those people, JD?" asked Amy.

"Only Tatum and the guy next to him. I have no idea who the others are. That's Mitch Hubbard, a former homicide detective. He lives in Warfield. I suspect the woman next to him is his wife."

Pickens rolled up to a stop far enough away from the site so as not to disturb the ground near it. Marge pulled up beside him. Pickens and Amy climbed out of his SUV. Marge and her team got out of their van.

"What's your first order of business?" asked Pickens.

Marge surveyed the area. "First, we'll walk carefully to where they found the hand, and then we'll need to set up a perimeter. If you've got tape, you can do it, but not until we know what we have. If the hand is part of skeletal remains, we're going to be here all day. If so, I'll call my mother and tell her we may be home late."

"If you're here, we're here, too," said Pickens and turned to Amy. "I hope you don't have plans for this evening."

"I did, but I can change them."

Marge glanced at her team. Morgan nodded yes. The two criminalists waved their hands and picked up their crime scene kits. Betty-Jean raised the camera that was dangling from her neck. Andy Doring, the other criminalist, who had a duffel bag strapped on his shoulders breathed a sigh of relief that he'd soon relieve himself of it.

Marge and her team slowly walked through the wiregrass. Pickens and Amy followed.

When they were within ten yards of Tatum and his party, Tatum started to approach them.

Pickens raised his hand. "Stay where you are, Bo. We don't want the scene to be disturbed any more than it already was."

Tatum held his ground.

"Show us where the hand is. No, stay where you are."

Tatum froze. "How the hell am I going to show from here?"

"Do the dogs know where it is?"

"Both know."

"Have them both go to it and point. We'll go to them."

"Coco, Rocker, go find." Tatum pointed in the direction of where the hand was. "Go find that damn hand. Go," he shouted.

The two dogs took off and ran to the site where the hand was, stopped, pointed and barked.

"Good dogs. Now stay." Both dogs obeyed.

"JD, you and Amy wait with the others. If we need you, we'll let you know," said Marge and turned to her team. "Let's go and watch where you walk." Then she said to Pickens, "You guys watch, too."

Pickens joined Tatum and the others.

"Bossy ain't, she?" remarked Mitch Hubbard.

Pickens grinned. "Yeah, and she's my wife. Good to see you, and who are these people?"

Hubbard extended his hand, and the two men shook. "Good to see you, too." He turned to the woman beside him. "Meet my wife, Donna." The woman nodded.

"Nice to meet you, Mrs. Hubbard." Pickens turned toward Amy. "Meet my senior deputy Sergeant Amy Tucker."

Amy feigned a salute. Hubbard did the same.

"Gonna be a long day, JD," said Hubbard.

"Too damn long," shouted Wiley Baxter.

"JD, meet the Baxters. Wiley and Harley," said Tatum. "Any idea how long we have to wait?"

"Hard to say, Bo. Depends on what the ME finds."

As soon as Marge and her team reached the site, Tom Morgan held up his hand, and everyone stopped. Their first thought was *snake*.

Morgan took a fleeting look at the scene.

"What if it's a burial ground or a . . ." asked Morgan.

Marge quickly surveyed the area.

"Or a boneyard?" Marge replied. "First let's see what we have and then we'll determine what we do next."

Morgan continued surveying the field for possible burial markers or gravesites.

Andy took the duffel bag off his shoulder, set it on the ground, reached in and took out a set of yellow stake flags. He handed one to Morgan who placed it in the ground near the hole.

"Wonder what made the dogs dig here?" asked Morgan.

"They're hounds, maybe they smelled the remains of something," replied Marge. "First, take some pictures of it, then I'll probe the ground to determine the soil's density."

Morgan raised the 35-millimeter camera that hung from his neck and snapped several photos. Then he paused, his eyes gazing at the ground.

"Strange, the vegetation seems dense here as compared to the rest of the area," Morgan said. "It's as though something in the soil caused contamination."

"You're right," said Marge. "Andy take a soil sample and a sample of the vegetation. We'll analyze them later."

Andy took both samples, put them in bags and marked them.

"Now give me a probe, a trowel, a brush, and a strainer," said Marge.

Andy took out the instruments and handed them to her. The T-shaped probe was a thin steel rod with a handle welded across one end. Marge stuck it in the ground.

"That was easy," she said. "Maybe whatever's buried here kept the soil moist, or it rained recently. Hey, Tatum, did it rain out here recently?"

"Yeah," he shouted. "Tuesday night. It came down in buckets."

"That explains why the dogs had no problem digging," said Morgan.

"Let's see what we have," said Marge.

She meticulously scrapped away the dirt around the fingers until she had a fully disclosed hand. She brushed it off, then stepped aside so Morgan could take more photos.

"Looks like a left hand based on the location of the thumb," said Morgan.

"Can't they go any faster?" yelled Baxter.

"No, we can't," Marge shouted back.

Pickens saw Hubbard's nostrils flare. Like him, Hubbard

knew Marge was correct, and that Baxter's remarks were out of place. He sensed Hubbard was losing his patience.

"Wiley, shut your damn mouth," said Hubbard. "Exhumations take time and can't be rushed."

"I don't give a shit, I got someplace I need to be," yelled Baxter.

Hubbard glared at him. "During my experience as a homicide investigator, I found that the person or persons who were impatient, they generally had something to hide."

Baxter froze.

"You know something about what's out there?" said Hubbard.

Pickens carefully observed the interaction between the two men; so did Amy.

Because of her suspicious nature, Amy made a mental note of it for future reference in case it was important. She also noticed Baxter's wife backed away from the conversation and seemed uncomfortable.

"Hell no," said Baxter. "What's the matter with you, Mitch?"

"Just making an observation."

"We got a flight to Vale this evening and have to drive to Orlando, and I don't want to miss it."

"Then you should have stayed home," replied Hubbard.

Marge continued painstakingly scraping away dirt until she uncovered the radial and ulna bones of a forearm. She backed away so Morgan could take photos.

"What do you think?" asked Morgan.

"Quick glance tells me it's either an adult female or a child based on the size and structure of the hand. The position of the hand suggests the body is on its back."

"Let's hope there is just this one and not a killing field," said Morgan.

"Yeah," said Marge. "We'll worry about that after we finish

with this one. It's going to be a long evening. We'll need to establish a perimeter and maybe set up lights."

"How wide a perimeter?" asked Andy.

"Should I set up a sieve, too?" "Let's presume the body is no more than six-feet long and set up a ten-foot radius just to be safe," answered Marge.

"Not yet," Marge replied. "We may need to do it later. For now, we'll use the small strainers."

Andy and Betty-Jean grabbed the set of stake flags and marked off a ten-foot circle. When they finished, they stood by waiting for an assignment.

"Ever done this before, Marge?"

"Once after I graduated from medical school. What about you?"

"Twice," Morgan replied. "Two tours in Afghanistan digging for remains from a suicide bomb attack." He took a deep breath. "It was horrible, mostly women and children. I never want to do that again. It was awful."

"Let's hope we don't have to do this again."

"I did it once," said Betty-Jean. "As a volunteer at a disaster site my sophomore year in college."

"Same here," said Andy. "It was in my junior year. I'll never forget it."

"Hey, you gonna stand there and talk or get this over with?" shouted Baxter.

"Shut up, Baxter, or I'll cuff you and lock you in my SUV," said Pickens.

"Or I'll shut you up myself," said Hubbard.

It was enough to make Baxter shut up.

"JD, can you come here?" yelled Marge. "I want you to see this."

Pickens carefully approached, stopped near the site, and looked down. "Tell me that doesn't belong to a kid," he said.

"Could be a teenager," replied Marge

"What can I do?"

"It's going to take us most of the day and into the evening. Send those people home, especially that loud mouth so we can do our work without interruptions."

"Anything else?" he asked.

"Yes, call my mother and tell her we'll be late and to look after Sarah."

"Is this gonna take all weekend?"

"No, we're just going to exhume whatever remains there are and get them to the morgue. We'll work on them after the holiday. No sense in spoiling everyone's Christmas."

"Amy and I are staying as long as you are. Let us help you any way we can."

"Thanks, we're going to need help digging up the remains. Hopefully, the six of us can get it done quickly without doing any damage."

Pickens turned and walked back to the hunting party.

"Bo, you can take your party back to their vehicles. Make sure you stay far enough away from the scene. Amy get everyone's info. You folks have a Merry Christmas. Amy, we're staying until Marge finishes here."

Amy nodded her head, took her pad from her shirt pocket, and started writing down their names and information.

"JD, I can stay if you need me," said Hubbard. "Baxter can give Donna a ride home."

"Not on your life," said Hubbard's wife. "If you're staying, I'm staying."

Pickens smiled. "Thanks, Mitch, but it's not necessary. If you want to help, I could use your experience once we know what we're dealing with."

"You got it. Ain't done it in a while, but I can't wait to get back to investigative work. Retirement is okay, but I miss the work. And I still have lots of contacts that would come in handy if and when we need them."

"Great, I'll call when I need you. Merry Christmas."

"You, too. Let's go, Bo. And keep your mouth shut, Wiley."

"Hold on a sec," said Pickens. "Bo, I don't want to read about this in the newspaper." He glanced at the field and waved his hand. "As far as your eyes can see, it's all an active crime scene so keep your mouth shut, or you'll have hell to pay from me." Pickens glowered at Tatum. "Understand?"

"But, JD, I got hunts planned for next week."

"Cancel them. No one's getting on your property until I say so. Until we know what we're dealing with, we have to assume there may be more bodies. Do you understand?"

"I do, but I don't like it."

"Deal with it." Pickens stared at the Baxters. "Same goes for the rest of you." The Baxters nodded their heads. "Good. Have a Merry Christmas."

They climbed into Tatum's vehicle, and he slowly drove away.

"What do you think of that Baxter guy, JD?" asked Amy.

"Complete asshole."

"Definitely, and I think he and his wife are hiding something. Just an observation."

"I agree, and we'll file that away until we need it. I'll call Ritchie and tell him it's going to be a long evening. I'll call Billy and have him send someone to relieve him."

Pickens called his deputy, advised him of the situation, and told him to string crime scene tape across the road. Next, he called Billy, had him schedule relief for Ritchie, and advised him that not to let anyone on the property.

CHAPTER 4

PICKENS AND AMY carefully approached the scene and stopped when Marge held her hand up.

"That's close enough," said Marge. "We've got a lot of work to do, and I don't want you interfering. You can observe from where you are."

"So, how does this work?" asked Pickens.

"We apply basic anatomy principles," answered Morgan. "We use the forearm as a start and then using its length, we determine the location of the shoulder, and mark it."

"Then we make rough calculations for the shoulders, hips, and feet," said Marge. "From there we stake out an outline of the remains. It's not exact science, but it's the best we can do under the circumstances. We weren't expecting to do an exhumation. A forensic anthropologist team would have better equipment and could do it more accurately. Andy will dig a shallow trench around the outline, so we can start uncovering the remains."

Pickens listened, but he wasn't content being on the sideline instead of leading the investigation. He wanted to do more than watch. He wanted a more active role. Pickens knew he had to be patient, but patience was something he had difficulty doing at times.

"Is there anything more I can do besides stand here?" Pickens asked.

Marge raised her eyebrows and gave him a glassy stare. "No, but we will need your help getting the remains into the van. For now, just watch."

"I'm just frustrated. What with Bo and Baxter, I want to do something."

After Marge, Morgan, Betty-Jean, and Andy finished outlining the remains, Andy dug the trench. Then all four got down on their knees and began exhuming the remains. Marge worked the left side, Morgan the right side, and the criminalists started at the feet working their way up to the waist.

"We got shoes," said Betty-Jean and held one up. "At least what's left of them. Mid-heeled and dark gray. We'll bag them."

Morgan finished uncovering the right hand and held something between his fingers.

"Got a wedding band," he said. "Means we got an adult female."

"If there is a date inscribed, won't that suggest her age?" asked Pickens.

"Yes, provided it's her ring and not placed on her finger to prevent identifying her," replied Marge.

Morgan checked the ring and said, "December 11, 1986. Presuming she was in her early twenties when she married, she'd be in her fifties now. Betty-Jean put this in an evidence bag."

"Her age won't tell us how long she was in the ground," said Marge. "But it might help once we examine the remains at the morgue, and it might help with facial reconstruction."

With the ring properly placed into evidence, Marge and her team continued exhuming. When she was ready to unearth the skull, Marge had Morgan assist her. They carefully scraped and swept dirt from it until it was completely exposed.

Marge rotated the skull to its right.

"Blunt force trauma judging by the injury," Marge said. Morgan took a closer look.

"I agree. Is she the only victim, or are there others buried out here?"

"What are you suggesting?" asked Pickens.

"That this may be a boneyard," said Morgan and looked out at the field of wiregrass. "We'll have to search the property for more bodies."

"Save it for next week," said Marge. "Right now, we have to get the remains to the morgue."

"When will you start on the remains and do facial reconstruction?" asked Pickens.

"Probably Tuesday," said Morgan. "We'll inspect the bones for anything that might help determine how long she was in the ground and her age."

Marge was about to add a comment when something shiny in the dirt caught her eye. She scooped it up with the strainer. "Got an earring," she said. Marge carefully sifted through the dirt on the opposite side of the skull. "Got the other one. If we're lucky, there might be DNA on them, too." She handed both earrings to Betty-Jean to put into an evidence bag. "Tomorrow we'll process and catalog the remains and take DNA samples if my team can come in," she said. "If not, I'll process the remains and do what I can by myself. It's not going to be a Merry Christmas Eve."

"If mama bear is going to work tomorrow, so will papa bear," said Morgan.

"So will cub bear," said Betty-Jean.

"Same here," said Andy.

"Don't you guys have plans to be with family?" asked Marge.

"We are family and families work together even on holidays," said Morgan. "Right guys?"

"Right," replied Betty-Jean and Andy together.

"Besides," said Morgan, "I want to work this one. She was someone's wife and someone's daughter, and maybe someone's mother." He looked down at the remains. "She deserves to go home, and we can help her."

Morgan's comments brought on a moment of stillness.

After a long sigh, Marge said, "We're done. And just in time. We won't need to set up lights."

The sky had turned a dark gray, and the temperature had dropped into the low fifties.

"How do I search for more bodies?" asked Pickens, and he pointed to the field. "That's a hell of a lot of ground to cover."

"What about using a drone?" asked Andy.

"Now where the hell would I get a drone?" asked Pickens.

"Billy has one," said Betty-Jean. "So do Andy and me." Pickens' jaw dropped as did Marge's and Morgan's. "We belong to a club and Billy is the president."

"And he has the coolest drone of everyone," said Andy. "He can do a lot with it. I bet he has a *thermal imaging camera* and software on it. He might be able to locate any bodies out there."

"Deputy Billy Thompson? Our Billy?" asked Amy.

Billy Thompson was one of Pickens' deputies, and his desk area was the office's nerve center. Billy was also in charge of the 911 operators.

Pickens knew Billy had access to resources that he shouldn't have had. But since his office was limited in resources, Pickens turned a blind eye. The last time Pickens had to investigate a murder had been over a year ago. That case was about a serial killer and was eventually solved thanks to Billy's investigative and computer prowess.

"Yep," replied Andy.

"Let's get the remains in a body bag, carefully, and load it into the van," said Marge. "We'll catalog them tomorrow."

Like a team of pallbearers, they lifted the remains and set them in a body bag, and then loaded it into the van.

Except for frogs croaking, the only other sound was the van door when it closed.

"I'll see you at home, Marge," Pickens said in a hushed voice as if not wanting to disturb the dead.

"What did my mother say when you called her?" asked Marge.

"Shit," he whispered. "I forgot to call her."

"Then you better pick up something for us."

"After I drop off Amy, I'll talk to Billy about a drone."

"Might want to wait until tomorrow to talk to him," said Amy. "He has a date tonight, and I'm sure he's gone home already." She nodded slightly in Betty-Jean's direction.

Pickens grinned. "I'll wait until tomorrow."

"If you know anyone who has cadaver dogs," said Morgan, "ask if you can borrow them. They'll make the search easier in addition to the drone."

"Cadaver dogs? Why?" said Amy.

"Because if this was a *boneyard,* and there were any recent or other bodies buried, they might be able to locate them."

"Is that what you think?"

"Yes," said Morgan, "but it's only a supposition. In a field like this, where there's one, there's possibly more. Anything's possible."

"We don't know anyone who has them."

"No," said Pickens, "but I know someone who might."

"Not Tatum?" said Amy.

"No, Mitch Hubbard. Remember he was a homicide detective, and he may have used them."

Marge and her team climbed into the van. Pickens and Amy got into his SUV. They made a U-turn and slowly worked their way back to Grange Road.

CHAPTER 5

S ATURDAY MORNING, PICKENS and Marge had coffee with her father before her mother got out of bed. They wanted to be out of the house before Marge's mother could start questioning them again about why they were late yesterday and why they were going to work on Christmas Eve.

Marge left it with her father to tell her mother that Pickens was going fishing with his dad, and she had some last-minute shopping to do before attending a luncheon at the Senior Center, then dropping off gifts at elderly citizens' homes who couldn't attend the luncheon. Both excuses were believable. Pickens sometimes fished on weekends with his father, and the luncheon was something she did every year with Sarah and Bailey, just not this year.

When Marge pulled into the parking lot at her office, it was empty. In the morgue, she flipped the light switch. The overhead fluorescents reflected off the pristine autopsy tables. The first thing she smelled was the clean scent of lemon. It was eerily quiet like before a viewing at a funeral parlor. She only came in this early on rare occasions. Today was a rare occasion because it was Christmas Eve and she wanted to get a head start before the others arrived.

Marge glanced around. There were no autopsies to be done. The last two were in drawers waiting to be picked up by

Jacobson's Funeral home. Both were elderly and had died of natural causes. They each had names and stories.

A third drawer contained the skeletal remains of the unknown woman. She had a story, too. It was up to Marge and her team to discover it.

She set her purse on the floor beside her desk and opened her laptop. She pulled up a blank case file and inserted a case number. Where it asked for a name, she entered *Unknown Female*. She hoped before the year ended, they'd have an actual name for her. Under Cause of Death, she inserted blunt force trauma. Marge was interrupted by the voices of her team as they arrived.

Marge watched as they donned lab coats and latex gloves. They went right to one of the autopsy tables and wheeled it over to the drawer with the skeletal remains. They pulled it out, carefully set the remains on the table, and wheeled it back under the lights and a microscope light. Next, they turned, stood at attention, and awaited Marge.

As a token of appreciation, Marge clapped softly, bowed her head, put on a lab coat and latex gloves, and joined them.

She picked up a headlamp and put it on. "Let's begin," she said. She and Morgan turned on their recorders.

"December 24, 2017." Marge looked at her watch. "Time eight-forty-five. Dr. Marge Davids and Dr. Tom Morgan processing skeletal remains found off Grange Road on Friday, December 23, of an unknown female."

Morgan handed her one end of a tape measure. They stretched it the length of the remains.

"Approximately five-feet-six allowing for postmortem shrinkage," said Morgan. "Let's measure the skull."

They moved to the skull.

"Definitely female and Caucasian," she said, "based on the

angle of the teeth and jawbone." She stepped back. "Betty-Jean take your measurements for facial reconstruction."

Betty-Jean leaned over the remains and started measuring. She called out the numbers and locations to Andy who put them in Betty-Jean's laptop.

"I'll enter this information into the program," Betty-Jean said, "and I'll add photos of the skull, too. I can't wait to do my first real facial reconstruction." Betty-Jean had been assigned the new software and had completed the necessary coursework but had only worked on ceramic cadaver skulls. Andy had also completed the requirements as her back up.

"You can have the skull once we're done with it," said Marge.

"Cause of death," said Morgan, "blunt force trauma to the left parietal of the cranium. She was struck twice with a flat object."

Next, they probed the remains for signs of physical trauma. Morgan carefully studied the left tibia using the magnifying lamp.

"Slight evidence of a fracture that occurred a while before her death?" he said. "Could've been ten years or more before she died?"

"I don't see any more," said Marge as she checked the arms and rib cage. "And there are no signs of beginning arthritis."

They moved to the pelvis and checked for fracture.

"So far, the remains appear to be that of a healthy female in her late twenties or thirties," said Morgan.

"She's starting to talk to us," said Andy.

"A little," replied Marge. "but she has to tell us more if we're going to identify her."

"Based on her wedding date and the condition of the remains, I'm willing to make a supposition she was in her late-thirties," said Morgan.

Marge glanced at the others to see what they were thinking. Betty-Jean and Andy tilted their heads as if they agreed.

"I haven't reached that point yet," she said. "I need more information, but I'm willing to consider it."

"If we could do carbon dating," said Morgan, "we could be more positive. But we'd have to send a sample of the remains to a lab that does it, and it would take at least two weeks. That's if they have the time to do it."

"She's been in the ground for some time now, what's two more weeks if it will help determine her age?" asked Betty-Jean.

Morgan took a deep breath and sighed. "If she was your mother or sister, would you want to keep waiting, or would you like to know something now? Definitive age is one thing, but that's not the only thing we need to identify her."

Betty-Jean stared down at her feet, regretting her words. "I'm sorry, you're right. I just wanted to help her. And, yes, if she were my mother, I'd want to know sooner than later," she shot back.

Marge sensed her team's emotions were beginning to wear on them. It was Christmas Eve, and they wanted to return the dead woman to her family. She did, too, but forensic analysis took time.

Marge glanced at her watch. "It's almost noon," she said. "Why don't we call it quits for the day. We have enough to do further analysis on Tuesday. I sense you all want to give this woman a name, but we need more data. At least we have an approximate age." She looked at Morgan. "I'm willing to accept your supposition, Tom. Tuesday we can determine how long she'd been in the grave. Betty-Jean can start facial reconstruction. Once we have that and how long she was in the ground, we can give that information to Sheriff Pickens, and he can do his investigation." She waited for a response, but all were silent.

"Look, guys, it's Christmas Eve. Let's enjoy the holiday and not let death ruin it."

One by one the others looked at each other for a decision.

"Okay," said Morgan, "but if you don't mind, I'm going to stay and do some research on forensic analysis. I have a colleague that I worked with on a dig, and I want to call him. He might be able to help."

"Won't he be enjoying the holiday?"

Morgan grinned. "He's a confirmed bachelor and a forensic anthropologist. He doesn't celebrate any holiday. But he may be off on an investigation or a dig. That's his meaning of a holiday."

Marge smiled. "Okay, but please don't spend the weekend here."

"I won't."

"Betty-Jean, you and Andy go home too, and don't come back until Tuesday."

Both criminalists grinned. "We promise, boss," said Andy.

"Good, now let's put our lady back in her drawer where she'd be comfortable."

In the short time that Marge and her team had worked with the skeletal remains, they'd come to see her as a person not just a batch of bones. Marge wondered what the woman's family was doing on Christmas. Would they be celebrating like her and Pickens? Would they have a tree decorated and presents under it? Would they open the presents tonight or wait until in the morning to open the gifts to the sounds of excited grandchildren? Or would they be mourning the loss of their mother?

After the remains were put back in the drawer, Marge got a phone call.

"JD, are you still at the office?"

"Yes, but I'm about to leave. How about you?"

"Me, too. I was hoping to get to the Senior Center in time for the luncheon, but it might be too late."

"How about I meet you there? That way you could still make it."

"I still have to drop presents off."

"I'll go with you. We can spend the afternoon together."

He waited for the silence to end before she replied.

"What the heck, it's Christmas Eve. Let's do it. I'll see you at the Senior Center."

CHAPTER 6

BEFORE GOING TO the office that morning, Pickens had stopped at Lydia's Bakery and purchased a dozen bagels. They were fresh out of the oven, warm in the bag, and smelled good. He'd eat at least two and leave the rest for whoever was on duty.

He was surprised to see Billy at his desk, busy on his computer.

Billy looked up when he saw Pickens enter. "Sheriff, I'd thought I'd come in and get a head start on the case. Betty-Jean filled me in during dinner last night on what happened at Tatum's place."

"You always talk shop on a dinner date? Doesn't sound romantic."

Billy smiled. "Nah, it just came up. We have similar interests, and sometimes work-related things come up. But they don't interfere with—"

"I get it," he said and walked to the break room, set the bag of bagels on the table, put two on a paper plate, and poured a cup of coffee. He ate one, sipped his coffee, and then went to Billy's desk.

"There's bagels in the break room. Help yourself." Pickens looked at the emergency operator on duty and another deputy on call. "Help yourselves guys, there's plenty." He sat next to Billy. "So, what have you done so far?"

Billy pointed to the screen. "I started a case file. Gave it a number, gender female, name Jane Doe, and COD blunt force trauma."

Pickens reviewed the information. "Good start, anything else?"

"Betty-Jean said there was a wedding band. I was just about to start a search of marriage licenses issued around the date. Hopefully, I'll have a possible name for the victim."

"Provided she was married in this county and not somewhere else."

"Got that covered," Billy said. "I'll search state records, too."

"Good work, but don't spend the whole day on it. It's Christmas Eve, and you should take some time to shop for that date of yours." Pickens smiled. "Speaking of Betty-Jean, she said you had a drone."

"Uh yeah I do," he said. "Why? You getting one for Sarah.

Pickens grinned. He suspected Billy knew what he wanted but went along with Billy's act. "No, I want to search the field where we found those remains. Any chance your drone has a camera with thermal imaging?"

Billy thrust his shoulders back and smiled. "I have the software, but I haven't used it in a while. It wouldn't be a problem to activate it. Let me know when you want me to."

Pickens rubbed his chin contemplating when. "After the weekend. I don't want to spoil your Christmas. Maybe Tuesday you and I can go out there."

"Maybe I'll go with you," said Amy, who had just arrived.

"What are you doing here?" asked Pickens.

"Same thing as you and Billy. Working. I came in to help Billy plan the schedule now that we have to post someone at Tatum's place."

Pickens shook his head. "I suppose it would be a waste of time to order you both to go home?"

Amy smiled. "It would be as far as I'm concerned, and I bet it would be with Billy." Billy grinned and nodded his head.

"Fine, do what you have to, but don't take all day." Pickens took a bite of his bagel and a sip of coffee. "I have to make a phone call. I'll be in my office."

Pickens sat at his desk and scrolled through his cell phone contacts. When he came to Mitch Hubbard's name, he pressed *call*. Hubbard answered after three rings.

"It's JD, Mitch."

"Hey, JD, how did the exhumation go?"

"It went," Pickens said. "My first one."

"That bad, huh? First time for me was . . . borrring."

"Same here."

"You calling to wish me a Merry Christmas or got something on your mind?"

"You know where I can get cadaver dogs?"

"You think there are more bodies in that field?"

"Don't know, but I have to check."

"I used dogs a time or two when I worked homicide. But you're not gonna like where I got them from."

"Shit, not Tatum?"

"Yeah, Tatum," Hubbard answered. "Sorry, JD. He trained and supplied them. Don't know if he still does or if he has any in his kennel, but you can call and ask."

"Guess I have no choice. I'll do it Tuesday."

"Good luck and Merry Christmas. If you need my help, call me."

"Thanks, I might just do that. I could use your wisdom and experience."

"Don't know about wisdom, but I got the experience."

After Pickens ended the conversation and stepped out of his office, Amy was waiting.

"I gave Billy the info on the witnesses from yesterday. Anything you want to do with it?"

Pickens scratched his chin. "Nothing on the Hubbards and Tatum but do a background check on the Baxters. Something about them bothers me. Especially Harley, the wife."

"Me, too. She seemed on edge. I'd like to know her background. You know anything about them?"

"Only that they're friends of the Hubbards. She did seem agitated. Billy, dig deep into her background." Pickens grinned. "I'm headed home. Don't hang around here too long."

CHAPTER 7

CHRISTMAS MORNING WHEN the doorbell rang, Pickens opened the front door. Standing there were his parents. Both had their arms full.

"I would have picked you up, Dad."

"You got your hands full. Merry Christmas, and I'm old enough to drive myself."

"Quit yakking." His mother stepped toward the door. "I'm gonna drop the desserts."

Pickens reached for them, but she dodged him and marched to the kitchen, the scent of freshly baked pie wafting after her.

"Stubborn," said his father.

"Just like you," said Pickens. He noticed his father's eyes knitted.

"Want me to take those, Dad?"

"Nah, I want to see the smile on Sarah's face when she sees her gifts."

"Me, too. Can I get you something to drink?"

"What are you drinking?"

Pickens breathed a heavy sigh. "A beer."

"This early? What's Marge's dad drinking?"

"A highball. I can make you one."

Mr. Pickens lifted his chin in thought. "It's Christmas, so I guess a highball won't hurt. But make it extra light, and don't tell your mother it's for me."

Pickens drew a finger across his lips. "Stephen and Sarah are in the living room. Say hello. I'll be right there with your ginger ale." He winked and went to the kitchen.

Mr. Pickens went to the living room. When Marge's father saw Pickens' father enter, he stood to greet him.

"Merry Christmas, Russell. You need help with those presents?"

"I got it. Besides, they're for Sarah."

Sarah stood up. "Grandpa, are they really all for me?"

"Yep, but you have to give me a hug before you can have them." She rushed over and wrapped her arms around him. "Let me set them under the tree. You can open one, but don't tell your grandmother I let you."

She put a finger to her lips. "I won't," she whispered.

He set the presents on the floor. Bailey sniffed them. "There's one for you, too. First I want a paw." The dog lifted a paw, and Mr. Pickens shook it, then sat.

"How was your cruise, Stephen?"

Mr. Davids drank the last drop of his highball. "It was a nightmare. Stranded on a ship with seven mystery buffs. Everyone and everything was a mystery to them. I'll never take a vacation with Marjorie's mystery book club again."

Mr. Pickens smiled.

"I'm going to freshen my drink. Can I get you one, Russell?"

"JD's fixing one for me the way I like it."

"Extra light, like ginger ale," said Mr. Davids, and he winked. "I'll fix it for you." Mr. Davids headed for the kitchen.

In the kitchen, Pickens' mother and his mother-in-law were exchanging greetings. Pickens was about to fix his father's drink when his phone rang.

It was Amy. "Please tell me you're calling to wish me a Merry Christmas."

"I'm out here on Grange Road, and I got Nosey in handcuffs."

Jimmy Noseby was the local newspaper reporter.

"Wait, you're where, and you what? Why aren't you home or somewhere celebrating the holiday?"

"Because we got married deputies who have families. Billy and I arranged for them to spend the morning opening presents with their kids."

"But I thought you had plans, and that Billy was spending Christmas with his parents?"

"My plans are for this evening. Billy relieves me at noon, and he gets relieved at four. Plenty of time to be with his family. What should I do with Nosey? He was trying to sneak onto the property and take pictures of the grave."

"How did he know about it. Did Tatum tell him?"

"Says he saw us leave Friday and followed us. He figured no one would be here Christmas morning. He figured wrong. It wasn't Tatum."

"I'll be right there." When Marge heard him, she tightened her eyes. "I gotta go. It's an emergency."

Marge understood. "Go. But try and be back before dinner."

"Does this have anything to do with why you two were late on Friday and worked yesterday?" asked Mrs. Davids.

Just then Mr. Davids entered the room. "Give it a rest, Marjorie," he said. "You've been badgering them all weekend."

"But . . ."

"You heard me. Go say Merry Christmas to Russell and play with Sarah."

"But . . ." she said again.

"I said now," he scolded.

"Oh, pooh," she said and stormed out of the kitchen.

"Don't mind her, JD, she'll get over it. I'll fix your father's ginger ale." He winked.

"Thanks, Stephen." Pickens looked at his mother.

"A sheriff's work doesn't stop just because it's Christmas," she said with a smile.

Pickens waved and left.

After Pickens left, Mrs. Pickens asked what she could do to help with dinner.

"I'm glad you're here," Marge replied. "I love my mother, but her idea of helping in the kitchen is to talk and talk." Mrs. Pickens smiled. "She was never one to cook. Mom and Dad always ate dinner out."

"Well, I'll talk if you want, but I'd prefer to do something, anything."

"You can start the veggies and check on the ham."

"I got it. When are your parents leaving?"

"Tuesday. I'll miss their watching Sarah since school is out."

"Russell and I wouldn't mind watching her. As long as you bring Sarah and Bailey to our house."

"That's wonderful," said Marge. "JD can drop her off first thing, and I'll pick her up after work."

"But I have one condition."

Marge's look expressed concern.

"You have to stay for coffee with me and no talk about work."

Marge smiled. "I can handle that."

CHAPTER 8

WHEN PICKENS ARRIVED on Grange Road, he parked behind the reporter's vehicle, sandwiching it between his SUV and Amy's patrol car.

"Where's Nosey?" Pickens asked.

Amy nodded toward the rear window of her patrol car. "In the backseat, handcuffed," she replied. "He's been screaming that he has rights, that I had no right to cuff him, and I'm an old Scrooge to do this to him on Christmas."

Pickens laughed.

"What should I do with him?" Amy asked.

Pickens looked in the rear window. The reporter shouted at him.

"Where's his hat," Pickens asked.

Noseby, the reporter, always wore a red ball cap turned backward. It was his signature.

"It's in his car," she said. "It fell off when I made him get out of it. I tossed it on the front seat."

Pickens then noticed a thermos and empty candy wrappers on the front seat.

"Is that your Christmas breakfast? How long have you been here?"

Amy grinned. "Since six-o'clock. Did you know the sunrise

here is amazing?" She took a deep breath. "And so is the fresh air. What do we do with Nosey?"

Pickens scratched his head. "We could let him stay where he is until Billy relieves you. Then again maybe not. Let's get him out but don't uncuff him. I'll give him a stern warning and promise him the scoop of his lifetime."

Amy opened the rear door and helped the reporter out.

Jimmy Noseby looked weird without his hat. He rarely took it off. He was short and lean and always wore a suit and tie.

"This isn't fair, Sheriff. I didn't do anything wrong."

"Shut up, Nosey."

"It's Noseby, Sheriff."

Nosey was the nickname given to him in high school when Noseby was the school newspaper reporter and stuck his nose in everyone's business.

"What did I just say? Say another word, and I'll book you for trespassing on private property, hindering and interfering with an investigation, and anything else I can charge you with." Pickens threat was enough to silence the reporter. "You'll spend the holiday in a cell, and you probably won't be arraigned until Tuesday. That's if the county prosecutor isn't still on holiday."

"You can't do that, Sheriff. I'm supposed to have dinner with my parents." He turned to Amy. "Please, Sergeant Tucker, tell him not to do that."

Amy coughed into her hand to stifle a laugh.

"Okay, I'll see what I can do," said Amy. "JD, let's talk."

Pickens clenched his jaw and kept a stern face.

"Why not," he said. "But in private." He motioned her to follow him. They stepped out of hearing range from the reporter and pretended they were having a lengthy conversation. When they finished, they walked back to the reporter.

"Here's the thing, Nosey," said Pickens. "We got an anonymous tip that there were bodies buried in that field, and we've just started an investigation." Amy turned her head and stifled a laugh. Pickens bit his lip and kept his stern face. "So far all we've found were animal remains, but we're bound by law to complete a thorough investigation. Keep your mouth shut, and if we find any human remains, I'll call you and give you the biggest scoop you ever had."

The reporter's eyes lit up. "You're not just saying that to fool me are you, Sheriff?"

"Did I lie to you last time?"

Again, Amy turned her head.

"Say yes, and Sergeant Tucker will uncuff you, and you can be on your merry way."

"Does he mean it, Sergeant?"

"He does," said Amy.

"Okay. I won't say anything. I promise. Can you uncuff me now?"

Amy uncuffed him.

"Have a Merry Christmas, Nosey."

"It's Noseby, Sergeant Tucker."

"Whatever," she replied.

"Be careful when you turn around, Nosey," said Pickens. "And lose the hat. You look ridiculous."

The reporter frowned and got into his vehicle. Pickens and Amy smiled.

Amy backed her patrol car thirty feet from the reporter's. Pickens directed him as he made a U-turn and drove back where he came from, narrowly missing scraping Pickens' SUV.

Pickens walked toward Amy as she got out of her vehicle.

"Think he bought it?" she asked.

"He did. He enjoys the spotlight," said Pickens. "Damn, that was fun. Now I gotta call Tatum and warn him not to say anything in case Nosey calls him."

Pickens dialed Tatum. He answered after several rings.

"Bo, it's Sheriff Pickens."

"Hey, JD, Merry Christmas. You calling to tell me I can have my property back?"

"No. I'm out here on Grange Road. We had a visit from Nosey, the reporter . . ."

"I didn't call him, JD, I swear."

"I know. He was snooping on his own. I gave him a bullshit story about finding animal remains and threatened to put him in jail for trespassing. If he should call you, tell him as far as you know, that's all we've found. And you have no comment. Understood?"

"Understood. Again, Merry Christmas."

"Yeah, you too. Before you hang up, Bo, you may want to put a real fence with a lock and a large 'no trespassing' and 'private property' signs. That link of chain doesn't cut it." Pickens smiled and added. "You need something better to stop the teenagers from trespassing."

"I'll have someone out there Tuesday. Just make sure your deputy doesn't arrest him."

"No problem. Hold on. I need a couple of cadaver dogs. Know where I can get them?"

"Cadaver dogs? What for?"

"To search your property for more bodies."

"You serious?"

"Yes, so can you help me?"

"I got two. They're old, but they can do the job. When do you want them?

"Maybe Tuesday. First, we're gonna do a drone search."

"Sounds serious. Does that mean I won't get my property back until next year?"

"I wouldn't plan anything before then. I'll call you Tuesday and let you know. If not Tuesday, then Wednesday."

After he hung up, Amy said, "Think he got the message?"

"He got it. Tell Billy Merry Christmas for me. I gotta get home before dinner."

"Wait," she said. "What was that about teenagers? How do you know they use his property?"

Pickens grinned. "I did it when I was one, before Tatum owned the property."

*   *   *

At home, Pickens found Marge in the kitchen checking the ham in the oven. She turned around. "Everything okay?"

He nodded. "Yeah, a trespasser on Tatum's property."

"You sure that was all it was?" asked Mrs. Davids, who had just walked into the kitchen.

Marge's mother was a pain in the ass when she wanted information she could use for her mystery book club meetings. She never let up.

"That's all it was."

"I don't believe you. I think it had to do with a case you two are working on."

"Marjorie, are you at it again?" said Mr. Davids as he walked into the kitchen. "It was bad enough on the cruise, but this has to stop. If you don't quit, we're going home."

Mrs. Davids' chin trembled. "You wouldn't really make us go home, would you?"

Mr. Davids gave her a stern look. "If you're not going to help in the kitchen, then go back into the living room. Now."

Mrs. Davids sighed and stomped out of the room.

"Sorry about that," Mr. Davids said.

"It's okay, Dad, she means well," said Marge. "She can't help it."

"It's that damn book club of hers," said Mr. Davids. "I'll make her a highball. It'll calm her down."

While Mr. Davids made a couple of highballs, Pickens got himself a beer from the fridge.

"Don't drink anymore after that one, JD, you'll spoil your appetite for dinner," said his mother.

Pickens held the bottle up. "Last call." He winked at Marge and took a sip of beer. "Wish me luck."

Later Pickens and his family sat down for Christmas dinner. After dessert, Sarah opened the rest of her presents. It wasn't a custom for the adults to give each other gifts.

After his parents had gone home, and Sarah was all tucked in bed, and Marge's parents had retired for the night, Pickens gave Marge her present.

CHAPTER 9

MONDAY HAD STARTED as a pleasant morning until Marge's mother woke, had breakfast, then started badgering Pickens and Marge about what they did Saturday and about Pickens' trip to Grange Road yesterday.

Pickens did his best to ignore her by playing with Sarah and taking Bailey for a walk. But Marjorie was relentless. He finally lost his patience and left the house and went to his parents.

Marge was left to take the brunt of her mother's constant interrogation. She pleaded with her father to make her stop. Marge had never had cross words with her mother and didn't want to have them now, the day after Christmas. She was fortunate that her mother was there to celebrate Christmas with her unlike the woman lying in the morgue alone on Christmas day with a mother or daughter wondering what had happened to her. It was enough to keep Marge from lashing out at her mother.

But Marge's father had had enough. When Marjorie saw the bags by the door, she panicked.

"What are those doing there?" she asked.

Mr. Davids crossed his arms. "We're going home," he said. "I warned you yesterday if you didn't stop, we'd leave. I packed everything except your pocketbook. It's in the bedroom. Get it. I'll wait for you in the car."

Mrs. Davids clutched her necklace, worried that he meant it. "You're not serious, are you?"

"Yes, I warned you, Marjorie. You ruined our Christmas and Marge's." He set his jaw.

"Get your purse, now."

"But . . ." Marjorie said.

"Now," he said.

"Well, I never," she said and stomped off to the bedroom.

Marge was dumbstruck. She'd never seen her father angry with her mother as he was then.

"You don't have to leave, Dad."

"Yes, we do. She won't quit, and it would only get worse. I'm sorry, Marge. Please apologize to JD." Sarah was behind her mother the whole time. "Sarah, I'm sorry you had to hear this. Your grandmother means well, but sometimes she gets carried away and I have to stop her." He reached out his arms. "Come give me a hug." Sarah tentatively walked to him and let him hug her.

Marge walked to him and hugged him. "I love you, Dad. I'll call Mom tomorrow."

"Whatever," he said and then picked up the bags and left the house.

Mrs. Davids came from the bedroom. Marge was about to say goodbye, but her mother gave Marge an icy stare. "Bye, Sarah," she said and left the house.

Later Pickens called. "Is it safe to come home?" he asked.

"Yes," said Marge, "they're gone."

"Gone? What does that mean?"

"Dad was fed up with Mom's questions. He packed their bags and they left. Mom's mad at me."

"She'll get over it. I bet she calls tomorrow and apologizes."

"Mom doesn't apologize. She acts as if nothing happened

and expects you to apologize. I'm not going to do it, JD. I didn't do anything wrong."

Pickens breathed a heavy sigh. He felt sorry for Marge and knew she was hurting.

"And Sarah saw the whole thing," Marge added. "She didn't understand, but I did my best to explain that sometimes adults get angry at each other." Marge went silent. "JD, are you okay with leftovers for dinner? I don't feel up to cooking."

"That's fine by me. If I knew there was a restaurant open, I'd take you out to dinner or pick something up."

"I'd rather we ate here as a family. I love you, JD."

He sensed the heartache in her voice. "Love you, too."

CHAPTER 10

TUESDAY MORNING AFTER breakfast, Pickens dropped Sarah and Bailey at his parents' house. He didn't get out of his SUV. Instead, he waved to his mother as Sarah and Bailey met her on the porch. Pickens had done it purposefully to avoid any discussion about his in-laws.

Marge had left a bit later than usual. She wanted time by herself to forget what happened the day before with her mother. Marge also wanted to prepare herself to deal with the remains of the woman in the drawer at the morgue. That woman was probably a mother and the daughter of a mother who was grieving her disappearance. The last words the woman may have had with her mother might have been harsh. The thought made Marge decide to make amends for what happened between her and her mother. She couldn't make amends for the woman's words if they needed it, but hopefully, she could return the woman to her mother.

The drive to her office was a somber one for Marge.

When Pickens walked into the office, Amy and Billy were waiting. Billy was smiling, Amy had a huge grin.

"I guess you two had a Merry Christmas by the look on your faces," said Pickens.

"I had a great one," said Billy, "and I've got a present for you."

"Billy, Christmas was Sunday, and we don't exchange gifts. You know that," said Pickens.

"Not that kind of present, JD," said Amy. "Wait till you hear what he has."

"Okay, let's have it."

"I know you wanted me to wait until today to do a drone search, but I couldn't wait," Billy.

Pickens' forehead wrinkled. "What does that mean?"

"Betty-Jean and I went to the field yesterday and did a drone search."

"You what?" said Pickens.

Billy ignored him and continued. "We did a drone search using *thermal imaging.* TI works best when there's a body, but we tried anyway. I covered the entire field then concentrated on the area where you found those remains." Billy paused and raised an index finger. "I think we found something not far from Friday's gravesite."

Pickens interest piqued. "How far from it?"

"About thirty yards. I had to keep the drone low to the ground for the camera to work. It's not perfect, and they're only images, but they could be human. It's the best I could do."

Pickens' eyes widened, and he scratched his head. He was amazed by Billy's knowledge and skills in the use of drones and search procedures.

"Whatever you say, Billy. Just show me."

Billy had already downloaded the images from his drone camera onto his laptop. He opened the file marked 'Drone Search – December 26, 2017.' "If you look closely, you'll see that the shapes in this image look more like human then animal."

Billy turned the laptop, so Pickens had a better view.

"Animals would look smaller," said Billy. "And what looks like arms and legs tell me their human."

Pickens and Amy leaned in closer.

"Looks like they could be two adults and a child, JD," said Amy, who was no longer grinning but frowning.

"Shit," said Pickens. "I hope those remains weren't put there by the same person who put the woman there. If so, we got a boneyard."

"What are you gonna do?" asked Amy.

Pickens rubbed his head. "Call Tatum and have him meet us there with his cadaver dogs. And make sure he understands not to call Nosey. What does the military say when something like this happens?"

"We got us a real cluster fuck," answered Amy.

"Yeah, a big one," said Pickens. "Good job, Billy. We'll need that search info to aid the dog search." Pickens paused. "I got an idea. We'll schedule the search for tomorrow morning. I want to bring Bailey along. He might be helpful."

"Won't he interfere with the cadaver dogs?" asked Amy.

"I'll keep him away from the dogs until after their search," said Pickens. "I'll call Tatum. Billy, any luck on a marriage license that matches the date on the ring?"

"Not yet," said Billy. "I'm still searching. I got one in the county for Charles Dernim and Amanda Wilcox. She's not the woman we're looking for. Amanda Dernim has a current driver's license, and her DOB is July 15, 1962. Makes her fifty-five now." Billy pulled up the license. "That's her photo. Want me to call her, Sheriff?"

Pickens scrutinized the license. "No, and I don't think the skeleton is hers. We'll wait until after the ME's office completes facial reconstruction. If there is any resemblance, I'll call her in the event she's a twin or a sister. Keep searching the state records."

Pickens went into his office and called Tatum.

"Bo, it's Sheriff Pickens."

"Hey, JD, I got someone putting a gate and proper signs at

the entrance to my property. I'll give your deputy a key to the lock."

"Good," said Pickens. "I need those cadaver dogs. Can you meet me at your property tomorrow morning?"

"No problem."

"I'll have my dog with me. Is that gonna be a problem?"

"As long as it doesn't interfere with my dogs."

"He'll only be there to observe. I'll keep him close by me. You don't need to search the entire property. I'll let you know where to search. And, Bo, let me remind you again, don't call Nosey and don't talk to him. Understood?"

"Understood. I got your message last time."

"See you tomorrow, Bo," Pickens said and ended the call. Next, he stepped out of his office. "We're all set for tomorrow, Billy. Amy, you ride with Billy. Bailey will be with me."

"Fine," said Amy.

"Sheriff, I also started a background search on the Baxters that Amy asked me to."

"Anything yet?" asked Pickens.

"Not much. But I just started. I figured you'd want the marriage license search first."

"You figured right. Can Amy help?"

"Um," Billy glanced at Amy. She saw his worried expression.

"I don't have the software on my laptop, JD, so I'm of no use," Amy said. She turned her head so Pickens couldn't see her wink at Billy.

"Then find something else you can do that's helpful," said Pickens.

"Would you like me to order lunch and go get it?" asked Amy.

"Smartass. Maybe you should, and pay for it, too." Amy's jaw dropped. "Just kidding," Then Pickens added, "Maybe the

ME will have something for us before the day is over. I sure hope so because I hate waiting."

"Amy," said Billy, "you can help me with the Baxters. You can start with a public records search."

"I can do that," Amy replied. "I'll start with Harley Baxter."

*   *   *

Marge knew that her entire staff had already arrived when she saw their vehicles in their designated parking spaces. She parked, checked her makeup in the mirror, got out of her car, and walked to the entrance. She greeted her office assistant and headed for the morgue.

Morgan was at the desk jotting down notes. Betty-Jean and Andy were in the lab. Betty-Jean was working on the facial reconstruction. Andy was working on DNA and soil samples.

"Looks like you guys were anxious to get a leg up on our lady," said Marge.

Morgan dropped his pen and turned. "You startled me. I hadn't realized you were here yet."

"I was anxious to get started but not as anxious as you. What are you working on?"

Morgan raised both hands. "Now don't get annoyed, Marge."

She raised her eyebrows. "Annoyed at what?"

"Remember Saturday I said I had a colleague who was a forensic anthropologist?" Marge nodded slowly expressing interest. "His name is Jonathan Vadigal. He has a Ph.D. in anthropology, archaeology, and human osteology. And has experience in all of those things. He is also knowledgeable and experienced in chain-of-evidence procedures."

"Impressive."

"I mentioned we found remains of a female in a field. He became interested and asked for details."

Marge knitted her eyes.

"I invited him for Christmas dinner and showed him the photographs from the gravesite."

"But, Tom, it's our case and he's not involved. You may have violated protocol and tainted evidence."

Morgan took a deep breath. "I know, but Dr. Vadigal is a well-respected forensic anthropologist and has worked with numerous law enforcement agencies."

"So?"

"We could always say we asked him for a consultation because of his expertise."

"Okay, I'll buy that. What did he say?"

"After reviewing the photographs, he was impressed with how we mapped the gravesite and asked to see the remains. Yesterday, I showed him them, and again he was impressed. His words, not mine. 'Not bad for novices.'"

Marge's jaw dropped.

"I know, it annoyed me too. But that's how he is. He didn't mean it negatively. It's just that he's a consummate professional and believes he's above everyone else. It's because of his experience, and you know what? He has the experience to back it up."

"Okay, so he's an egomaniac."

"That, too."

"What else did he say?"

"He inspected the remains for *adipocere*, the wax-like substance that forms in corpses." Marge nodded indicating she knew what *adipocere* was. "He wasn't surprised there wasn't any given the location, climate and the length of time for decomposition."

"Did he offer any conclusion?"

"Dr. Vadigal agreed that the remains were of a Caucasian female and that based on her bone structure she was a healthy one, possibly athletic. We extracted bone marrow and gave it to Andy for DNA. Dr. Vadigal would have taken it to his lab for analysis, but he's leaving for a dig tomorrow. He said DNA wouldn't be helpful unless we have a family member to check it against. When and if we do, we'll have the results by then. What teeth were left suggested she was in her late-thirties."

"Same as we thought. Anything else?"

"His educated guess is the remains were in the ground at least twenty years, possibly longer."

"That saves us a lot of time. At least we have something to give the sheriff. It's not much, but it's helpful. He'll find out who she was."

"And we'll have an idea what she looked like after Betty-Jean finishes with the skull."

"That, too. But let's not rush Betty-Jean. We want a good picture of who she was." Marge paused. "By the way, where does Dr. Vadigal live?"

"Pittsburgh. With the promise of a pair of prime steaks and a bottle of choice scotch, I lured him here."

Her mouth fell open. "Pittsburgh? How did he get a flight out of Pittsburgh so quick? And, Tom, you don't eat steak."

Morgan cleared his throat. "I don't. The steaks were for him and his lady friend. He was staying with her in Tampa before flying to Brazil for a dig. They drove here Christmas morning and left early this morning."

"So, this Dr. Vadigal is also a ladies' man besides being an egomaniac."

"Sort of." Morgan's phone pinged. "It's a text from Vadigal. He e-mailed a summary report as an attachment. He'll collect his fee next time he's in Florida."

"His fee? I thought . . ."

Morgan smiled. "Steaks and scotch."

"Oh." Marge's phone chirped. She took the phone from her pocket and answered. "JD, I was . . ."

He interrupted her. "We have more remains."

Marge stiffened. "How many?"

"Three sets."

"Hold on let me put you on speaker phone. I want Tom to hear this." Morgan gave her an incredulous look. "Okay, we're listening."

"Billy did a drone search on his own yesterday." He didn't want her to know about Betty-Jean being with Billy because Marge might not approve of Betty-Jean visiting the site without her or Morgan. "I'm looking at the image from the camera. I see three skulls." He paused and breathed a sigh. "And, Marge, I'm no expert, but it looks like one set might be a kid."

Marge almost said the expert had already left.

As if reading her mind, Morgan texted Dr. Vadigal that they had found more remains. He showed her the text. She nodded agreement.

"What's your plan?" she asked.

"Billy and I are meeting Tatum tomorrow morning. Tatum's bringing two cadaver dogs. Billy will use his drone to pinpoint the exact spot. It's yards from the gravesite. And I'm bringing Bailey."

"Why Bailey?" asked Marge.

"Just a hunch I have," answered Pickens, "I want him to get a dog's read on the site."

"Tom and I will meet you there. We'll stake out the location and then formulate an excavation plan. JD, won't Bailey be a distraction for the cadaver dogs?"

"No, he'll wait in my SUV until their done."

"Okay, I was going to call you and tell you what we've got so far."

"Let me have it."

"The remains were of a Caucasian female, height five-foot-seven, possibly athletic, and age thirty-five. Batty-Jean is working on facial reconstruction. She'll have something soon, and we'll have DNA results by Friday, hopefully."

"That's great. I'll give that info to Billy. He's doing a marriage license check. So far, he only turned up one name in the county, but she's still alive. He's searching the state. Once Betty-Jean finishes the reconstruction, have her e-mail me a copy."

"I will."

"If only we had Dr. Vadigal," Marge said to Morgan.

Morgan pointed an index finger. "Hold on, got a text from him."

Marge muttered, "*Please.*"

"He's canceling his flight and delaying the dig. He'll be here tonight. He wants to help." Morgan laughed. "Same fee."

"Does he like barbecue?"

"We can ask."

CHAPTER 11

PICKENS GAVE BILLY the information about the skeletal remains. As Billy entered the data into the case file and Amy researched Harley Baxter in public records, Pickens paced in his office and deliberated a decision. After reaching a conclusion, he slammed his fist on the desk, stepped out of the office, and into the bullpen.

"How would you guys feel if I brought in outside help?" he asked.

Amy and Billy stopped what they were doing and froze.

"You mean the Feds?" said Amy.

She looked at Billy, who was shaking his head.

"Don't, JD," she said.

Pickens waved his hands. "Not the Feds. Mitch Hubbard."

Amy breathed a sigh of relief.

"He was a homicide detective with the experience we need." He held his hand up. "I know he's retired, but that's good. It means he'll have the time to work with us. We got four sets of remains that we have to identify, and that means a lot of casework. Besides, I bet he has the contacts with resources that we don't."

"As long as the Feds don't get involved, it works for me," said Amy. "He was at the scene Friday." Amy pursed her lips and pointed a finger. "He also knows the Baxters."

"You thinking he may provide some background on them?" asked Pickens

"Exactly," Amy replied.

"His wife is friendly with Mrs. Baxter, and you're suspicious of her," said Pickens. "Mrs. Hubbard might help if Mitch asked her."

Amy nodded.

"Does that mean you're okay with Hubbard working with us?"

"Yes." Amy looked at Billy. He nodded. "So is Billy."

"Good, I'll call him."

"You may want to call and alert the county commissioners, JD."

"I'll do that later."

Pickens dialed Hubbard.

"Mitch, it's JD Pickens, I need your help."

'Oh, oh, sounds like you got a big problem with those remains. Okay, what can I do for you?"

"We found three more sets of remains. Same location. I need that expertise of yours."

"You got it. Anything you need; I can't wait to get back in the saddle again. What do I do?"

"We're going out to Grange Road tomorrow morning. Can you meet me there?"

"Just give me a time."

Pickens knew he had to drop Sarah off at his parents, pick up Billy at the office, and then go out to Grange Road. He'd need a good hour. "Nine-thirty. If I'm not there, wait by the gate. I'll alert my deputy to give you access."

"I'll be there. Anything else?"

Pickens scratched his chin. "Yeah. I'd like to know more about the Baxters, especially Harley. Any problem with that?"

"You don't think they're involved do you?"

"It's just a hunch. My deputy has a feeling about her. Trust me on this."

"Okay, but they're still in Vale and won't be back until after the New Year. I'll talk to Donna and see what she thinks. She and Harley are good friends. Other than hunting, I don't have much contact with the woman. We both can't stand Wiley, but we tolerate him because of Harley."

"Thanks, Mitch. I'll see you tomorrow."

CHAPTER 12

WEDNESDAY MORNING, MARGE waited for Morgan and Vadigal. She was expecting a late-forties, good-looking, sophisticated professorial individual. But when Dr. Vadigal entered the morgue, he was anything but. At some point, he may have been in his forties and maybe good looking. But the Dr. Vadigal she was looking at looked more like an Old West prospector. He wore crumpled trousers tucked into weathered boots and held up by suspenders and a shirt that looked like the top from a pair of long johns. His beard was mostly gray and large enough to hold a bird's nest. His head was covered by a khaki colored twill hat that looked like it had been stuffed inside his pocket.

Marge extended her hand. "Dr. Vadigal, I'm Dr. Davids. It's nice to meet you."

Vadigal held her hand gently in his. Marge thought he was going to kiss it.

"The pleasure is all mine, Dr. Davids." Vadigal smiled.

A flirt too, Marge thought. "Would you like to change into coveralls?"

Vadigal grinned. "I'm fine, Dr. Davids. These are my working clothes."

Marge lifted her eyebrows.

"I get the same reaction wherever I work. Most people

expect someone who spends their days behind a podium at a university. That's not me."

Morgan grinned and said softly, "He cleans up nicely."

"I heard that, Dr. Morgan." Vadigal grinned. "I would like to see your lab before we go out to the site."

"Sure," Marge said, "but it's not like your lab in Pittsburgh. We're a small county with a limited budget."

Vadigal smiled. "I can assure you, Dr. Davids, I rarely work out of that lab. Most times I share space in a funeral home or a table outside under a canopy if I'm lucky." Vadigal held his hand out. "Shall we?"

Marge smiled. "Follow me." She led him in and went right to the morgue. "This is it," she said.

"Impressive, Dr. Davids. Can I see your facial re-construction area?"

"Right this way."

Vadigal followed her. Morgan followed behind them. Betty-Jean was working on the reconstruction.

"Betty-Jean Carr is doing the reconstruction," said Marge.

Betty-Jean nodded and continued working.

Dr. Vadigal walked over near the criminalist. "Narrow the cheeks," he said. "Her mandible and zygomatic bones suggest her face was thinner."

Betty-Jean glanced at Marge. Marge nodded affirmative.

"Much better," said Vadigal. "Dr. Davids, where do you do lab work?"

"That would be Andy's table next door. Care to look?"

"Please."

Marge led him to where Andy Doring was doing lab work. Vadigal looked in but didn't enter.

"I'm impressed, Dr. Davids. I look forward to working with you and Dr. Morgan. But could we use first names? I'm not used to being addressed as Dr. Vadigal by colleagues."

"I'd prefer we stayed on a professional name basis if you don't mind."

Vadigal hunched his shoulders. "Works for me," he said. "Shall we go out to the site now, Dr. Davids?"

"I hope you don't mind riding in a coroner's van," Marge said.

"Won't be the first time. I've ridden on horses and donkeys to get to a site."

Marge turned to Morgan.

"I might learn to like this guy, Dr. Morgan," said Marge.

"He's a likable guy and grows on you," said Morgan.

They left the morgue and got into the van. Morgan let Vadigal sit up front next to Marge. He sat behind them on a makeshift seat that the criminalists used. It would be an uncomfortable ride for him.

"What was it before it became a coroner's van?" asked Vadigal.

"An EMT bus," replied Marge. "It made the conversion easier."

When Pickens and Billy turned onto Grange Road, the new gate was open, and he proceeded to the site. Marge and Hubbard were already there. Bailey sat up front with Pickens in the SUV. The drone was in the rear. Pickens drove past Hubbard's truck and parked behind the coroner's van. Pickens and Billy got out, and Billy removed the drone from the SUV.

Introductions had already been made. Marge introduced Pickens to Vadigal, and Pickens introduced Billy to everyone.

"That your dog in the SUV?" asked Vadigal.

"Yes, sir, his name is Bailey."

"Mind if I say hello? I make it a point to say hello to every dog at an excavation site," said Vadigal. "Been doing it since 9/11, starting at Ground Zero."

"Be my guest. He doesn't bite."

Vadigal walked over to Pickens SUV, placed his hand on Bailey's head and petted him. He let Bailey lick his face.

"Good dog," he said and walked back by Pickens. "I can tell he's a special dog. I'm glad you brought him along."

Pickens looked at Marge. Her eyebrows contracted as did Pickens. Both wondered what he meant.

"He is. He's special to my daughter," said Pickens.

Tatum got the crates with the cadaver dogs off his truck, let the dogs out, and leashed them.

"Female's name is Grace," Tatum said, "male's name is Max. Both are chocolate labs. I trained them myself. Ain't done a search in a while, but they know what to do. Just be patient, they move kinda slow."

"We're in no hurry, Bo," said Pickens. "Billy, show Dr. Davids the search you did."

Billy handed Pickens the drone, opened his laptop and pulled up the search. He angled the monitor so Marge, Vadigal, and Morgan could see it.

"I crisscrossed the property," said Billy. "I scanned a three-mile area. I even searched the lakeshore." He pointed to the monitor. "Those are the only sites of possible human remains I captured."

"You covered three miles?" said Tatum. "Hell, my property ain't that big. If you did, you covered ground that I don't own. And the farther you go into my property, you take a chance on getting bogged down. Soil don't drain well. First time I was out there, needed a tow truck to pull me out. Don't think anyone would be dumb enough to bury bodies that far out. You covered more than enough property, boy. And I ain't taking a chance on getting my dogs bogged down in the mud."

"You won't need to, Mr. Tatum," said Vadigal. "I'm betting there aren't any more remains. If your dogs can point us to the spot, we'd appreciate it."

"We walking out there or riding?" asked Tatum.

"We'll take the van," said Marge. "JD, you can take Mitch in your SUV. We'll go as far as the open gravesite. That okay with you, Dr. Vadigal?" He nodded affirmatively. "Then let's go. Tatum, you bring your dogs in your truck. But no one goes past the open gravesite."

Hubbard got in Pickens SUV. Billy put the drone in the rear and climbed in the backseat. The convoy then proceeded to the gravesite.

"What do you think of Vadigal, JD?" asked Hubbard.

"Reminds of the cook on that sixties era television series *Wagon Train.*"

"Yeah, me too."

When the convoy reached the gravesite, everyone got out of their vehicles. Billy retrieved the drone.

"Billy, send your drone out and pinpoint the location so Tatum can send his dogs out," said Marge.

Billy fired up the drone and let it fly over the area. When it reached the site where the remains were, he made the drone hover over it.

"Okay, Tatum, let's see what your dogs can do," said Marge.

Dr. Vadigal watched Marge as she took command of the situation. He let her be in charge since it was her investigation.

Tatum released the dogs. They slowly walked the area. It seemed like they were barely able to walk. Age had taken a toll on them, most likely arthritis of the legs made it difficult to walk. But the dogs lumbered on. They stopped at the open gravesite and sniffed.

The image from the drone camera showed how close the dogs were to the remains. When the dogs were approximately fifteen-feet from the spot where the remains were, they froze and refused to advance any closer.

"Go dogs," shouted Tatum. But the dogs just sat. "Damn dogs, go, I said." But they refused to move.

"Easy, Tatum you'll spook them," said Hubbard.

"Spook them? I'll show them who's boss," said Tatum.

"A moment please, Mr. Tatum?" asked Vadigal.

Tatum's head jerked back. "A moment? What the hell does that mean?" he said.

"Easy, Bo," said Pickens. "Hear what the doctor has to say."

Tatum threw his hands up.

"Thank you, Sheriff," said Vadigal. "Mind if I let your dog out?"

Pickens hunched his shoulders. "If it will help, go ahead."

Vadigal opened the door to Pickens SUV and let Bailey out. He rubbed the dog's head.

"See if you can get those dogs to move, Bailey," Vadigal said. "We need your help."

The dog looked at Pickens. "Go ahead, boy," said Pickens.

Bailey walked over to the cadaver dogs. The dogs laid down. Bailey barked and pointed to the field. The dogs didn't move. Bailey took a step forward. Grace yelped. Bailey stopped, turned around and sat.

"What the hell?" said Tatum.

"Just as I thought," said Vadigal. "The dogs won't move. They sense *evil* and want no part of it. Don't blame them."

"So, what do we do?" asked Hubbard.

"We'll let Billy guide us," answered Vadigal. "When we reach the spot, we'll map it out. That okay with you Dr. Davids?" He was putting Marge back in command.

"Yes," she replied. "Just the three of us. JD, you, Mitch, Billy, and Tatum stay here."

Pickens raised his palms up. "You're the boss, Doc." Marge shook her head.

Billy lowered the drone and watched his monitor. When he did, the dogs started barking.

They're afraid of what's there," said Vadigal. "Let's go, and slowly."

Marge, Morgan, and Vadigal started toward the spot where the drone hovered.

When the three reached the exact spot, Billy called out, "You're standing on top of the remains."

The three doctors stood side by side. Marge felt an icy chill.

"Did you feel that?" she said.

"I did," said Morgan. "Like a sudden change in temperature."

"It's because you're standing where something horrible happened," said Vadigal. "*Evil* was here. Let's map the site and get away from here. We can do an excavation another day."

"I agree," said Marge. "JD," she shouted, "in the van, there is a stack of yellow flag stakes. Bring them to me."

"Got it," Pickens replied and opened the back door to the van. He saw the stakes and grabbed a batch. Next, he walked out to the doctors and handed the stakes to Marge. Pickens rubbed his arms. "Damn it's cold here," he said, then turned and walked away.

The doctors mapped out the area using Billy's thermal image as a guide. When they finished, they joined the others.

"What next?" asked Pickens.

"We'll come back tomorrow or Friday to do excavation," said Marge.

"We'll need a backhoe and an excellent operator," said Vadigal.

"Any idea where we can get one, JD?" asked Marge.

"I do," said Tatum. "Best damn backhoe operator in the county. Used him myself. When do you want him?"

"How soon can you get him?" asked Marge.

"If he ain't out of town, tomorrow. Latest, Friday morning. He owes me a favor. Hold on, I'll call him."

"I noticed you called the sheriff by his first name," said Vadigal. "Are you two . . . ?"

"He's my husband," Marge answered.

"Not only a small county but a close-knit one too."

"Yes," Marge said, "especially when it comes to law enforcement."

"Interesting," said Vadigal. "Reminds me of a town in Tennessee where I did a forensic analysis on a serial murder case."

Tatum reached into his jacket pocket, took out his phone, and dialed. He stepped away, so his conversation was private.

When Tatum finished his call, he said, "Tomorrow morning, but not before ten. I'll meet him here."

"Thanks, Tatum," said Marge.

"My pleasure, Doc. Say, JD, four dead bodies in less than a week. I'm gonna have to shut down permanently."

"Hold on, Bo. After tomorrow, I'll work in town." Pickens looked at Marge. "Unless the ME needs me to, I'll cancel my deputy and remove the crime scene tape."

Marge turned glanced at Vadigal.

"We'll work from the office, too," said Vadigal. "You can have the backhoe operator fill in the holes."

Tatum smiled. "Good. Say, Doc, how long have those bodies been in the ground?"

"Quick guess, at least twenty years," Marge replied.

"Before my time," Tatum said. "I bought the property fifteen years ago. Got a good deal. Weren't no road, just a beaten path. I graded it and called it Grange Road." His eyes sparkled. "Now the property is Tatum's Hunting Resort and Lodge."

Tatum then loaded the dogs. The doctors got into the

coroner's van. Pickens, Bailey, Hubbard, and Billy got into the
SUV. Pickens stopped by Hubbard's truck and let him out.

"You doing anything the rest of the day, Mitch? I could use
your help at the office."

"Donna doesn't expect me until dinner time." Hubbard
grinned. "I'm all yours."

Hubbard got into his truck, and the convoy left Grange
Road.

CHAPTER 13

BACK AT THE office, Pickens and Hubbard set up a murder board. Across the top, they drew in four heads. They labeled the lone female—*Victim #1*. The others—*Victims 3-4*. Under number one, they put COD-BFT. Under 3-4 COD-UNK.

"It's a start," said Hubbard. "We'll add more as we go."

"After tomorrow," said Pickens, "we'll add COD for the other victims. If Donna can help us, maybe we'll learn more about number one from Harley."

"Hopefully," said Hubbard. "Billy and Amy learn anything yet?"

"I found some stuff on Harley," said Amy who stood behind them. "Marriage certificate lists her maiden name as Gasden."

"That's her previous married name," said Hubbard. "Baxter is her second marriage. Donna might know her original maiden name. I'll ask her."

"In the meantime, I'll try Harley Gasden."

"Good," said Pickens. "Billy, you got anything yet?"

"Thirty-five marriages in Florida on December 12, 1986. It'll take a while to narrow the search."

"Have you tried missing persons?" asked Hubbard.

Billy's face reddened. "I didn't think to," he said.

"Try it," said Pickens. "Maybe there will be one from this county."

"You have a missing person's file, JD?" asked Hubbard.

"If we do, it's boxed up in a storage locker somewhere. When we moved to new quarters, a lot of records got lost. Twenty years ago, I was still in college."

"How about your predecessor? Think he might know?"

"Might, if he can remember. Shit, I hate having to ask him. There's no love lost between us."

Hubbard put a hand on Pickens' arm. "I'll go with you. Maybe he'll talk to me."

"Maybe. I'd call him, but he'd probably hang up on me. If you got time tomorrow, we could go out to his place after I return from the excavation. Unless you care to join me at the site?"

"No thanks, I'll wait here. Maybe I can help Amy or Billy."

*　*　*

At the medical examiner's office, the three doctors were in the morgue preparing to go over the remains of the unknown female.

"If you don't mind, Dr. Davids," said Vadigal, "I'd like to spend some time observing the facial reconstruction. You two are capable of handling the remains."

"That's fine. Maybe you can offer advice to Betty-Jean."

Vadigal nodded and went to join Betty-Jean while Marge and Morgan would get the remains, finish their analysis, and entered the information into the file.

Vadigal pulled open the door to the room where Betty-Jean sat at a computer working on the image of a woman's head, smooth and without distinct features, on her screen.

"Hello, Dr. Vadigal," said Betty-Jean. "Did you find more bodies?"

Vadigal grinned. "We found remains, but we have to unearth them. How is the reconstruction going?"

Betty-Jean pointed at her monitor. "Slow, I've got a lot to grasp with this software, but I'll get it."

Vadigal reviewed her work. "Are you using the latest version of that software?"

Betty-Jean hunched her shoulders. "The only one we could afford. Is there a better version?"

"Hmm," Vadigal said and rubbed his chin. "There is. Have you had lunch yet?"

"I was going to eat at my workspace. Why?"

"Is there a place in town that sells computer monitors?"

"No Walmart or Best Buy, but there's a small computer store not far from here."

"Save your work, then let me use your computer."

Betty-Jean glanced around as if looking for someone's approval.

"Don't worry. I know what I'm doing."

She saved her work, logged out of the software, and stepped aside.

Vadigal brought up the internet and did a Google search. He typed in the software's manufacturer and searched for the current version of the facial reconstruction software. He purchased it using his account and downloaded the current version.

"Next time you log in, you'll have the newer version."

Betty-Jean gasped.

"Now, let's go to lunch. Come on. I won't bite."

Betty-Jean grabbed her purse and followed him.

Vadigal walked by Marge and Morgan and momentarily stopped.

"Dr. Davids, I'm taking this young lady to lunch. Is that okay?"

Marge tilted her head. Betty-Jean hunched her shoulders. "Sure," she replied.

Vadigal and Betty-Jean left. They stopped at Leroy's restaurant. She ordered a pulled pork sandwich. He ordered a small portion of ribs. After lunch, Betty-Jean drove to Marcin's Electronics on Dugan Street in downtown. Vadigal purchased a thirty-four-inch LED monitor and paid with his credit card.

"Now you'll be able to see your work," he said. "That tiny screen you have doesn't cut it." Betty-Jean smiled.

They drove back to the ME's office. Betty-Jean carried the box with the monitor into the building and took it to her workspace.

"What's that?" asked Andy.

She grinned. "A thirty-four-inch LED monitor. Dr. Vadigal bought it for me."

"Holy crap. I'll help set it up."

"Thanks. He also updated my facial reconstruction software. Wait until you see what I can do now."

While Betty-Jean and Andy set up the monitor, Vadigal joined Marge and Morgan.

"I hope you don't mind, Dr. Davids, I bought your criminalist new software and a larger monitor."

"You what?" said Marge.

"If she's going to work on the new remains, she'll need the current version and the larger monitor will aid in the visual results. If I'm going to help you, you need the better tools. Don't worry. I paid for them."

Marge was dumbfounded.

"Better get used to it, Marge," said Morgan. "He's known for doing it."

"You should have asked me first," she said.

"Would you have said no?"

Marge threw her hands up.

"I thought so." Vadigal smiled.

With assistance from Dr. Vadigal, Betty-Jean finished the facial reconstruction. She emailed the image to Billy. Pickens added it to the murder board. On a hunch, Marge had her print a copy for her.

Later, when Marge arrived at Pickens' parents' house, she sat in the kitchen with her mother-in-law. Over a cup of coffee, Marge decided to ask her mother-in-law if she would look at the image.

"Jeanette, remember Thanksgiving you mentioned a woman you met at a church social?"

"The one whose daughter just up and left?"

"Yes." Marge took out the image and set it on the table in front of Mrs. Pickens. "Does this look anything like her?" Marge had asked Betty-Jean if she could age the image. With the help of Vadigal, the image was aged to look like an elderly woman.

Mrs. Pickens picked up the image and studied it.

"Let me get my cheaters," said Mrs. Pickens. She went into the living room and came back wearing glasses. She picked up the image again. "Much better." She extended her arms, brought the image up close, and looked from left to the right of it. "It's possible," she said. "It looks a little like her. Why?" Marge hesitated. "Is she?"

"No, we're trying to identify a woman, and I thought she might be that woman's daughter."

Mrs. Pickens cupped her mouth. "That means that woman is dead, doesn't it?"

"Yes," replied Marge. "Is there any chance you could identify the woman you met? It would be very helpful to me and JD."

Mrs. Pickens removed her glasses and took a sip of coffee. "I don't think so. I haven't seen her since. I'm not even sure she's a member of our parish."

"Have you ever seen her in town?"

Mrs. Pickens looked down in thought. "No. She may not even live in Creek City." Mrs. Pickens scratched her chest. "She might live in Warfield and belong to a parish there. Have JD look into it."

Marge grinned. "I will. Thanks, Jeanette."

Mrs. Pickens smiled and placed a hand on Marge's hand. "You're welcome. You and JD will find out who this mystery woman is."

Later that evening, Marge told Pickens about her conversation with his mother. She piqued his interest.

"Mom thinks this mystery woman lives in Warfield?" said Pickens.

"No. She said the woman might. Have you had any luck identifying the remains?"

"Not yet. We're working on it. Why?"

"Take the image and go to Warfield and ask at churches there. You might get lucky."

Pickens shook his head. "Are you suggesting I don't know how to do my job? Or are you becoming a sleuth like your mother? By the way, how is she?"

Marge took a deep breath. "I don't know. I haven't called her. We've been busy with remains in case you've forgotten," she snapped.

"I haven't forgotten. I've been busy, too." Pickens held a palm up. "Okay, I'll ask Mitch to do it since he lives near Warfield and may go to church there. I'll have him be discreet. No sense in alarming anyone."

"I'm sorry I snapped at you."

"It's okay. We're both a little on edge. I need to talk to Sarah."

"About Bailey and those cadaver dogs?"

"Yes."

In the living room, Sarah was playing with Bailey. Pickens and Marge joined them.

"Daddy, Bailey told me about what happened today," said Sarah.

Pickens and Marge weren't surprised. They knew that Sarah was capable of communicating with creatures large and small. She'd inherited the gift from her maternal great-grandmother who was a renowned veterinarian and was able to do the same. It wasn't the first time Sarah used that ability with Bailey. She once used it to help Pickens solve the mystery of a serial killer.

"What did he tell you?" asked Pickens.

"He said the other dogs didn't want to go near the spot Mommy wanted them to. He didn't want to go either. Bailey said something *bad* had happened there. Something *evil*. You're not angry with him, are you, Mommy?"

"No, sweetheart. I'm not. Neither is Daddy."

"Good. Bailey said he doesn't ever want to go back to that awful place."

"He won't have to," said Pickens.

CHAPTER 14

THURSDAY MORNING WHEN Pickens arrived at the office, Mitch Hubbard and his wife were getting out of Hubbard's truck.

"Hey, Mitch, what brings you here this early? We're not going to talk to my predecessor until after lunch."

"I know," Hubbard replied. "Donna wanted to get an early start talking with Amy about Harley. She's got something she has to do this afternoon."

"Amy is already here, so it won't be a problem." Pickens rubbed his chin. "Say, Mitch, I got something else for you to do. I've got this image of an elderly woman. Would it be possible that you could show it at the churches in Warfield? Discreetly of course."

"You think this woman might be related to the remains from Friday?"

"It's just a hunch. Marge gave me the idea."

Before Hubbard could respond, Mrs. Hubbard interrupted him. "May I see it, Sheriff?"

Pickens hesitated. "She's good with faces," said Hubbard.

Pickens handed the paper to Mrs. Hubbard. She unfolded it and studied the image carefully.

Mrs. Hubbard lightly tapped the image. "I've seen this

woman at the Senior Center. She plays bingo on Wednesdays. She's there with her husband. They keep to themselves. Come to think of it, they weren't there yesterday."

Pickens' eyes bulged.

"Don't be surprised, JD. Donna runs the Senior Center."

"More like I'm a paid volunteer," said Mrs. Hubbard. "I'm good with seniors. It's what I did for a living."

"Maybe Donna should ask about the woman," said Hubbard.

"If you could spare a female deputy, Sheriff, she could go with me next Wednesday."

Pickens breathed a sigh. Marge's hunch might pay off. And he had someone who could help determine if the mystery woman was related to the woman in the morgue.

"Sergeant Amy Tucker would be perfect," said Pickens. "In fact, she's the same person you'll be speaking with about Harley Baxter."

"Wonderful, I can't wait to meet her. If you don't mind, I'll hang onto this picture." Pickens nodded. Mrs. Hubbard put the picture in her purse.

"What are you gonna do while your wife talks to Sergeant Tucker, Mitch?"

"I'll hang around until you need me," replied Hubbard.

"Why don't you come with me to Grange Road. Your wife can go home when she's finished, and I'll take you home."

Hubbard glanced at his wife.

"Go ahead, Mitch. I know you want to."

"You sure, Donna?"

Mrs. Hubbard narrowed her brows. "Do I look like I'm not?"

"Uh," said Pickens, "why don't I introduce you to Sergeant Tucker."

Hubbard took a deep breath. Pickens led them into the office and called to Amy.

"Sergeant Tucker, you got a minute?"

Amy's jaw dropped surprised by Pickens' formality. "Yes, Sheriff Pickens."

Pickens nodded at Mrs. Hubbard. "This is Mrs. Hubbard, Mitch's wife. She came to talk to you about Harley Baxter."

Mrs. Hubbard extended a hand. "It's Donna, Sergeant Tucker. I'm pleased to meet you. What's your first name?"

Amy looked at Pickens. He tilted his head.

"It's Amy." She shook hands with Mrs. Hubbard. "I'm pleased to meet you. We have a conference room where we can talk. Would you like a cup of coffee?"

"I'd love one." Mrs. Hubbard addressed the two men. "You boys go do whatever you had planned. Amy and I will be just fine. And, Mitch," Hubbard stepped back, "I can drive myself home."

Hubbard shook his head. Then he and Pickens left.

In Pickens' SUV, Hubbard said, "Donna sort of takes charge. I just let her be. Makes for a good marriage."

"I know what you mean. Marge does it sometimes."

"JD, you never said what your predecessor's name was."

"It's Bascom," Pickens said and clenched the wheel so tight it almost broke. "Floyd Bascom. If it weren't important, I'd stay clear of him."

Hubbard noticed that Pickens stilled clenched the wheel.

"I take it there's no love lost between you," said Hubbard.

"You could say that. I wouldn't be surprised if the bastard was drunk and didn't remember me." He loosened his grip. "We'll see."

Pickens was grateful that Hubbard let the conversation go, and the ride out to Grange Road was a silent one.

When Pickens turned onto Grange Road, his deputy opened the gate and waved to him. Marge was already at the site with Vadigal and Morgan. Dr. Vadigal was talking to the backhoe operator, a solidly built man by the name of Dixon. Pickens drove his SUV to the site and parked, and he and Hubbard got out.

"Looks like they started without us," said Hubbard. "What's the professor telling the backhoe operator?"

"Probably giving instructions. I told Tatum to tell the operator that the professor discovered hundred-year-old Indian remains and the ME's office was helping excavate them. I don't want the operator telling people we're digging up new remains."

"Good thinking, JD."

Pickens and Hubbard watched as the backhoe, under Vadigal's directions, started excavating. As the bucket dug, Vadigal would signal when to stop and start. Dixon emptied each bucket of dirt in a pile to the side and away from the grave. When Vadigal decided the grave was deep and long enough, he signaled for the operator to stop and back away.

Vadigal got down into the grave and carefully inserted a probe. When he hit something solid, he used his hands and scraped away the dirt. What the probe hit was inches below.

"Can you scrape away six inches more?" he asked the operator.

Pickens wasn't sure, but he thought he saw the operator spit tobacco juice.

"Ain't gonna be easy," said the operator. "I can if you want me to, but you have to watch the bucket to be sure I don't go too deep. Whenever you're ready, Doc."

Vadigal climbed out of the grave and signaled for Dixon to lower the bucket. As soon as the bucket entered the ground, Vadigal signaled to stop.

"That's deep enough," he said.

Dixon carefully scraped the bucket over the surface until it reached the end of the grave. Then he scooped up the dirt and emptied the bucket on the pile of dirt.

"Need me to dig anymore, Doc?" asked Dixon.

"No, you did fine. Thanks for your help. When we're finished, you can fill this hole and that other one."

Dixon backed the backhoe away from the gravesite.

Vadigal, Marge, and Morgan climbed into the grave and finished unearthing the remains.

"Two adults and a child," said Marge. "Someone took the time to bury them near each other."

"As if they were a family," said Morgan.

"No wonder the dogs didn't want to approach the site," said Vadigal. "Someone *evil* put them here. I saw this once before." Vadigal shook his head. "It was done by a family member. That's what *evil* does."

The three doctors completed the unearthing and loaded the remains into body bags and the coroner's van.

"We're done," said Vadigal. "You can fill in the holes, Mr. Dixon."

Dixon fired up his backhoe and turned it around. It was equipped with a blade for bulldozing. Dixon leveled the gravesites. When he finished, he loaded it onto his truck and left.

"You need me anymore, Doc?" said Tatum.

"No, we're done," answered Marge. "The field is all yours."

Marge waved to Pickens, and then the three doctors got into the van and left.

"Guess we're done here, too," said Pickens. "Let's go talk to Bascom. "Hey, Bo, we're done here, too. I'll tell my deputy he can leave. Remember, Bo, don't say anything about what took place here. Especially, not to Nosey."

"I told you I wouldn't, JD. You don't need to remind me."

"Just making sure. Happy New Year, Bo."

"Same to you."

Pickens and Hubbard climbed into Pickens SUV and left. When they reached the gate, Pickens told his deputy to remove the crime scene tape and take off.

* * *

At the sheriff's office, Amy and Mrs. Hubbard were in the conference room. Amy had started the interview.

"So, tell me, Amy, why is JD really interested in Harley Baxter?"

"Actually, I'm the one who is interested," replied Amy.

"Why?"

"Call it my suspicious nature, but last Friday she seemed upset when we discovered the remains. It made me think she might know something about them."

"Does it have to do with this picture JD gave me?" She reached into her purse, took out the sheet of paper, and unfolded the image.

Amy studied the image. It wasn't the one she had. Hers was the younger version.

"I haven't seen that picture. The one I have is of a much younger woman. We think it may be of the victim we found."

Mrs. Hubbard folded the picture and put it back in her purse. "May I see it?"

Amy set a file on the table, opened it, took out the original picture of the mystery woman, and handed it to her.

"Could be the same woman only much younger. You think Harley might know her?"

Amy wrinkled her forehead. "It's a possibility," Amy said and steered the conversation back to Harley Baxter. "How long have you known Harley?"

"Since middle school. We lived in Apopka. In high school,

we hunted quail together with our dads. We went to FSU together. Harley majored in education and I majored in social work. After graduation, Harley took a teaching position in Warfield. She taught elementary school and a few special classes in middle school. Warfield's education budget was tight, but Harley enjoyed being a teacher." Amy listened with intense curiosity. "She met her first husband, Carl Bishop, there. He was a high school teacher. They didn't have children because Harley couldn't conceive. Her students were her children. She loved them all as if they were hers." Mrs. Hubbard paused and wiped a tear. "Harley and Carl had thirty-three happy years together until Carl had a stroke that killed him. She met Wiley Baxter years later. Harley was lonely, and Baxter seemed like someone she could share the rest of her life with." Mrs. Hubbard shook her head. "I'm not so sure he is. Mitch and I put up with him because of Harley."

Learning that Harley Baxter was a school teacher was a surprise to Amy, and that Mrs. Hubbard had known Harley since middle school was enough to satisfy Amy about Harley but not Wiley Baxter. She'd wait and see if Billy turned up something on him.

Amy breathed a sigh of relief. "Not about Harley, but about the woman whose remains we found. If Harley recognizes her when she sees the facial reconstruction image, she might have taught the woman in elementary school."

"Or her children," said Mrs. Hubbard.

"There's that possibility," said Amy. "If she did, then at least we'll have a name for the victim. Harley might even know what happened to her." Amy realized she wasn't making herself clear. "Not what killed her, but about her disappearance."

"It's certainly a possibility. Unfortunately, Harley is still in Vail and won't be back until Tuesday. I'll call her early Wednesday morning and set up a meeting with her. But it will have to be at my place. Harley won't come here. Wiley won't let her."

Amy wasn't surprised. She suspected something was troubling about Baxter.

"I can do that," said Amy. "After we talk with her, we can have lunch together before going to the Senior Center."

"Excellent idea, Amy." Mrs. Hubbard checked her watch. "I've got time for a quick bite. Would you like to have lunch with me? My treat."

Amy smiled. "Excellent idea, Donna."

CHAPTER 15

PICKENS TURNED INTO the long narrow driveway that led to Floyd Bascom's house. As he and Mitch got out of the SUV, Bascom's wife was walking toward her car.

"JD Pickens, what the hell do you want?" yelled Mrs. Bascom.

Like her husband, Mrs. Bascom was in her mid-sixties. Age hadn't been kind to her. She had once been a good-looking woman, but fifty years of being married to Floyd Bascom had taken a toll on her. She was still a heavy smoker and drinker. It was probably what kept her sane after putting up for years as the wife of a bigoted and heartless sheriff.

"Ain't you caused enough trouble for Floyd by forcing him to retire?"

Pickens hadn't forced Bascom into retirement. The citizens of the county did by not re-electing him.

"Just want to talk to him, Mrs. Bascom."

"About what?"

"Something that happened over twenty years ago," Pickens replied.

She crossed her arms and tilted her head. "He's around back chopping wood." The woman smiled. "Be careful he don't chop you up, Pickens. Now move your fucking vehicle, so I can go into town."

Pickens climbed into his SUV and made room so Mrs. Bascom could drive past him. He gave her a phony salute. She gave him the finger.

Pickens got out of the SUV.

"I take it she doesn't love you, JD."

"Feeling's mutual."

The two men walked around to the back of the house. Floyd Bascom was chopping wood. As soon as he saw Pickens, he stopped and held the ax above his head.

"Well if it ain't JD Pickens. You son of a bitch, what do you want?" Bascom held the ax in both hands and stood ready for a fight.

Pickens instinctively put his hand on his gun. Hubbard did the same but realized he didn't have one and crossed his arms instead—ready for a fight.

The three men eyed each other like gunfighters on the streets of Dodge City sizing up their opponent—waiting to see who was first to draw.

"That your muscle, JD?"

Hubbard stood calmly like a Mafia bodyguard.

"Looks too old for one. Plus, he ain't carrying."

Pickens raised a palm. "Just want to talk, Floyd. I ain't here for trouble."

Bascom slammed the ax into the chopping block and held onto the handle.

"About what?"

"About a case you may have worked over twenty years ago."

"Twenty years ago? Hell, you think I remember that far back? I barely remember what happened last week." Bascom pointed to his forehead. "Missus says I got early onset dementia. Whatever the hell that means."

"Show him the picture, JD, maybe it will help him remember," said Hubbard.

"What picture?" said Bascom.

"This one," said Pickens and took the paper with the image on it from his pocket, unfolded it, walked over and handed it to Bascom. "We found remains of a woman on Bo Tatum's property last week."

"Bo Tatum?" Bascom interrupted. "That son of a bitch still alive?"

Pickens took a deep breath. He was starting to get frustrated. "He is. Take a look at the picture. See if you recognize her. Maybe she was a missing person's case."

Bascom reached down and picked up a pack of cigarettes off the ground, took one out, and lit it. He took a long drag and exhaled.

"I think better with one of these." Bascom studied the picture. "Nope, can't say that I recognize her." He took another drag and exhaled. "Hold on. There was a case of a missing woman in Warfield. That was over twenty years ago. I didn't work the case. It was Chief Nolan's case. You remember him, don't you? He died after you disbanded his department."

"I didn't disband it, Floyd. The city council did and put the sheriff's office in charge of law enforcement."

"Same thing," said Bascom with a mean look in his eyes. "Too bad Nolan is dead. You could ask him."

"Any suggestions where I might find the case file?"

Again, Bascom took a drag and exhaled. "You could try the city clerk's office. She might know." Bascom's nostrils flared. "Or you could ask that girl you replaced Nolan with. Maybe their kind can find them, but I doubt it."

Pickens' face turned an angry red. "What kind is that, Bascom?"

Bascom put his foot on the chopping and pointed to his boot. "That kind."

Pickens' nostrils flared. "You're a son of a bitch, Bascom.

For your information, her name is Sergeant Dunne. And those women you referred to as girls, are decorated veterans, and each has more intelligence than you and Nolan combined. Neither of you could hold a candle to them."

Sergeant Dunne was in charge of the Warfield office and was the second female that Pickens hired after he was elected.

"Fuck you, Pickens. We're done talking." Bascom grabbed the ax handle. "Get off my property before I throw this ax at you."

Pickens crossed his arms and stood his ground—daring Bascom to try.

After a moment where nothing happened, Pickens said, "Let's go, Mitch, we're done here."

Pickens and Hubbard backed away until they were out of range of Bascom's throwing ability. Then they turned and walked away. Behind them, they heard the sound of wood splitting and Bascom's cackle.

"Seems like you're about as welcome as a zit on a teenager's face," said Hubbard.

"Dumb son of a bitch," said Pickens.

When they were on the road, Hubbard asked, "What do you want me to do tomorrow, JD?"

"How about I call Sergeant Dunne and tell her you'll meet her at her office tomorrow. Then you and she can go to the clerk's office and ask around if anyone knows where the old files are. If you locate them, you and Dunne can go through them. If not, I could use your help at the office."

"Anything I should know about Sergeant Dunne?"

Pickens grinned. "Yeah, she's a no-nonsense law enforcement officer, and you have to call her Sergeant Dunne."

"A hard nose for formality," said Hubbard.

"Something like that, but I trust her with my back and have on occasion. Like I said, if you don't find the files, come to my office. We can work the murder board, add whatever Amy learned from Donna, and whatever Billy found."

"That kid has a way with the keyboard, doesn't he?"

Pickens shook his head. "Yeah. He does things I don't want to know about."

Hubbard grinned.

"You hungry, Mitch?"

Hubbard smiled. "Am I hungry?" He looked at his watch. "I ain't had lunch. There's plenty of time until dinner—damn right I'm hungry."

Pickens smiled. "Bartley's Country Store is on the way. How about we stop there?"

"Oh yeah, beer and a sausage dog on the porch. That's what country living is all about, boy."

"It sure is, Pa," said Pickens. Both men laughed.

After they ate, Pickens dropped Hubbard off at home and then drove to the ME's office.

When Pickens entered the morgue, Marge, Morgan, and Dr. Vadigal each hovered over a set of the recent remains. Pickens thought they looked like the *Three Amigos* dressed in similar garb and gesturing as they talked to each other.

"Anything yet?" Pickens asked.

Marge abruptly turned.

"What are you doing here?" she said. "I thought you were going to see Sheriff Bascom."

"Done. I took Mitch Hubbard with me and drove him home. I showed the image to his wife. She thinks she knows who that elderly woman is." Pickens smiled. "I did what you asked, and Amy is going to Warfield Wednesday to investigate." Again, he smiled. "So, you got anything for me?"

"All three were Caucasian," said Dr. Vadigal.

"Two females and a male," said Marge. "One female was an adult and one was a child. All three were Caucasian."

"The child wasn't more than ten years old based on the *tibia* and the higher number of bones, whereas the adults have only two-hundred and six—which is normal for an adult," said Morgan. "Plus, her wisdom teeth weren't fully developed."

"Based on the density of the adult bones," said Dr. Vadigal, "both were in their early forties and if you look at the spines, there is some indication arthritis had started."

Pickens felt like he was taking machine gun fire as the doctors fired answers at him. He rubbed the back of his head.

"We found striations on the rib cages of all three, which suggests they were stabbed with a sharp object and not just once," said Marge.

The thought of a child being brutally murdered sickened Pickens.

"Whoever did this, did it out of rage. What kind of person does something like that?" Marge asked.

"Someone sick in the mind," said Vadigal. "And someone extremely *evil.*"

Pickens winced. "Any idea how long they were buried?"

"Over thirty years," said Marge, "based on Dr. Vadigal's estimation."

"Betty-Jean will start facial reconstruction tomorrow," said Morgan.

"When you have a report, send it to Billy," said Pickens.

"We will," replied Marge.

"Uh . . . I gotta go." said Pickens overwhelmed with information. "I'll see you tonight, Marge." He exhaled and rubbed the back of his head as he left.

Later, when Pickens arrived at the office, Amy told him about her interview with Mrs. Hubbard, and her upcoming trip to Warfield Wednesday to meet with Harley and then visit the Senior Center.

"Sounds like you've got a good plan," said Pickens. "Mitch

is going to Warfield tomorrow to meet with Sergeant Dunne. They're going to check with the city clerk's office for old missing persons files. He'll call if he finds anything."

"Sounds like you've got a good plan too," said Amy.

Pickens smiled. "Yeah, I do. I stopped by the morgue. The doctors have started examining the remains. Two adults and a ten-year-old child." Pickens breathed. "Betty-Jean should be able to start facial reconstruction soon."

"Have her do the child first and send Billy a copy of the image. I'll take it with me Wednesday and show it to Harley."

Pickens furrowed his eyebrows.

"Harley was a schoolteacher. Maybe the child was one of her students."

"I'll call Marge and ask her to do it. Billy, you have anything to add?"

"I did another search on Harley based on the information Amy gave me. She's clean. Everything Mrs. Hubbard told Amy checks out."

"Good. If Mitch learns anything tomorrow, we'll update the murder board with what we have. After you finish in Warfield, Amy, we'll add that info." Pickens frowned. "It's almost New Year's Day, and we might have to wait until next year to finish our investigation. Shit."

CHAPTER 16

FRIDAY MORNING, MITCH Hubbard met Sergeant Mia Dunne at her office in Warfield. She was everything Pickens had described. African-American, wearing a bright, clean, white blouse, both trousers and blouse neatly pressed, and spit-polished shoes.

At Sergeant Dunne's insistence, they took her patrol car to the city clerk's office.

Vonti Johnson, an African American whose smile warmed the heart of many a man, greeted Dunne and Hubbard. She dressed in casual clothes since it was Casual Friday.

"Sergeant Dunne, it's good to see you again. You and hubby planning a New Year's celebration?"

Dunne smiled. "Not this year. It will just be our family. What about you?"

"Same here. What can I do for you?"

Dunne pointed her thumb at Hubbard. "This is Mitch Hubbard. He's helping Sheriff Pickens. We need to look for some old case files from twenty years ago."

Johnson grinned. "I know who Mitch is. He's been in here before with his wife." She nodded at Hubbard. He nodded back. "Twenty years ago? I'm not sure we have any. That would be during Chief Nolan's time, and he wasn't much for keeping records. If there are any, they'd be in the storage locker the city maintains."

"Any chance we could look in the locker?" asked Dunne.

"Sure, let me lock up here, and I'll go with you."

"Thanks, Mrs. Johnson. We'll take my patrol car."

Johnson smiled as did Hubbard. "If you say so."

Johnson locked up the office, and Dunne drove the three of them to the city's storage locker. Johnson unlocked the door and raised it up.

"If there are any files, they'd be in the right rear corner. You're welcome to look," Johnson said.

Dunne nodded and then she and Hubbard made their way to the rear of the locker and rummaged through a bunch of boxes searching for old case files.

Twenty-five minutes later, Hubbard said, "Doesn't look like there are any files. It was a waste of time. Any suggestions, Sergeant Dunne?"

"Not that I can think of. I wasn't around back then. How about you, Mrs. Johnson?"

"Me? I wasn't around either. You could ask one of the old police officers if you could find one."

"We could if there are any alive and they'd talk to us," said Dunne.

"Another waste of time," said Hubbard. "I don't expect they'd help with a sheriff's investigation. I'll call Sheriff Pickens and tell him we didn't find anything. Thanks, Mrs. Johnson, you were very helpful."

"Yes, thank you," said Dunne.

They stepped out of the locker; Johnson put the door down and locked it. Dunne drove Johnson to her office and Hubbard to his vehicle.

"Thanks for your help, Sergeant Dunne."

Dunne gave him a three-finger salute, and Hubbard drove off. He called Pickens on his cell phone and advised him of his visit with Sergeant Dunne.

*   *   *

At the morgue, the doctors wrapped up their analysis of the remains. Marge sat at the desk and typed up her report. She pulled up a case file and entered the information on the three sets of remains. When she finished her report, she e-mailed a copy to Billy.

Morgan busied himself getting the remains into drawers. Vadigal helped Betty-Jean with her facial reconstructions.

After Betty-Jean finished the one of the child, Vadigal okayed it and then she e-mailed the image to Billy. When Betty-Jean was well on her way toward completing the adults, Vadigal left her alone.

"Dr. Davids, I guess I'm no longer needed here. It's been a pleasure working with you and Dr. Morgan." He bowed his head. "I bid you a fond farewell and a Happy New Year."

Marge smiled. "Same to you, Dr. Vadigal. It's been a pleasure working with you. Are you off to a dig?"

Vadigal grinned. "Not yet. I'm going to celebrate the New Year with a lovely friend of mine in Tampa. If I leave now, I can be there this evening. Dr. Morgan, thanks for accommodating me."

"You're welcome," said Morgan. "Come back and see us anytime."

Vadigal nodded. "I will, and Dr. Davids, if you ever need my help, feel free to call."

Not expecting he could, Marge took a chance and asked, "Can you help me get DNA results in a hurry?"

"I can," said Vadigal. "Overnight your samples to my lab in

Pittsburgh. I'll call and tell them to expect them." He smiled. "You'll have the results by the end of next week. Is that soon enough?"

Marge nodded. "It certainly is."

Dr. Vadigal smiled and left.

At the sheriff's office, after Hubbard had called, Pickens stood in front of the murder board pondering it. Amy walked over and joined him.

"Any thoughts, JD?"

Pickens shook his head. "Not a one. We have four sets of remains and not a clue as to who they belong to." He rubbed the back of his head. "Four bodies in less than a week. Damnedest thing. Maybe Tatum was right, and he should shut down permanently. Worse yet, I may have to call Nosey and give him a scoop."

"You sure you want to do that? It might tip the killers off."

"And what? They'll flee? I don't think so, but it might make them nervous."

"And nervous people make mistakes," said Amy.

"Mistakes are what help us," Pickens replied. "Call Nosey and tell him to be here Tuesday morning. I'll give him just enough to ruffle some feathers."

"But not enough to jeopardize my talk Wednesday with Harley and those other people."

"Don't worry. I wouldn't do that. You might learn enough . . ."

Just then Hubbard arrived.

"I thought we'd work the board together, JD. You starting without me?"

Pickens shook his head. "No, Mitch, we were talking about giving that nosey reporter a scoop about finding the remains. Just enough to warn the perpetrators we're on to them."

"Good idea. I did that several times myself. Causes perps to make mistakes which is what you want."

"Something like that," said Pickens.

Billy walked over with Marge's report and the image of the child.

"I just got these, Sheriff." He handed Pickens both. "I've put them in the computer."

"Thanks, Billy." Pickens handed the image to Mitch. He shared it with Amy while Pickens read the report.

"Billy, print me a copy of the image," said Amy. "I'll take it with me when I speak with Harley. She may have taught the girl." Billy walked away, printed another copy, and handed it to Amy.

Pickens handed the report to Mitch.

Hubbard scanned it. "Thorough, especially the ages of the remains and the length of time in the ground." Hubbard clenched his jaw and shook his head. "But multiple stabbing of a child, now that's sick."

"It is," said Pickens. "We're looking at a thirty-year-old murder, and I'm not asking Bascom about it. Not after yesterday."

"I agree," said Hubbard. "Let's update your board and wait until Wednesday after Amy and Donna talk in Warfield."

"Might as well, and I'll wait until Wednesday morning to give Nosey his scoop. For now, we're done here unless something happens. Everyone goes home and celebrates the New Year. We'll start again on Tuesday. You got plans for tomorrow night, Mitch?"

Hubbard exhaled. "Unfortunately, yes. Donna's making me go with her to the New Year's Eve party at the Senior Center."

"Lucky you," said Pickens. "Marge and I are celebrating at the annual neighborhood party. How about you, Amy?"

Amy smiled. "I'm celebrating."

"So am I," said Billy then hesitated. He wasn't about to say with who.

"Um-hum," said Pickens.

Saturday night, Pickens and Marge attended the neighborhood New Year's Eve party at the Klugerman's house. Sarah and Bailey were at home with a neighbor's teenage daughter watching them.

At the stroke of midnight, everyone kissed and sang *Auld Lang Syne*. Pickens and Marge stuck around until one in the morning, then said Happy New Year to their neighbors and went home.

Once in the house, Pickens paid the sitter, tucked Sarah in with Bailey beside her, and then went to their bedroom, undressed, got into bed, and turned the light off.

"So, how was it working with Dr. V?" asked Pickens.

"It was enlightening. I learned something, and Dr. Vadigal learned something. He's considering making me his protagonist in his next novel." Pickens' mouth opened and Marge continued. "He's also a writer of mystery novels based on forensic anthropology." Marge gave him a coy smile. "Are you going to talk all night or fool around?"

"What do you think?"

Monday, Pickens and his family had New Year's Day dinner at his parents' house. While Pickens and his father watched bowl games, Marge helped his mother in the kitchen.

"Have you spoken to your parents, Marge?" asked Mrs. Pickens.

"I have. I called this morning and wished them a Happy New Year."

"How is your mother?"

Marge cleared her throat. "Fine. She didn't mention what happened Christmas, and neither did I." Marge exhaled. "It's typical of my mother."

Mrs. Pickens put a hand on Marge's arm. "Mothers have a way of forgiving and forgetting." Marge smiled. "I don't mean to pry, but did I help with that picture of the woman I met?"

"You're not prying. Yes, you did. The woman lives in Warfield. JD is sending someone to talk to her Wednesday."

"Good." They heard shouting from the living room. "It sounds like a game is over. Let's call the boys in."

Marge smiled, then called Sarah and the men in for dinner.

CHAPTER 17

WEDNESDAY MORNING, AMY left for Warfield to meet with Donna Hubbard and Harley Baxter. Pickens called Noseby the reporter and told him to come to the office. He had a scoop for him.

Pickens no sooner hung up the phone when Noseby walked into the office.

"That was quick," said Pickens.

Noseby smiled. "I've been scouting your office ever since Christmas Eve. I was across the street waiting for your call." He took out his pad and a pen. "I'm ready for my big scoop."

Without mentioning particulars or Amy's visit to Warfield, Pickens told Noseby that human skeletal remains had been found on Tatum's property. His office had not yet identified who they belonged to and was actively investigating them as a homicide.

"That's it, sheriff?" said Noseby. "Nothing more?"

Pickens crossed his arms and grinned. "That's it, Nosey, take it or leave it. When I know more, I'll call you."

Noseby shook his head. "It's Noseby, Sheriff."

Pickens tilted his head and smiled. "Whatever," he said. "You want it?"

"I'll take it. But promise me you'll call me when you know more."

Pickens grinned. "Absolutely."

Noseby put his pad in his jacket pocket and left.

Later, when Amy turned into the Hubbard's driveway, there was a car parked near the house. It had a bumper sticker that read, *Guns don't kill. People do.* Amy suspected the vehicle belonged to Harley Baxter. She had hoped to meet with Mrs. Hubbard before Harley arrived so they could strategize their conversation. Now Amy would have to go with her gut feeling and be blunt when questioning Harley.

Amy rang the doorbell and waited.

Donna Hubbard opened the door and greeted her.

"Sergeant Tucker, good morning."

Amy nodded.

"Come in. Harley is in the den. I took the liberty of telling her why you wanted to talk to her, and I mentioned I had told you about her past. I hope you don't mind."

Don't mind? Amy said to herself. *Of course, I do.* Then she realized that Mrs. Hubbard was the wife of a retired homicide detective, and by association probably knew how to question a suspect. But Harley wasn't a suspect, and she wasn't even a person of interest. When they go to the Senior Center, Amy would have to take the lead.

Amy waved her off. "That's fine. It'll help when I question her."

"Good. Introduce yourself while I put up a fresh pot of coffee. I have muffins that I'll heat in the oven. I'll join you when they're ready."

Amy smiled, entered and went to the den. Harley sat in a leather chair fiddling with her cell phone.

"Harley, I'm . . ."

The woman raised an index finger. Amy waited. And waited. Amy was surprised that, with her age and background,

Harley had joined the rude crowd that was oblivious to their surroundings and those around them and continuously texted on their phones.

Amy sat in the other leather chair with the file folder she had with her and waited. Harley continued texting. Amy got up and paced around the room, stopped and admired the trophies in the trophy case—quail hunting for Donna and target shooting for Mitch. She moved on to the pictures of game birds on the wall.

Harley continued texting. Amy started to feel like an expectant father waiting to hear news of his firstborn.

Mrs. Hubbard entered the room carrying a tray of warm muffins, cups, and a carafe of coffee.

"Harley, stop that," said Mrs. Hubbard. "You can do that later. Don't be rude. Sergeant Tucker doesn't have all day."

Harley stopped texting and looked up. It didn't take much for Amy to notice that Harley had recently had an emotional event and was wary. She looked from left to right as if expecting someone and her eyes narrowed as if in confusion.

Mrs. Hubbard set the tray on the coffee table.

Harley glanced at Amy. "I know who you are, Sergeant Tucker."

Amy decided to be direct and avoid Mrs. Hubbard taking control of the situation. "Then you know why I'm here," said Amy.

"You want to question me about that body you found. Am I a suspect?"

"No, Harley, she just—" said Mrs. Hubbard before Amy interrupted her.

"I'll take it from here, Mrs. Hubbard." Mrs. Hubbard frowned then poured three cups of coffee, took one and sat. "You're not a suspect, Harley."

"Then what am I?"

Mrs. Hubbard was about to respond, but Amy cut her off again.

"I just want to ask you some questions, that's all."

"About what?"

Amy exhaled. She was starting to get frustrated. Amy had brought a folder with three images of the dead woman. The original and two aged. Amy opened the file folder and took out the image of the dead woman. "Do you know this woman?" Amy handed the image to Harley.

"Should I?" asked Harley before looking at it.

Mrs. Hubbard didn't know about the reconstructed image of the dead woman only the one of the woman they planned on meeting at the Senior Center. But it was her idea to have Amy talk to Harley at her house.

"Just look at it, Harley," said Amy.

Harley studied the picture. She tilted her head left, then right and scrunched her nose.

"She looks familiar. I don't think she was ever a student of mine, but she may have been a parent of one." Harley continued to study the picture. Suddenly as if a light bulb turned on, Harley cupped her mouth and gasped. "I know her," she said. "I taught her children. Jeremy and Jenny Wilson."

"Do you remember her name or anything about her?" asked Amy.

"Is she the body you found?"

Amy wasn't about to mince words. She needed answers.

"It wasn't a body. We found skeletal remains."

"Oh my God," cried Harley, "so that's what happened to her."

Both Amy and Mrs. Hubbard's mouths fell open.

"What happened to her?" asked Amy.

"Those poor children. I helped counsel them after their

mother disappeared. It was over twenty years ago. The police investigated it as a missing person case. Her husband first said he thought she was on a business trip. When Chief Nolan questioned him, he admitted that she took numerous business trips and suspected she had a lover somewhere. But I never believed his story. Neither did her mother. I met this woman numerous times, and I can honestly say she was devoted to her children and would never run off without them." Amy stopped making mental notes and feverishly made written ones. "That idiot Nolan believed the husband and dropped the case."

Amy reached into the folder and took out the image of the elderly woman.

"Do you know this woman?" she asked and handed Harley the picture.

Harley took a quick look and said, "Yes, that's Mrs. Henderson, Mrs. Wilson's mother. She lives here in Warfield. I occasionally see her."

"We're going to talk to her at the Senior Center after lunch," said Mrs. Hubbard.

"Then you had better take me," said Harley. "I know her, and I should be the one to tell her that her daughter is dead. Otherwise you'll frighten her, and trust me she'll have a heart attack."

Mrs. Hubbard looked to Amy.

"Please, Sergeant Tucker. But you have to tell her it's only a possibility."

Amy indeed wasn't about to be the cause of an elderly woman's death, and she could use all the help she could get.

"Okay," said Amy. "We can't make a formal ID based on a facial reconstruction photo." Then, on the off chance, Amy reached into the folder and took out the image of the child Billy had given her. "Do you recognize this child?" she asked and handed the image to Harley.

Harley took one look, dropped the photo, cupped her mouth and gasped.

"What's the matter, Harley?" said Mrs. Hubbard.

"I . . . I . . . I know her," stuttered Harley. "I'm good with faces, but sometimes I can't remember names. This one I remember. It was Celia. Such a sad child. I taught her in elementary school." Harley crossed her hands over her chest. "Please don't say she's dead."

Amy hesitated. Mrs. Hubbard shot Amy an angry look. Another photo she didn't know about. Amy ignored her.

"Please," said Harley. "She was in my class. I remember. It was thirty years ago. Then suddenly one day, she stopped coming to class. After a week, I went to her house. There was no one home and no sign that anyone lived there. I called the police, and they checked." Harley took a deep breath. "The whole family just disappeared and were never heard from after that." She shook her head. "Strange, isn't it?"

"It is," said Amy. "I'm sorry to say we found her remains and probably those of her parents."

Harley made the sign of the cross. "What about her brother? Did you find his, too?"

Amy gave her an incredulous stare. "Her brother? No, just hers and her parents. Do you think he may be alive?"

"Maybe, but if he is . . . Where?"

"Can you describe him? I know it was thirty years ago, but we might be able to create a sketch of him, then age it."

"I don't know. I wish my late husband were here. He'd be able to. Carl taught him in high school. That was years before the school was shut down and consolidated with the county school system. After that, Carl taught what they now call middle school." Harley grinned.

Amy listened patiently as Harley went on about how she met her late husband and what Amy learned from Mrs. Hubbard.

Amy picked up on the mentioning of Harley's late husband, not her first husband, and how Harley's disposition had improved, unlike Harley's wariness when Amy first met her.

"Anyway," continued Harley, "I'm rambling. The boy was sixteen at the time. Carl said he had troubles, as did most teenagers." Harley tilted her head and gazed up as if trying to remember something. "If you could locate yearbooks from the old high school, his class picture might be in one of them. I might be able to recognize him."

"Where would we get old yearbooks?" asked Amy.

"How about the library?" said Mrs. Hubbard. "They might have some."

"It's worth a try, Sergeant Tucker," said Harley. "If you'd like, I could check."

Amy had enough on her plate with talking to the parents of the mystery woman—which would be more of notification of death than a conversation. She had done a number of death notifications during her career, but not one where there was no body, just twenty-year-old skeletal remains. It would be quicker if Harley checked the library, and maybe it would be easier if Harley helped with the death notification since she appeared to have a bond with the parents.

"That would be helpful, Harley."

Mrs. Hubbard checked her watch. "It's about time we left for the Senior Center. Harley, why don't you join us? We can discuss how to approach those people."

Amy wondered if Harley's husband allowed her to be away from home so long.

Harley curled her lip. "Those people have names, Donna. Virginia and Gerald Henderson. And, yes, I'd be happy to join you."

Before the tension in the room got any worse, Amy spoke. "I'd better call Sheriff Pickens and update him." She stepped away, called Pickens, briefed him on what she'd learned, and said she'd give him a full report when she was finished in Warfield and returned to the office.

After her call, Amy followed Mrs. Hubbard and Harley to the Senior Center.

* * *

Right after the reporter left, Mitch Hubbard strolled into the office. He pointed his thumb over his shoulder as if hitchhiking.

"Who was that guy?" Hubbard asked. "He had his fists high over his head like *Rocky* on the steps in the movie." Hubbard shook his head.

Pickens smiled. "That was Nosey the reporter. I gave him something to write about. I didn't give him details, just enough for him to consider it a scoop."

"Well, he was happy. I'd swear he was humming the tune from the movie."

Pickens laughed. "I'm waiting to hear from Amy."

Hubbard bit his lip and shook his head. "Don't get your hopes up high, JD. Harley might not be helpful."

"Why? Didn't Donna say she would talk to Harley?"

"She did, but Harley's in a bad situation. The vacation in Vale didn't go well. Baxter not only couldn't control his mouth, but he couldn't control his drinking. He embarrassed Harley the whole time they were there."

"That must have been terrible. What did Harley do?"

"She's staying with us until she can get her own place. Harley's filing for divorce. She's already contacted a lawyer."

Pickens shook his head. "What a shame. I feel sorry for Harley."

"Me too. So where are we at?"

Pickens walked over to the murder board. "We have four unknown victims, one from blunt force trauma, three from multiple stabbing, and no suspects. Not much to go with. Any suggestions?"

Hubbard scratched his chin. "If Amy gets anything from Harley, we might have something. And if Donna and Amy get something from that couple at the Senior Center, we may have the identity of the mystery woman."

"Hopefully. Maybe I should put Amy's name on the board since everything hinges on what she learns." Both men grinned.

"Why don't we start with what we have," said Hubbard. "Make two big circles and inside each one, put smaller circles representing the victims. At least it's a start."

"Good idea," said Pickens. "Once we hear from Amy, we'll add whatever she's got."

Pickens erased the board, picked up a marker, and was about draw a circle when his phone rang. It was Amy calling.

"Did you learn anything from Harley?" Pickens asked.

"And how," replied Amy. "Harley was a trove of information." Amy gave him a summary of what she learned about the mystery woman and the child. "I'll fill in the details when I finish here."

"Okay," said Pickens. "I gave Nosey his scoop."

"Did he buy it?"

"Oh yeah, without a doubt. See you later."

Hubbard waited to hear what Pickens had learned.

"You were wrong about Harley, Mitch. She identified our mystery woman, the elderly couple and the little girl. Amy will give us a detailed report later. Meanwhile, we've got something to add to the board."

Pickens drew two circles, labeled one *mystery woman* and the other *mystery family*. In the woman's circle, he drew a head and labeled it *Wilson*. In the second circle, Pickens drew four heads and labeled them *unknown*. In the fourth head, he wrote *son* and a question mark.

When he finished, Pickens put the marker down and stepped back to admire his handiwork.

"What do you think, Mitch?"

"Terrible artwork, but it's a good start. Except for one thing."

Pickens raised his eyebrows.

"Now you have two cases to work." Hubbard looked around the room. "You don't have the manpower to work them." Hubbard smiled. "Fortunately, I'm an experienced detective." Hubbard's smile widened. "You have to hire and deputize me."

Pickens jaw dropped.

"Don't worry. I'm cheap. Just keep me in food and an occasional beer. But don't tell Donna about the beer. We got a deal?"

Pickens grinned and shook his head. "I thought I already deputized you." He extended a hand. "Deal."

They shook hands then stood in front of the murder board and pondered their next step.

"Let's start with Billy searching the names Amy gave you," said Hubbard. "Later, she can add more."

"While Billy is doing that, I have a good idea for us." Pickens smiled. "Let's go to lunch. The cases aren't going anywhere, and we need Amy's full report."

"Works for me."

*   *   *

At the Senior Center, Mrs. Hubbard introduced Amy and Harley to her assistant, then they ordered lunch. Amy had to settle for meatloaf, mashed potatoes, and collard greens. It was the only thing on the menu. They filled their trays and sat in the rear of the dining room at a table for five.

"Wednesdays, we have a busy lunch crowd since it's bingo day," said Mrs. Hubbard.

"Oh look," said Harley, pointing to the entrance. "That's

Mr. and Mrs. Henderson. We're in luck. Let's wave them over before they order lunch."

"Maybe we should let them have lunch first," said Mrs. Hubbard.

"Nonsense," said Harley. "It would be better if we talk to them before they ate lunch. Wait here, and I'll go get them." Harley excused herself, got up, and left the table.

"Do you think it's a good idea to talk to them before lunch, Sergeant Tucker?" asked Mrs. Hubbard.

"It's probably better that we do. We don't want to spoil their lunch. It might make them ill."

Harley returned with the Hendersons. All three were smiling. Mrs. Henderson frowned when she saw Amy.

"Sergeant Tucker, meet the Hendersons," Harley said to Amy who then stood. "Of course, you both know Donna Hubbard."

Mrs. Henderson smiled at Mrs. Hubbard. "It's good to see you, Donna." Mrs. Hubbard smiled. Mrs. Henderson wrinkled her nose as she looked at Amy. "Sergeant Tucker, are you here to arrest me?"

Amy's head snapped back.

"She's just kidding," said Mr. Henderson. "We're pleased to meet you, Sergeant Tucker. Please, sit down."

"Please join us," said Harley. "We'd like to talk to you."

Mrs. Henderson's gaze focused on Amy. "But we haven't ordered lunch yet," she said.

"I'll order it for you," said Mrs. Hubbard. "Please sit down."

Amy stood and pulled out two chairs that were between her and Harley. Mrs. Henderson turned to her husband. He tilted his head.

"Might as well," said Mr. Henderson, "since Donna's buying."

Mrs. Henderson looked around her as if expecting someone or something. She breathed deeply then sat as did her husband.

"Is there a reason why you asked us to join you, Harley?" asked Mrs. Henderson, "other than just lunch?"

Mrs. Hubbard was standing near the meal line and looked back at the table. Amy nodded, signaling for her to hold off ordering lunch.

Harley hesitated.

"There is, isn't there?" said Mrs. Henderson. "We've known you a long time, Harley. You were there for Jeremy and Jenny, and you've been there for us. Just be honest, please."

Harley placed her hand on Mrs. Henderson's.

"Mrs. Henderson," said Amy. "I'd like to talk to you. That's why Harley asked you to join us."

Mrs. Henderson's lips trembled. "About what?"

Amy reached into the folder and took out the image of the mystery woman as she would have looked today. Harley glanced at Amy and shook her head. Amy ignored her and handed the picture to Mrs. Henderson.

"Do you recognize this woman?"

Mrs. Henderson took a quick glance at the picture and shook her head. "No, should I?"

Mr. Henderson snatched the picture from his wife. "Let me see it." Mr. Henderson studied the picture, moving it closer to his eyes and then away. "Hmm," he said, "looks to me like a younger version of you, sweetheart." He pointed to the nose. "See she has a nose like you do and her chin could be yours."

Mrs. Henderson grabbed the picture. "Let me see that. No. She doesn't look anything like me." Suddenly her face paled. "Oh my god, you're right she does." She looked closer at the image. "That's Annie, that's my Annie." She dropped the picture and glanced at Amy. "Did you find her, Sergeant Tucker? Tell me, please. Where is she? Is she all right?"

Amy winced at Mrs. Henderson's rapid fire of questions.

Mrs. Henderson covered her mouth with both hands. "She's dead, isn't she? Don't lie to me. She's dead, isn't she, Sergeant?"

Amy dreaded the moment. All law enforcement officers did. No amount of training and experience could prepare someone for it. As an experienced grief counselor, Amy dealt with the emotional grief of family members under challenging circumstances, but she didn't like it. People reacted differently. Some broke down, and some, like the elderly, were stoic. Which one would Mrs. Henderson be? Amy made direct eye contact with Mrs. Henderson so the woman could see the sincerity in her eyes.

"I'm sorry to say she is." Amy wondered why law enforcement used that phrase. It could be interpreted that you were sorry because you were responsible for what happened. But Amy felt it was better than the alternative, 'I'm afraid she is.' Afraid of what? Afraid because—it was your fault?

Amy steeled herself for the questions that routinely followed.

"When did you find her body? Where did you find it?" asked Mrs. Henderson.

The worst of the questions that were always asked.

"The Friday before Christmas. In a field not far from here."

Amy dreaded the next two.

"How did she die and how long has she been dead, Sergeant?"

Amy glanced at Harley. Harley had tears in her eyes. She would be no help to Amy. Amy could say *blunt force trauma to the head* or *a fractured skull*. Neither would be dealt with lightly by the dead woman's parents. But *fractured skull* sounded better than *blunt force trauma*—which she would have to explain.

"Her skull was fractured. She was killed over twenty years ago." Amy waited to see how they would handle her response.

Mrs. Henderson took a deep breath, and her eyes went cold and hard.

"I knew she didn't up and disappear and leave her children behind," said Mrs. Henderson angrily. "I never believed that cockamamie story her husband told." She pointed a finger at Amy. "He killed her, and you better arrest him and give my Annie justice. You hear me, Sergeant Tucker? You better do it."

"Easy, Virginia," said Mr. Henderson. He put his arm around his wife. "You'll give yourself a heart attack. I'm sure Sergeant Tucker will investigate. Won't you, Sergeant?"

Mrs. Henderson brushed his arm away. "Don't tell me to take it easy, Gerald. I don't want an investigation. I want that bastard who killed our Annie arrested." Mrs. Henderson started to sob. "Don't you understand what I went through all those years?"

"I do, and I went through them too. But we don't want to rush to judgment for our grandkids sake."

"Grandkids?" said Mrs. Henderson. "When's the last time we heard from our grandkids? They've forgotten all about their mother and wanted me to forget about her, too. But I never did."

Mrs. Hubbard waved to Amy. Amy shook her head so Mrs. Hubbard would know to forget lunch.

"Can we see her, Sergeant Tucker, please?" asked Mr. Henderson.

Fortunately for Amy, Harley recovered from her grief and said, "Gerald, you and Virginia don't want to see her body. It's best you remember Annie the way she looked the last time you saw her."

"Maybe we should forget lunch and bingo and go home, sweetheart? I'm not in the mood for either," said Mr. Henderson.

Amy hoped they would. She also wasn't in the mood for lunch.

"Maybe we should," replied Mrs. Henderson.

Mr. Henderson stood and helped his wife out of her seat.

Without another word, the Hendersons turned and walked away. Amy felt sorry for them.

"I've lost my appetite, how about you?" asked Harley.

Amy breathed a sigh. "Same here. I think I'll go back to Creek City. Thanks for your help, Harley."

"I don't think I was much help, but I'm glad I met you. If you need any help, feel free to call me."

"I will. I'll say goodbye to Mrs. Hubbard." Amy got up, walked over to Mrs. Hubbard, thanked her and said goodbye.

It was going to be a long drive back to Creek City.

CHAPTER 18

WHEN AMY WALKED into the sheriff's office, Pickens, Hubbard and Billy were huddled around Billy's desk like three guys hanging out at the water cooler discussing the bowl games and Monday morning quarterbacking.

Still carrying a heavy heart, Amy approached them.

Pickens was the first to notice her. "Welcome back. How'd it go?"

Amy shrugged. "It ended up being a notification."

"Oh man," said Hubbard. "I dreaded doing them and don't miss it."

"I could have done without it," said Amy as she glanced at the murder board. "Is that Sarah's artwork?" Hubbard and Billy laughed. "I hope you're better at diagraming plays, JD."

"Ha, ha," said Pickens. "Very funny. We updated the board with what you gave me. Anything you want to add?"

The lighthearted moment eased Amy's wariness. "Put Celia for the girl's name and age ten, and age sixteen for the boy." Pickens picked up the marker and added it to the board. "Now, erase mystery woman and put Anne Wilson. Also, add twins Jeremy and Jenny ages ten." Pickens did it.

"Anything else?"

"Might as well add Virginia and Gerald Henderson, Wilson's parents."

Pickens added the names. "Now we divide and conquer. Two cases, two investigations."

"I want the lead on the Wilson case," said Amy.

"Since you're up to date on it, you got it. Mitch and I will handle the unknown family case. And, Amy, I want Sergeant Dunne brought up to date and involved." Amy nodded. "Mitch will act as a consultant on both cases."

"I thought I was a deputy," said Hubbard.

"You're now an unpaid consultant. It's a position that I don't need approval for from the commission."

"Works for me. And speaking of Sergeant Dunne, she's chummy with the Warfield city clerk. Maybe she could ask the clerk to search old property records, utility records, tax rolls, even voter registrations."

Pickens and Amy raised their eyebrows.

"What? You've never worked a cold case before?"

"Just one," replied Pickens. "The file is on my desk buried under other files. I haven't looked at in two years and may never look at it again."

"Novices," said Hubbard. "I always get novices. I'll have to teach you a thing or two."

Pickens frowned. "Fine, but can you help me find a lead or two?"

"A lead or two? JD, you've got a treasure chest of leads." Pickens' head jerked back. Hubbard looked behind him at the murder board. "Help me turn this thing around and get me a piece of chalk."

Billy handed him a yellow chalk stick.

"Now, pay attention while I list your leads. First, we put *Unknown Family* on the left side and then *Identified Woman* on the right." Hubbard wrote the information as Pickens and his deputies eagerly waited to see where he was going. "Now, in the center we put *Commonalities*."

"Commonalities?" said Pickens. "What do the cases have in common?"

"Pay attention, and you'll learn," replied Hubbard. "The first commonality we have is . . ." Hubbard wrote a name on the board.

"Tatum?" said Pickens. "What's he got in common with the victims?"

Hubbard shook his finger. "Both sets of remains were found on his property and were buried there before he owned it. Which means the killers knew about the access road."

"Which means," added Billy, "they were familiar with the area and probably from here."

"Very good, Billy." Hubbard wrote *suspects local* under each case. "Now we come to Harley. She's going to be central to the investigations."

"Because she was familiar with the children of the victims and their parents. And the grandparents," Amy added.

"So, we add *familiarity* next to Harley," said Hubbard.

"Which reminds me of something I forgot to ask Harley and those parents. What year did the victims go missing?" said Amy.

"And if Harley can remember," said Billy. "then we have an approximate TOD."

Hubbard nodded. Pickens stepped back, amazed at how his deputies were coming up with leads.

Hubbard wrote TOD on the board. "And we have COD."

Pickens was about to say *blunt force trauma* but realized the causes were different.

"*Brutal homicide*," said Amy. "Possibly *vindictive*, too."

Hubbard wrote both on the board.

"Now back to Harley. If she could remember the names of

other students and their parents from both cases, we'd have names of people to talk to about the victims. More leads." Hubbard wrote *information*.

"Let's not forget colleagues and known associates," said Pickens. "What kind of work did Wilson do?"

"Hold on," said Billy and pulled the file up with the information gleaned from what Amy had told him. "She was an audiologist. Her office was less than a block from her husband, Daniel Wilson's office. He was an ENT specialist."

"Excellent," said Hubbard and added *Audiologist* to the board. "Wouldn't hurt to check for former associates. No pun intended, but she might have heard something she shouldn't have." No one laughed.

"Which might provide a motive," said Amy.

"Possibly," said Hubbard, "but let's hold off on a motive for now."

"What about suspects?" asked Billy.

"What about them? Anyone have any suggestions?"

"Spouse or family members are initially prime suspects," said Amy. "Based on what Wilson's mother implied, I'd put the husband at the top of the list."

"Okay, suspect number one—the husband," said Hubbard.

"I'll call the husband," said Amy, "and invite him here to let him know we found his wife's remains. I'll shoot for tomorrow."

"Good," said Pickens. "The sooner, the better."

"Now that that's taken care of, any more suspects?" asked Hubbard.

"Based on the ME's explanation that whoever killed the family did it out of rage . . ." Pickens started to say.

"The son," said Amy. "Or another family member if there was one."

Hubbard wrote *suspect 1-the son*.

"Which means we need to know if he's alive or dead," said Pickens. "If alive, we need to find him and quick."

"What about witness protection?" asked Billy.

"Witness protection? Why?" asked Hubbard.

"Maybe the whole family was in protection, and whoever they were hiding from found them and killed them. The son might have escaped and is now in WITSEC."

Billy's comment caused everyone to stop and think.

"You have any sources in WITSEC, Mitch?"

Hubbard rubbed his chin. "I don't think so, but I do with the FBI and the U. S. Marshall's office. I'll check around." Hubbard wrote *WITSEC* as a motive under the family.

Hubbard stepped back and admired the board. "Is that enough leads for you, JD?"

Pickens raised his palms. "More than enough. Thanks, Mitch."

Hubbard checked his watch. It read 5:30.

"No problem. By the time this is over, you three will be excellent homicide detectives. I'm afraid I have to leave. We'll pick this up again tomorrow." Hubbard smiled. "*Adios,* detectives," he said and left.

"He's something, JD," said Amy.

"He has the knowledge and experience. Now, unless you need me, I'm taking leave; so should you two."

"I'm hanging around to write up my report. I'll put a copy on your desk and give Billy one so he can add it to the case file."

"I'm visiting Mrs. Gronfein at her house to check on her and her dog. You remember them?" said Billy.

"From the last case we worked," said Pickens.

"And you're hoping for a free meal too," said Amy.

"That too," said Billy, and he smiled.

"In that case," said Pickens, "*adios,* deputies."

At home, Pickens set his keys on the kitchen counter, kissed

Marge on the neck, then went to the bedroom, put his gun in the safe, and returned to the kitchen.

"What's for dinner?" he asked.

Marge smiled. "Thanks for the kiss." Pickens grinned. "You have a choice between heated leftover ham and vegetables or cold ham sandwiches. We have to finish the leftovers from New Year's Day."

"I'll have a sandwich. I had a big lunch. How was your day?"

"Nothing exciting happened. Betty-Jean finished the reconstructions of the two adults. She'll email them to Billy in the morning. How was your day?"

"Productive. Amy talked to those folks you wanted me to. They're the parents of the dead woman, and we now know her name. Harley identified the parents and also identified the girl. Just the first name. And Mitch worked up a case profile for us."

"So, Mitch was the coach and you sat on the sideline. How did that feel?"

Pickens smiled. "Like you probably felt sitting on the sideline with the professor." Marge grinned. "Mitch has more experience than I do, and I have to admit it was a terrific learning experience."

"Same as it was for me with the professor. Say hello to Sarah and Bailey. I'll call you when your sandwich is ready."

CHAPTER 19

Thursday morning, when Mitch Hubbard walked into the sheriff's office, he went right to the chalkboard, picked up the chalk stick, circled TOD under both cases and put a question mark on the line for the family and *1995* on the one for the woman. Then he pointed at the board with the chalk stick.

Pickens, Amy, and Billy gathered around him.

"I talked with Harley last night," Hubbard said. "Don't look surprised, Sergeant Tucker. Harley's staying with Donna and me while she goes through her divorce." Amy now understood why Harley was distant when she first met her at Hubbard's house. "Anyway," continued Hubbard, "she remembered the years the victims went missing, and I got an idea. Isn't Sergeant Dunne's husband the principal at the Warfield middle school?"

"So?" said Amy.

"Maybe he has access to old school records, maybe old yearbooks. Plus, he could check the student list and see if any parents of the kids at the middle school attended the high school before it was shut down."

"One of those parents might remember the girl, her brother, or both," said Pickens.

"They might remember the last name," said Amy.

"And they might have an old yearbook," said Hubbard. "If they do, maybe they'll let us borrow it, and Harley could look through it."

"Betty-Jean sent the reconstructed images of the man and woman from the second gravesite," said Billy. "Maybe Sergeant Dunne's husband could show those pictures to parents of current middle school students and their parents. It's worth a try."

"Great idea, Billy," said Pickens.

"Maybe it's time you gave that reporter something, JD," said Hubbard.

Pickens eyed Hubbard skeptically. "Like what?"

"Let him run the picture of the girl and an article about her. He could lead off with a headline that says, 'Do you know this girl?' We may get lucky. Someone may, and we might get a few calls."

Pickens scratched his head. "I hate to give him more. I just gave him something. He'll want even more. You don't know how he is" Pickens picked up the morning's issue of the newspaper and pointed to the frontpage headline. "Wasn't that enough?"

"No," said Hubbard. "The new one would be better. You want to solve this case, don't you?"

Pickens shook his head and bit his lip. "Okay, I'll do it. But I'll have him run it in the weekend edition. It might attract more attention. And the ME said she'd have the DNA results tomorrow. Come Monday, maybe we'll know who the family was. Maybe even what happened if we're lucky. I'll call Nosey tomorrow. I'll call Sergeant Dunne and ask her about her husband."

"She might not like doing that, JD. Sergeant Dunne doesn't like mixing family with business," said Amy.

"I'll explain that we need the information. She might know

some of those parents through the Parent Teacher Organization and won't have to involve her husband. If she does, she could ask if any of them were in school during the mid-eighties, knew the girl or boy, and have yearbooks."

"It would save us a lot of time," said Hubbard. "I'll ask Harley if any of her students became teachers. She could ask if they knew those kids."

"That's better than involving Sergeant Dunne's husband," said Amy.

"Billy," said Pickens, "you start digging deep into both Wilsons. I want to know everything about them. Where they ate, where they socialized, with whom, did they belong to a country club. Anything you could learn about them, I want to know." Amy leaned against a nearby desk, crossed her arms, and furrowed her eyes. Pickens noticed. "And then give it to Amy, since she's the lead on the Wilson case, and she can work up a preliminary profile." Amy uncrossed her arms but still frowned.

"And do it on the QT," said Hubbard. "We don't want anyone to get wind that we're investigating the husband."

"Got it," said Billy. He tapped his fingers on the keyboard.

Pickens called Sergeant Dunne and explained what he wanted.

"There's a PTO meeting next week," said Dunne. "I'll ask around. If I turn up something, what should I do?"

"You're going to be involved in both cases, so take the lead and find out what you can, especially a last name and yearbooks. Mitch Hubbard is working this case with me. You can call him or me. Thanks, Sergeant Dunne."

"It's what I get paid to do. Thanks for getting me involved and not my husband."

After he finished talking to Dunne, Pickens called Noseby and invited to come to his office Friday morning. He'd have something for the reporter. Noseby agreed and sounded as giddy as a bride at her wedding reception.

Friday morning, Dr. Vadigal came through as promised. Marge received the DNA result on all four victims. The two adults and the child were a match proving they were family members. The unknown female who now had a name, her DNA was a match for Anne Wilson who was in the system. Her DNA could be matched to her parents and children when the time came.

Marge put the results into her case files and sent the information to Pickens who gave it to Billy to input into their case files.

Noseby strolled into the sheriff's office looking like a man who had just learned that he'd become a daddy. All he needed to complete the look was a cigar hanging out of his mouth. He wasn't wearing his red ball cap. He wore a dark fedora and a bow tie—a poor imitation of Jimmy Olson, the cub reporter in *Superman.*

"I'm here, Sheriff," said Noseby. "Ready for my big story. I even brought my large notebook to take notes and an Ipad." Noseby held up his briefcase. "Let's get it on."

Pickens shook his head and considered throwing the reporter out of his office and canceling the interview. But Hubbard and Amy extended their hands palms down to calm him.

"In my office, Nosey," said Pickens.

"Uh, Sheriff, it's . . ."

"In my office, now."

Noseby lowered his chin in defeat and followed Pickens into the office. Pickens closed the door.

"Sit, Nosey. This won't take long." The reporter was about to object to the mispronunciation, but Pickens put a finger to his mouth and shushed him. "Sit." Noseby sat. "Listen carefully. I want you to run an article in the weekend edition." The reporter grabbed his pen and pad and started writing. "Keep it brief. The headline will read, 'Do you know this girl?' Use my personal number as the tip line." Pickens handed the reporter the sketch of the girl.

"Is that all? That's not much of a story."

"I don't want a story. I'm only interested in getting someone who knows the girl to call me. Say something like her relatives are looking for her. Nothing more, Nosey. Did I make myself clear?"

"It's . . ."

"Did I make myself clear, Nosey?"

The reporter slumped his shoulders. "Yes. I'll take care of it."

"Good. I promise I'll have a big story for you when the time is right."

The reporter smiled. "Thanks, Sheriff."

"Nice hat," said Pickens.

The reporter grinned. "It's my new signature."

Pickens waved him off.

After the reporter left, Amy asked if she could talk privately with Pickens. He pointed for her to sit. Amy closed the door behind her and sat.

"What is it, Amy? If it's about yesterday, I'm sorry."

Amy raised her palm. "It's not. Yesterday I had an ego moment. I'm over it. I may be the lead in the Wilson case, but you're the sheriff and responsible for everything about both cases. I got something else I want to run by you."

"Let me have it."

"I got a call from Anne Wilson's daughter."

Pickens shot her an uneasy look.

"Her grandmother called her and told her about her mother. The daughter lives in Jacksonville and will be spending the weekend with her grandmother. She wants to meet with me Monday. Is that okay with you?"

"It's your case, so run with it. But keep me apprised. What about the husband, have you contacted him?"

"I did. He's not available until Monday afternoon. I'm meeting with him at 2:30. Do you want to sit in? I'd appreciate it."

"No problem. I know I've said it before, but what would I do without you?"

Amy smiled. "Hire six Mitch Hubbards."

Pickens shook his head and grinned.

When Amy stepped out of Pickens office, Billy called out to her.

"Got something for you, Amy." Amy walked over to Billy's desk. "I finished my search on marriage licenses. Found one for Anne Henderson and Daniel Wilson in Marion County, December 11, 1986."

"That's them," said Amy. "Henderson's parents lived in Ocala. It's probably where the wedding was."

"Unfortunately, Facebook didn't exist in 1986, so there are no posts or wedding pictures."

"I'll ask her mother if she has any or a wedding album," said Amy. "I'd like to know who was in the wedding party. Maybe I'll ask Harley to do it since she's in tight with the mother."

"I ran a search on Daniel Wilson's business. The website lists a Lawrence Meade as his partner since the business started."

"What about the audiology business? Does it still exist?"

"No. But there's another one in Warfield. I figured you'd want something about it, so I ran it. The website lists Barbara Hobbs as the owner and Isabella Asado as an associate. Both worked for Anne Wilson before opening the new place."

"Interesting," said Amy. "Are they married?"

"I'll search both and get back to you. What about Meade? You want to know if he's married?"

"Yes. Also, did Wilson remarry?"

Billy's fingers sped across the keyboard. "I'm on it."

Amy called Wilson's daughter and scheduled a meeting for Monday at 10:00 at the sheriff's office. She couldn't wait to hear what the daughter had to say.

CHAPTER 20

MONDAY MORNING, WHEN Mitch Hubbard strolled into the sheriff's office, he went right to Pickens' office and sat.

"Morning, Mitch, what's up?"

Hubbard leaned forward and quirked an eyebrow. "I did some investigating over the weekend."

Pickens' eyes narrowed. "What are you talking about?"

Hubbard waved his hand. "Nothing to get annoyed about. I talked to Harley and asked her if she remembered where that family that disappeared lived. At first, she didn't think she'd remember because it was thirty years ago. We went for a drive around Warfield, and Harley was able to pick out the street. I drove down it, and she pointed to the house. I wrote the address down and thought maybe you'd want to talk to some of the neighbors. One of them may remember the family."

Pickens' eyebrows raised and he gave Hubbard a thumb up. "I like it, Mitch."

"I knew you would. So when do we knock on doors?"

Pickens scratched his chin. "Let's wait until Wednesday." Hubbard's head jerked back. "Hear me out, Mitch. The article was in the weekend paper. I might get some calls. If I don't by Wednesday morning, then we'll do some knocking. In the meantime, I'll have Billy run the address."

"Okay. We could wait until Thursday and see what Sergeant Dunne learns at the PTO meeting." Hubbard raised a finger. "Better yet, why not have Sergeant Dunne talk to the city clerk, and have the clerk do a records search. The records might show who owned the property in 1987."

"I like it, and it's not as if family members are waiting for an answer."

Hubbard raised his index finger. "The son might be."

Pickens exhaled. "He could be, but he could be the killer."

"Yeah, that too."

* * *

Amy watched as Jenny Wilson came through the door and asked where she could find Sergeant Amy Tucker. The day-time emergency operator/receptionist pointed to Amy. Amy had already made sure the chalk board was covered and tucked away out of sight. Next, she waved the woman over to the conference room.

"Miss Wilson, I'm Sergeant Amy Tucker." Amy extended a hand. "It's a pleasure to meet you."

"It's a pleasure to meet you, Sergeant Tucker."

"I reserved the conference room so we'd have privacy." Amy extended her hand toward the doorway. Wilson entered. Amy followed and closed the door behind her. Both women sat. Amy on one side of the conference table, the woman on the other.

Amy noticed the family resemblance. The woman looked like a much younger version of her grandmother. Same nose, same chin, and the same hazel eyes. Unlike her grandmother who'd had anger and resentment in her eyes, the woman's eyes reflected the sadness she felt learning that her mother was no longer missing but was dead. Amy felt sorry for the woman.

"I'm sure this was difficult for you, Ms. . . ."

"It's Miss Wilson, Sergeant Tucker. I never married." The

woman sighed. "Yes, it is. When my grandmother contacted me, I thought it was because she harbored ill will toward my father and refused to accept that my mother left her family." Her chin trembled. "But now this."

Amy felt like reaching out to the woman and holding her hand but knew she best not. The woman had to grieve in her own way.

"I understand. Does your brother know?"

The woman's expression was pained. "No, my grandmother said he refused to take her call. He still thinks my grandmother is harboring too much anger." She shook her head. "I never did. I always felt my grandmother was upset as any mother would be. She believes my father killed my mother." The woman made eye contact with Amy. "Do you think he did, Sergeant Tucker?"

Amy nervously ran her thumb across her fingertips. "We have to consider it a possibility, Miss Wilson."

The woman played with the locket hanging from her neck. "Then you need to know something." Amy reached for a pad and pen. "I overheard my parents arguing about divorce. My mother seemed to want it more than my father."

Amy wrote *divorce/motive* on the pad. The woman noticed.

"I told my brother, but he didn't believe me. Jeremy always sided with my father even after my mother . . ." A tear slid down her cheek. "I told Uncle Larry, and he said I must have been confused." She took a deep breath. "I wasn't confused. I knew what I heard."

Amy wrote *Uncle Larry/suspect.*

"Can I see my mother, Sergeant Tucker?"

Amy pursed her lips. "I don't think that's a good idea."

"Why not?"

Amy dreaded the moment but wanted to be honest. "Because we only found her skeletal remains. You should try to remember her as she was the last time you saw her."

The woman wiped her eyes. "It was that bad?"

"Yes, and we're treating her death as a homicide. Mind if I ask your Uncle Larry's full name?"

"Oh, sorry. Uncle Larry is my father's partner, Lawrence Meade. They went to college and medical school together."

Amy scribbled *partner*. Again the woman noticed.

"You don't think?"

"No, I'm just making notes. It's my nature as an investigator, but I may want to talk to him and your father at some point. Did your mother have any close friends that you know of? I know it was a long time ago, but it would help."

"Sorry, I can't remember any, but if I do, I'll call you. I'd still like to see my mother's remains. Can you arrange it?"

Amy felt an ache in the back of her throat as she dreaded agreeing to it. "I really think you shouldn't. If it were my mother, I wouldn't." Amy handed the woman the sketch of her mother at time of her death. "Think of her as she looks in that picture. We created it."

The woman looked at the picture. It took a moment, but she eventually smiled. "She was pretty, wasn't she?"

"Yes, she was. Remember her as that pretty woman and remember how she was your loving mother."

"I will. Thank you, Sergeant Tucker. I think I'll show this to my grandmother."

"Before you go, the only ID we have are the sketches you and your grandmother identified as your mother. We need a more positive identification. May I take a sample of your DNA? It would help."

"Of course, if it will."

Amy took a swab from the woman's mouth and placed it in the evidence bag she had with her.

"Thank you, Miss Wilson."

After the woman was gone, Amy sat and let her thoughts

race as she tried to comprehend why the father of that beautiful woman or his partner might have brutally killed her mother.

As soon as Amy came out from the conference room, Billy waved her to his desk. Amy raised a hand.

"One minute, Billy. I have something to do first."

Amy walked over to the chalkboard, uncovered it, wrote *divorce* on the motive line for Henderson, and *husband* and *partner Meade* as suspects.

Pickens and Hubbard came over beside her.

"*Divorce*?" said Pickens. "What's that about?"

"The daughter said she overheard her parents arguing about divorcing." Next, Amy told Pickens and Hubbard what the daughter had said. Meade saying she was mistaken, and her brother taking her father's side. "It's possible the father was having an affair, and his partner knew about it."

"It's also possible that the mother was having an affair, which was why she wanted the divorce," said Hubbard.

"The Uncle Larry thing makes me suspicious of him," said Pickens. "Maybe the husband and partner killed the mother."

"But why?" asked Amy.

"Money," said Hubbard. "It's always about money. Follow it."

"A divorce might have cost the husband a bundle," said Amy. "I'm gonna run with that."

Pickens tilted his head. "It's your case, just keep your options open."

Amy waited impatiently for Daniel Wilson to arrive. The appointment was scheduled for 2:30, and it was now 3:45. Wilson didn't say that he had appointments, but that it was his day off. Maybe the daughter or mother-in-law had contacted him and told him about his wife. It was possible he had contacted a lawyer, and both would show up.

At 4:15, Wilson walked through the front door with another man. Was he Wilson's lawyer? Or was it his partner?

Pickens was moving the board out of view. Amy signaled for him.

Daniel Wilson strolled up to Amy as if he didn't have a care in the world. He was shorter than Amy and had a smug expression as if he was better than everybody.

"Are you Sergeant Tucker?" asked Wilson.

"I am," said Amy.

"You wanted to speak with me? Was it necessary for me to come to the sheriff's office? I'm a busy man."

Amy made direct eye contact with him, letting Wilson know she wasn't intimidated.

"Yes, it was. This is Sheriff Pickens." Pickens nodded but didn't extend his hand. "We'd like to talk with you in private."

Amy eyed the other man.

"He's my partner, Lawrence Meade. Anything you have to say you can say in front of him."

"It's about your wife," said Pickens.

Wilson crossed his arms. "What about her?"

"Let's talk in the conference room. It's private," said Pickens and he directed the two men to the room.

Meade looked around the office. "It's probably better, Dan. Go ahead I'm right behind you."

Wilson stepped into the conference room. Meade followed. Pickens and Amy followed behind them.

"Have a seat, please, Mr. Wilson," said Pickens.

Wilson's expression hardened. He and Meade sat.

"Now, what about my wife? She left me over twenty years ago, and as far as I'm concerned she's dead."

Harsh words thought Amy, especially for someone who was about to learn that his wife was murdered and her body had been buried not that far from where he lived.

Pickens looked at Amy and tilted his head letting her know she had the lead.

"She is dead," said Amy abruptly. "We found her skeletal remains the Friday before Christmas in a field off Grange Road."

Wilson placed his hands on the table and leaned forward.

"What are you talking about?" said Wilson. "My wife abandoned her family and ran off with her lover. I had her declared dead after never hearing from her."

Amy had no sympathy for the man, and she considered him a viable suspect based on his attitude. Maybe his mother-in-law was right about him.

"You never heard from your wife because she was brutally murdered in 1995. We would never have found her remains if it weren't for a dog digging them up. I'm sorry for having to tell you."

Meade put his hand on Wilson's shoulder. "Did you have to be so blunt, Sergeant?"

"We're both sorry," said Pickens. "We would have liked to be more sympathetic, but Mr. Wilson didn't strike us as a man who cared that his wife was murdered."

"I care," said Wilson. "I thought she ran off with another man. Forgive me if I appear callous."

"You said you found skeletal remains?" asked Meade. Pickens nodded. "Then I guess there's not much to identify her. How can you be sure it's Anne?"

Amy held back her temper. "We did a facial approximation and showed it to Mr. Wilson's in-laws. They identified her." Amy took out the sketch of Henderson's wife at the time of death and handed it to Wilson. "This is what the initial reconstruction looked like. Do you recognize her, Mr. Wilson?"

Wilson glanced at the picture. "It looks like her. What do you think, Larry?"

Meade picked up the picture. "It's her, Dan. It's Anne."

"What happens with the remains?" asked Wilson.

"For now, they're evidence until we finish our investigation," said Pickens. "After that, you're welcome to bury them."

Pickens and Amy waited to see Wilson's reaction and if he'd want the remains so he could bury his wife.

"We'll get back to you," said Meade. "Thank you."

No reaction from Wilson. The two men stood and left.

After Wilson and Meade were gone, Pickens said, "What do you think?"

"Arrogant son of a bitch," said Amy. "He did it. He killed his wife. And I'm going to hang him for it."

"Easy, Amy. Finish your investigation before you condemn the man."

CHAPTER 21

TUESDAY MORNING, PICKENS, Amy and Hubbard were huddled around the chalkboard checking to be sure the investigations were up to date.

"We just about listed everything we know so far," said Pickens. "Maybe we should turn the board around and start using the murder board?"

"Might as well," said Hubbard. "It's probably easier than the chalkboard."

The two men turned the board around. Hubbard erased what they had previously written. He listed both cases separately with sketches of the victims under the case names.

Stacie, the daytime emergency operator, had answered the office phone and covered the mouthpiece with her hand.

"Sheriff," Stacie called out, "that reporter is on the line and wants to speak to you. He said it was extremely important."

Pickens scowled. "I'll take it in my office." He went into his office and picked up the receiver. "What is it Nosey? Did you get a call about the girl? The calls were supposed to come to me."

Noseby didn't even try to correct his name this time.

"No," the reporter answered. "I got a call from a Mrs. Henderson. She said she was the mother of Anne Wilson who went missing over twenty years ago, and you found her body.

Also, that you're investigating her son-in-law, Daniel Wilson, for murdering his wife. Is that true?"

Pickens' nostrils flared. "Listen, Noseby." Pickens used the correct pronunciation as he was going to need the reporter's cooperation. "You need to come to my office, and I'll explain. I don't want you writing anything until I talk to you. Can you promise me that?"

"But, Sheriff, she said if I don't write an article about her son-in-law being the suspect of her daughter's murder, she'd call the local news station."

Pickens rubbed the back of his head in frustration. "Don't worry about the news station. I'm good friends with the manager, and she won't do anything without calling me first. Get here as soon as you can, Noseby."

"I'm on my way."

After he hung up the receiver, Pickens stepped in the doorway and yelled. "Amy, get your butt in here now." Amy's head jerked back. "Now, Sergeant Tucker."

Amy frowned, left Hubbard and went to Pickens' office.

"Close the door," said Pickens.

"What's this about, JD? And why did you call me by my rank?"

Pickens pursed his lips. "What the hell were you thinking? I told you to finish your investigation before condemning Wilson."

Amy held a hand up. "Hold on, what are you talking about?"

"You told Wilson's mother-in-law that I was investigating Wilson for his wife's murder. And she called Nosey. As the lead investigator, you sure screwed up. Now I have to fix your mess."

"JD, I did no such thing. His daughter asked if I thought he might have killed her mother, and I said we have to look at every possibility. I never said we were investigating him. I told you that yesterday."

Pickens hadn't considered that a possibility. Now he had to. "The daughter must have told her grandmother and the woman took it the wrong way."

"Mrs. Henderson believed her son-in-law killed her daughter. The woman was upset after I talked to her, and she lashed out at her son-in-law. I can understand it. She just found out her daughter was murdered and needed to blame someone."

Pickens exhaled. "Now I have to stop Nosey from writing that we're investigating Wilson for the murder. He's on his way here, and I have to make up something."

"Tell him you're giving him a scoop. We found Wilson's remains and are investigating what happened to her twenty years ago when she went missing. We have no leads and no suspects yet. He'll buy it. Nosey loves a scoop."

Pickens rubbed his chin. "Maybe. It's worth a try. Sorry, I yelled at you."

Amy grinned. "It's not the first time, Sheriff."

When Pickens opened the door, the office was quiet. Everyone preoccupied themselves with something as if they hadn't heard Pickens dress down Amy. Hubbard had covered the murder board.

Standing near the office entryway was the reporter with a sheepish grin. He waved to Pickens.

Pickens signaled for the reporter to join him and Amy.

The reporter strolled past Billy's desk. Billy ignored him.

"Morning, Sheriff. Morning, Sergeant Tucker."

"Inside, Noseby," said Pickens.

The reporter entered the office and sat.

"Listen up, Noseby, I'm only going to say this once."

The reporter grabbed his pen and pad. Pickens told him what Amy suggested, but added a caveat.

"Put my number in the article, so I get all the calls. You got that?"

"Yes, but what about the Henderson woman?"

"Don't worry about her. Sergeant Tucker will take care of her." Amy looked befuddled. "Now go before I change my mind."

The reporter got up and left.

"What do you mean I'll take care of Mrs. Henderson?" asked Amy.

"You wanted to be the lead. Now you deal with the woman."

Amy left Pickens office and went to make a call. Pickens joined Hubbard at the murder board.

"What was that about?" asked Hubbard.

"A problem with the Henderson woman, and I gave that reporter another bit of information. Just enough to satisfy him." Pickens glanced at the murder board. "I see you've been busy with the board."

Hubbard had erased the board and started a new one. He divided it in two. Across the top, he wrote *Wilson - 1995* on one half and *Unknown Family -1987* on the other. In the center of each, he attached a copy of the images from each case. Wilson at time of death and Celia at her time of death for the family. He drew two circles to represent Celia's parents and attached their images. In each case, he wrote *Suspects*. For Wilson, the obvious one—the husband. Also, Lawrence Meade, the husband's partner, and Barbara Hobbs, the new owner of the audiology practice—with POI after it. In the family case, he wrote *Son*—with a question mark next to it.

"Beats your artwork, JD."

Pickens shook his head. "At least we have a good start. Now I have to do something I dread doing."

"What's that?"

"Talk to the widow of Chief Nolan. He might have kept files at his house." Pickens exhaled. "If he did, maybe there are files on both cases. You up for going with me?"

"Will it be like your predecessor?"

"I hope not."

Amy finished her phone calls and joined them.

"I called the granddaughter. She said she'd visit her grandmother and talk to her. I also called Harley. We're going to visit the Henderson woman and talk to her. I'm meeting Harley at your house, Mitch, after she finishes with her attorney."

Pickens nodded. "Good. Mitch and I are going to Warfield to talk to Chief Nolan's widow. I'll keep you posted, and you do the same with me."

In Warfield, Pickens drove up to a gray clapboard house on Pennington Drive. The landscaping was well taken care of, and winter annuals dotted the gardens. Someone had already removed the holiday ornaments.

"Nice property," said Hubbard. "Think she takes care of it?"

Pickens shrugged. "I don't know. But if she does, she does a good job. You ready for this?"

"Ready if you are."

Pickens walked up to the door and rang the bell. A seventy-something looking woman opened the door. She had gray hair and glasses on. The aroma of freshly baked pie wafted behind her.

"Mrs. Nolan, I'm Sheriff Pickens, and this is—"

"I know who you are, Sheriff. What can I do for you?"

"First, let me say. I'm sorry for your loss. I'd like to talk to you about a couple of old cases that Chief Nolan might have investigated. Mind if we come in?"

Pickens watched as she eyed him up and down, then did the same to Hubbard.

"Who is he?" she asked.

"Mitch Hubbard. He's helping me."

Mrs. Nolan smiled. "I know you. You're Donna's husband. You were with her at the New Year's Eve function, and you danced with all the women."

Hubbard grinned. "I did, and I danced with you. You sure know how to do the Lindy Hop."

Pickens saw the gleam in the woman's eyes from Hubbard's comment.

"Where are my manners? Come in. I made a fresh pot of coffee, and you have to eat a slice of pie." Mrs. Nolan stepped aside as Pickens and Hubbard entered. "Have a seat. I'll go get the coffee and pie."

Pickens and Hubbard sat in the living room. Pickens noticed the pictures on the mantle of Chief Nolan in uniform and others with his wife. Also, one with another police officer. Pickens didn't know who he was. Next to that one was a picture of the same men out of uniform and holding fishing rods.

"So far, it's going better than that sheriff visit," said Hubbard.

"I hope it stays that way."

Mrs. Nolan returned with a tray with cups of coffee and plates of pie and set them on the coffee table.

"First off, Sheriff, I got no qualms with you. I heard what happened when you went to Bascom's house. What happened to my husband wasn't your fault. If he would have retired when I wanted him to, he'd still be alive today. The stress of the job was eating at him, and I think something haunted him. Don't ask me what."

Pickens wondered what she meant by something haunted Nolan. Was it the cases or something else? If the cases, he wondered what about them bothered Nolan. He'd ask but didn't want to upset Mrs. Nolan and destroy any chance of looking for old case files.

Mrs. Nolan poured three cups of coffee, handed Pickens and Hubbard each a cup and a plate of pie. She set the other cup and plate in front of herself.

"What about his old cases, Sheriff? I don't know if I can help you. It's been a long time since . . ." Mrs. Nolan picked up her napkin and wiped her eyes. Pickens gave her time to compose herself. "I'm sorry. I didn't mean to cry."

"I understand," said Pickens. "Take your time. I can always come back another day."

"No, I'm fine." She raised her hand. "What cases are you asking about? Chief Nolan kept some boxes of files in the garage. Thad Underhill, he was the chief's best friend and worked for him until Thad retired, long before you came along. Anyway, Thad told me not to get rid of them. There might come a day when you might want them." Suddenly, the doorbell rang. "That must be him. I forgot he was coming for coffee and pie. He comes every other day. We're kinda—you know? Let me get the door." Mrs. Nolan went to answer the door.

"Did you notice the gleam in her eyes when she mentioned Underhill?" asked Hubbard.

"Yeah. Maybe he knows what's in those boxes and could help us."

Mrs. Nolan returned with a gentleman older than her. He was dressed in jeans, a flannel shirt, and wore glasses. He also walked with a cane. Pickens glanced at the mantel. The man only slightly resembled the man in the picture of Nolan and another man holding fishing rods.

"JD Pickens, I wondered how long it would take you to finally get here," the man said. "Thad Underhill. It's nice to meet you." He switched the cane to his left hand and extended his right.

"You looking for case files that Chief Nolan had pertaining to the bodies you found?"

Pickens' brows hitched.

"Hey, I read the newspaper, and I hear things. Ellie-Jane, get me a cup of coffee and some of that pie." Mrs. Nolan patted his arm and left. He looked at Hubbard. "You're Hubbard, Donna's husband. "What's he doing here, Pickens?"

"He's consulting with me on the cases."

"You got yourself a retired homicide detective to consult with you? Wish Nolan and I had one twenty and thirty years ago. So, you looking for old files?"

"What files did Nolan keep?"

"The Wilson case and the family disappearance. We both worked them. I had my suspicions about the husband in the Wilson case. So did Nolan, but we had nothing to go by. He waited over a week to call us, and then he said she was probably on a business trip. Then why call us and say she disappeared?"

"How about her office? What did they say?"

"Same thing. Except we had our doubts about her associate. The same thing with Wilson's business partner. Something didn't sit right with him."

"Did anyone suggest she had an affair?"

"Yeah, the husband and her associate. But they weren't sure. We checked the airlines, the trains, and buses. Got nothing. We even checked the cab company. Again nothing. Her vehicle was missing, but the husband said she probably left in it. We had no other choice than to close the case. Nolan was upset when, years later, the husband had his wife declared dead. I was, too. Everything you need is in the file."

"What about the other case?"

"The Groves family?" Underhill rubbed his neck. "That one really bothered Nolan."

Pickens made a mental note of the name Groves.

"Nolan didn't think we did enough on that one, but we had little to work with. If that little girl's teacher hadn't called us, we never would have investigated."

"How did you work it?"

"Like a missing person's case because of that little girl. Nolan might have come across as a hardass, but he had a soft spot for kids. We visited the house, walked through it, but it was spotless. The clothes closets were stripped clean like they'd took off in the night without telling anyone. Their car was gone. The neighbors said they knew little about the family as they kept to themselves. They'd only moved into the neighborhood five years before they disappeared. Came from some state up north. It's in the file."

"Did you talk to his POB, the school, anybody?"

"Of course we did. His POB said they hadn't heard from him in over a week. Naturally, we talked to the girl's teacher since she alerted us. We talked to the boy's teacher, too."

"Find out anything about the boy? We haven't found his remains, yet."

Underhill scratched his chin. "Hmm . . . I thought maybe you did. But Nolan and I were curious about him."

"Why so?"

"When we talked with his teachers, they said he was a loner. Didn't associate with the other kids. We talked to some of his classmates. Except for him being in their class, they had nothing to do with him and avoided him. A few said they'd saw him leave campus and meet up with an older guy. They'd take off in the guy's truck."

"Did you do a BOLO on the family's car?"

"Why? Other than the fact they up and disappeared, we had nothing to suspect something was wrong. We were a small police department, had minimal resources, and did the best we could. You should understand that. Look what you have to deal with."

"Yeah, I understand, but at least now we're better equipped. Better, but not that much better. That's why Hubbard is helping me."

"You're lucky, Pickens. Anyway, Nolan never could get that case out of his head because of that little girl. I hope you find her."

Pickens exhaled. "Unfortunately, we did. We found her skeletal remains and those of her parents buried on Bo Tatum's property around thirty years ago. We haven't released that information yet, so I'd appreciate it if you don't mention it."

"*Shit.* I hate to say this but thank goodness Nolan is dead."

Underhill turned to Mrs. Nolan as she returned with his coffee and pie.

"Sorry Ellie-Jane, it would have killed him to find out that little girl was dead and buried when we were investigating her disappearance."

"It's okay, Thad," said Mrs. Nolan, and she set his coffee and pie in front of him. "I know it would have."

"So, Pickens, anything else I can do for you?"

"Can I have the files?"

"After coffee and pie. Then I'll get them from the garage. They're in a box where Nolan kept them."

After coffee and pie, Underhill retrieved the box from the garage and handed it to Pickens.

"I hope the files are helpful."

"Thanks, Underhill, I hope so, too. At least we now have the last name. After I go through them, maybe I'll have a first name for the boy. Until now, all we had was the girl's first name."

"If you need anything else, call me. I ain't like Bascom. Never liked that asshole."

After they left the Nolan house, Hubbard said, "Nice people and nothing like the Bascoms."

"Yeah, and Underhill was helpful. Didn't know that Nolan had a soft spot for kids. If it weren't for his age and reputation, I might have kept him on the job."

"Don't think he would have stayed. He would have retired. After a while the job gets to you. That's why I retired. Just wait, JD, it will get to you, too."

"Any more cases like these, I might decide to become a fishing guide."

"Marge would love that. As long as you stayed busy."

CHAPTER 22

AFTER PICKENS AND Hubbard finished combing through Chief Nolan's files, they updated the murder board with Amy. They now had a name for the family and the boy.

Pickens erased Family and wrote *Groves*. He replaced "son" with *Jessie*.

"Thanks to Underhill and Nolan we've got more to work with," said Hubbard. "Billy can search the name Jessie Groves, and he might find something. Like Underhill, I have a suspicion about him."

"And I've got suspicions about Wilson's husband, his partner, and her associate. It's also possible Wilson had a lover no one knows about yet," said Pickens. "Amy, can you do a preliminary profile based on what we've got for both cases? And as far as Wilson is concerned, be open-minded."

"I'll do my best. Who's taking notes?"

"Billy will, and Mitch can scribble something on the board."

"I'll start with both cases, then do them individually. Since COD was violent, it suggests the killer or killers were enraged about something. A perceived wrong, an affair gone wrong, financial problems, a jealous lover, even abuse. All those things work in both cases. Now, in the Wilson case, we have all those things, including envy. The husband, his partner, and Wilson's associate fit that description. Remember, the daughter mentioned divorce. That would suggest financial or child custody. Wilson's associate might have envied her and wanted her business practice. If she did, she got it. If Wilson had an affair, then you have an unhappy spouse.

"As for the Groves, I'd rule out witness protection. They were running from something, and something *evil* found them. Violent rage killed them. It could have been the son and his unknown friend, or the son witnessed the murder and escaped never to be heard of again. It's a long shot, but maybe he's buried in that field or his backyard. Wouldn't hurt to use Billy's thermal imaging. This is a complicated case to profile, but I'm sure more than one person did the killings. I'm guessing, but I have a hard time thinking the boy killed his sister. He'd had to have a twisted mind to do it. One thing for sure, the killers were psychopaths, and it wasn't their first nor their last. This was premeditated."

Amy pointed at the Wilson case and continued. "I believe there were at least two people involved in the Wilson case. A woman could commit blunt force trauma, and it suggests it wasn't premeditated—but was spontaneous and in a fit of rage. Also, a woman wouldn't be able to bury Wilson's body by herself. She'd need help. So, you're looking for at least two people. One did the killing. The other helped bury the body."

Pickens' phone suddenly chirped. He checked who was calling. "That's good, Amy, but hold on, I got to take this call." He stepped away and answered. "Yeah. I see. Keep her there. I'll send Amy. Thanks."

"AMY, I thought you took care of the Henderson problem?"

Amy stiffened.

"That was Sergeant Dunne. She has the woman in custody. Wilson called her and said Henderson was picketing in front of his office with a sign calling him a killer. YOU CALL THAT TAKING CARE OF THE SITUATION?"

"STOP YELLING AT ME. I did take care of it. At least I thought I did. I called the granddaughter, and she said she'd talk to her grandmother. Both Harley and I talked to the woman. She'd been grieving the disappearance of her daughter for over twenty years and just found out that her daughter was murdered and buried not far from her. Her grief boiled over, and the woman struck out at the one person she believed killed her daughter. She's a mother who lost her daughter, her grandchildren dismissed her concerns, and she can't see her daughter's body. She's handling it the best she can. YOU'RE A MAN. YOU WOULDN'T UNDERSTAND HOW A MOTHER REACTS TO THAT."

Pickens kicked the nearest trash can then bolted for his office. The walls rattled when he shut the door. He sat at his desk with his head buried in his hands. He then picked up the phone and called the one person he knew would help him.

"Marge—I got a problem." He told her about going off on Amy and his office witnessing his tirade. "I need help."

"Take a deep breath, JD. First off, Amy will forgive you, and it's not the first time your office witnessed one of your tirades. As for the Henderson woman, I understand what she's going through. If it were my mother and something happened to me, the whole world would have hell to pay. The same goes for me if anything happened to Sarah. Your mother has the patience of a saint, but your father no way. If something happened to you or Sarah, it would take your entire staff to restrain him. Apologize to Amy and your staff, JD. Keep it brief and get on with it. We're all upset about the two cases. They both hit a nerve with us."

Pickens calmed. "Thanks, Marge, I knew you would know what I should do."

"Remember, brief and get on with it. Whatever you want me to do, I'm glad to help—I love you, too."

Pickens stepped into the bullpen. As always, everyone acted as if nothing happened and took care of other matters.

"Okay, let's not pretend nothing happened. Amy, I'm sorry for yelling at you. I'm sorry everyone had to witness my childish behavior. I can't say it won't happen again, especially with these cases. That said, Amy, I want you to go to Warfield and speak to Mrs. Henderson. Pick up Marge first."

Amy narrowed her eyebrows in confusion.

"Yes, she's going with you. You have to stop at the elementary school and get Sarah. She's going, too. It was Marge's suggestion since she's a woman and a mother." Without arguing, Amy nodded and left.

"Billy, print out Amy's profile and distribute it to everyone. We're going to use it and go all out in our investigation. Amy will continue to lead on Wilson. Mitch and I will assist her. He and I will handle the Groves case. Search everywhere and everything you can on both cases based on Amy's profile."

Hubbard surveyed the board. His left forearm was across his chest, and his right hand held his chin.

"You see something, Mitch?"

"Amy's profile intrigues me, especially how it might connect to the Groves case. I'd like to get a look in their old house and the backyard."

"I could try to get a search warrant for both, but thirty years have passed. What would I use as an excuse?"

"Yeah, there's that. But there's no reason we can't do a drive-by. See if you can get a warrant. Then let's visit the neighborhood. Maybe some of the neighbors were there when the Groves were."

"I'll make a call. You see anything about the Wilson case?"

"I'm intrigued about the husband and Hobbs, the audiologist.

You should consider inviting Wilson back for a long talk. Might also, invite Hobbs for a talk."

Pickens scratched his chin. "I'll call Wilson and let Amy call Hobbs. Anything else?"

"Nah. Make your call for the warrant."

Pickens dialed the county prosecutor. The call lasted less than a minute.

"No luck?" said Hubbard.

"Just as I suspected, she said we need more than a hunch. I'll try Wilson." He dialed Daniel Wilson's number. The call lasted more than a minute and irritated Pickens. "He's pissed about his mother-in-law picketing his office. I'd never call my mother-in-law what he called his. Long story short, he'll be here in the morning—when he gets here."

"Oh, oh, I sense a confrontation. Want me to sit in?"

"I'd better let Amy. You can sit in when she talks to Hobbs."

Billy stepped up, cleared his throat, and said, "Sheriff, I got something on Hobbs."

"What is it, Billy?"

"She got her Doctor of Audiology degree from the University of South Florida a year after Wilson got hers from UF. Hobbs was married to Kyle Barton and divorced in 2000."

"That's the same year Wilson declared his wife dead," said Pickens. "Are the divorce records available to the public?"

"Sheriff, anything is available to the public if you know how to get them."

Pickens raised both palms. "Don't tell me how. Just get them." Billy grinned and let his fingers do the walking across his keyboard.

"I didn't hear that conversation," said Hubbard. "Let's go visit Groves' neighborhood."

When Pickens and Hubbard arrived at the Groves house, there was a 'For Rent' sign on the lawn. The condition of the house seemed as though it hadn't been taken care of in a while. It needed painting, the roof had several shingles missing and looked like it needed replacement, and a front window had a piece of plywood as a window pane.

"We could walk around it," said Pickens. "Act like we're interested in renting. I'll call the rental agent and ask to get inside."

"Maybe he'll permit us to search the backyard. You could tell him about the Groves family, and that you're looking for the son's body."

"I could do that after we walk around. Hold on. Let's talk to that neighbor," Pickens said pointing to a man walking on the sidewalk. "He looks old enough to have lived here in the eighties."

They got out of Pickens' SUV and approached the man. He had a bald pate, walked with a limp, and a cigarette dangled from his mouth.

"Excuse me. Sir," said Pickens.

The man removed the cigarette and coughed. "Yeah. Whatever you're selling I ain't interested."

Pickens raised his hands. "I'm not selling anything. I'm Sheriff Pickens, and this is Mitch Hubbard. We'd like to ask you a few questions."

"About what?"

"About the house next door."

"Why don't you call the Realtor? He knows all about it."

"I'm not interested in renting or buying it. I'd like to know if you lived in your house when the Groves lived next door in the eighties."

The man took a long drag on his cigarette. "Them? Yeah, I lived here. Thank goodness they moved away. One day they were there, the next day they were gone. Good riddance to them. Especially their kid. He was a mean one. After they were gone, no more dogs died from poisoning in the neighborhood. Why you asking about them?"

"We're working a case that involves them. How long has the house been vacant?"

"It's always vacant. Ever since the Groves moved away. No one rents for long. It was for sale several times, but no one was interested in buying it. It's like it's haunted. I told the Realtor he should bulldoze it, but he said the bank won't let him. Anymore question? 'Cause I gotta walk around the block. It's exercise they tell me."

"No, we're good. Enjoy your walk."

The man hobbled down the street.

"Interesting about the house," said Hubbard.

"Yeah. Instead of walking around it, I'm going to call the Realtor and get permission to enter and search the ground out back. We might find the son or something. Interesting comment about the dogs, though."

"It was."

Pickens dialed the Realtor and left a message.

*   *   *

When Amy, Marge and Sarah entered the Warfield satellite sheriff's office, Sergeant Dunne and Mr. Henderson were having a discussion.

"Please, Sergeant Dunne, let me take my wife home. I promise she won't cause any more trouble."

"You'll do no such thing, Gerald. I'm making no promises. If Sergeant Dunne wants me to stop, she'll have to shoot me. I'll keep picketing that son of a—"

"Please folks, there's a child present," said Marge.

Mrs. Henderson gasped.

"Dr. Davids, thank goodness you're here," said Dunne.

"Dr. Davids? She's not my doctor," said Mrs. Henderson.

"Mrs. Henderson, I'm Dr. Marge Davids, Sheriff Pickens wife. I'm also the county medical examiner and the coroner. I'm the person who found your daughter. I'm responsible for the sketch that identified you." Marge then told Mrs. Henderson about the conversation with Pickens' mother, her suggestion that Pickens have someone show the sketch to someone in Warfield—which led to Mrs. Henderson's identification of her daughter.

"My husband is doing everything he can to find the person who hurt your daughter." Marge purposely avoided words like murdered, bodies, remains, and anything pertaining to the killing. Sergeant Dunne had earlier placed the picket sign in a storage closet so Sarah wouldn't see it. "This is my daughter Sarah." Sarah stepped forward. Her angelic expression calmed Mrs. Henderson. "If anything happened to her, I would be upset like you are. So would my husband, my mother and my mother-in-law. I have faith in my husband and trust he would do everything he could to bring that person to justice."

Sarah chimed in. "My daddy is the best sheriff in the whole county and has caught a lot of bad people. So have Sergeant Mia and Sergeant Amy."

Mrs. Henderson smiled. "Sergeant Dunne, I'm ready to go home now if you'll let me. I promise I won't cause any more trouble."

"You're free to go, Mrs. Henderson."

Mr. Henderson wrapped his arm around his wife and escorted her out of the sheriff's office.

"Thank you, Dr. Davids."

"You're welcome, Sergeant Dunne. Amy, let's go home."

On the way back to Creek City, Marge called Pickens and told him what happened.

CHAPTER 23

ANIEL WILSON NEVER returned Pickens call. But
Wednesday morning Wilson arrived at the sheriff's
office with another man in tow. They waited while
Stacey Morgan, the daytime emergency operator went to get
Pickens.

Both Pickens and Amy were surprised to see Wilson. They
covered the murder board and then had Stacey escort the two
men to the conference room.

"Interesting," said Pickens. "Wilson shows up accompanied
by someone other than his partner after I left a message
yesterday. I wonder if it's because of his mother-in-law picketing
his office and that's his attorney. He wouldn't be asking to have
her arrested, would he?"

"I wouldn't put it past him," said Amy.

"Let's go find out."

When Pickens and Amy entered the conference room,
Wilson didn't stand, but the other man did.

"Sheriff Pickens, I'm Robert Faller. I'm Mr. Wilson's attorney." Faller extended his hand to both Pickens and Amy. "Mr.
Wilson would like to make a statement off the record. Is that
okay with you?"

"It depends on what he has to say. Is it about yesterday?"

"Partially."

"What does that mean?"

"Dammit, Faller. Get on with it," said Wilson.

The attorney ignored Wilson. "Because of Mrs. Henderson's actions, Mr. Wilson would like to clarify his position as to the death of his ex-wife. Can we proceed off the record?"

"I'm listening."

"Daniel, go ahead. But remember what I told you and stay calm."

Wilson cleared his throat. "Could I have a cup of coffee, please?"

"Sure. Amy, get Mr. Wilson a coffee. How do you take it?"

"Black."

Amy left the room and returned moments later with Wilson's coffee.

"Thank you, Sergeant." Amy nodded. Wilson took a couple of sips, then set the cup down. "First off, I understand why my mother-in-law did what she did. I have no intention of pressing charges against her."

"Mr. Wilson, your mother-in-law won't be a problem anymore," said Pickens. "Sergeant Tucker talked to her, and Mrs. Henderson has agreed to leave you alone. Your daughter also talked to her."

"That's a relief. My attorney suggested that I might be a suspect in my ex-wife's murder."

"Careful, Daniel," said Faller.

Wilson ignored his attorney and proceeded. "I need to tell you something about our marriage. It was a marriage of convenience, and it wasn't perfect. Maybe it started that way. But it became a sham. By that I mean, both of us had an affair."

Pickens' and Amy's brows tightened.

"Surprising, isn't it?" Wilson said. "Hers started two years after we were married. I only know he lived in Warfield. Her former assistant might know who he was."

"When did yours start?" said Amy.

"Before we were married."

"Did it continue after your marriage?" asked Pickens.

"Yes. Anne and I acted as a loving couple up until the twins were born. I love my children, Sheriff, but Anne and I were living separate lives even though we remained under the same roof."

"Your daughter said she once overheard you and your wife arguing about divorcing," said Amy. "Is that true?"

"Yes. Larry told me that Jenny asked him about it. I thought it best if we didn't divorce because of the repercussions and how it would affect the twins. But Anne wanted it. We agreed to wait. Sheriff, I'm gay. I was bisexual before I met Anne." Wilson paused when he saw their reaction. "She had that same look when I told her I was gay. *Shock.*"

Pickens wondered what it would be like if he or Marge asked for a divorce. What would it be like for Sarah when it was revealed that the reason was infidelity? But Pickens' marriage was rock solid, and there were no skeletons in his or Marge's closet.

"It certainly came as a surprise," said Pickens. "You realize that makes you a prime suspect, and whoever your partner is, so is he."

"Wait a minute, Sheriff, just because my client admitted that he is gay doesn't make him or his partner prime suspects. A person of interest, maybe. There's still whoever his ex-wife had an affair with, and if that man was married, his spouse could have killed Mrs. Wilson in retaliation. Any good defense attorney would argue that."

"I'm just making an observation," said Pickens. "But I have to keep all options on the table."

"Do you have a time of death? It might help. My client might have a credible alibi."

"Come on, Mr. Faller. Be serious. It was over twenty years ago. All we have is sometime in November 1995 based on the time your client filed a missing person report."

Wilson sat back, crossed his arms, and smirked.

"Then you can't place my client at a crime scene. Can you? Anything else you want from my client?"

"Yes, I need to know who his lover is."

Faller glanced at Wilson and nodded okay.

"Lawrence Meade, my partner. We've been lovers since college. Anne found out about us after the twins were born. She overheard Larry and I talking about our relationship. That's when the talk about divorce started. I swear neither Larry or I had anything to do with what happened to Anne. Neither of us could murder the twins' mother. We both adore the twins and would do anything for them."

Pickens had hoped Wilson would reveal who his wife's lover was. It would add a new dimension to the suspect list.

"Is that all, Sheriff?" said Faller. "Otherwise, we're done. And I repeat, this conversation was off the record. You can understand why."

"For now, it is. But I might want to talk to your client again. I'd also like to talk to Meade."

"I'm representing Meade also. He'll say the same thing as Mr. Wilson. But it has to be off the record."

Pickens scratched his chin. "Okay, for now. But I'd like a DNA sample from both, and their fingerprints. It might help rule them out at some point in our investigation."

"You can have mine," said Wilson. "But I'm sure Larry and mine are already available since we had to give both in college. There was a rape on campus near our fraternity house, and the police had us give them as part of the investigation. All the fraternity members had to, and we were all cleared. But if you want my DNA now, here." Wilson grabbed his cup of coffee, lifted it, finished it, and then slid the cup across the table. "You got it."

"Are we done, Sheriff?"

"Yes, Mr. Faller, for now."

Wilson and Fuller left.

"That was revealing," said Pickens. "I didn't anticipate the gay thing. But it gives Wilson and Meade a motive. What do you think?"

"Arrogant son of a bitch," said Amy. "I still like him as his wife's killer, and I'm going to nail him for it."

"Hold on, cowgirl. Let's not forget the wife's lover and his wife. And Wilson's assistant. Did you get in touch with Barbara Hobbs?"

"She'll be here tomorrow afternoon. Are you sitting in on the meeting?"

"If it's okay with you, I'd like Mitch to be in there . . . Whoa, whoa, it has nothing to do with you. I'm getting heat from the county commission, and I need all the help I can get. With Mitch's experience, it can't do anything but help with the investigation. You can have him observe or let him ask some questions. Work it out with him before you meet Hobbs. Is that okay?"

Amy bit her bottom lip. "Do I have a choice?"

"No, you don't, Sergeant Tucker. Now get that cup into evidence, and let's get on with the investigations."

After Amy left the conference room, Pickens got a call. When he finished, he made a call, then went looking for Hubbard. He found him with Billy eyeballing Billy's monitor.

"Mitch, the Realtor returned my call. We're good to go. I called Tatum. He'll meet us there with a dog."

"No drone this time?"

"A cadaver dog is much quicker. Besides, Billy didn't bring his drone to the office today."

Billy smiled.

"Works for me. Billy did a property search on the Groves' residence. After the Groves disappeared, the bank foreclosed. The house never sold, and the bank still owns it." Hubbard grinned. "Maybe there is *evil* in it."

"Maybe. Let's go."

On the way to Warfield, Pickens was silent. Hubbard sensed something was bothering him.

"You going to tell me what happened in the conference room, JD? Or do I have to pry it out of you?"

"Amy wasn't happy when I told her you would be with her when she interviews Hobbs."

"I could bow out if you want."

"No. Amy is hung up on Wilson and has lost her objectivity. I need you with her. I'd do it, but I want you there to be sure she stays on target. I've never met Hobbs, but I've got a bad feeling about her. Don't ask me why."

"I'll keep an open mind. I'll also let Amy do the questioning and only stick my two cents in where necessary."

"That works. Wilson gave us a motive for him and Meade. They're gay and are lovers."

"Gay? Really. Did Wilson's wife know?"

"Yes." Pickens then reiterated the conversation with Wilson and whose idea it was for a divorce.

"That's motive enough for Wilson and Meade, and the wife's lover and his spouse. I understand why you think Amy lost her objectivity."

"Yeah." Pickens shook his head. "Anyway, we've got our work cut out for us on the Groves murders."

"Thank goodness Nolan had the sense to keep a copy of his files, and we now know they were killed sometime in October 1987. Thanks to his report."

"Doesn't help find the killer or killers, but it's a start. And what that neighbor said about the kid makes me believe he didn't just up and disappear. I'm beginning to think he was there and brutally stabbed his family. Which makes him a *demented* bastard."

"I would have said a *psychopath*. It fits with Amy's profile."

Pickens pulled into the driveway of what was once the Groves' residence.

"That's the Realtor. Tatum's right behind us," said Pickens.

Brett Sonjay, the Realtor, was pacing in the driveway impatiently when Pickens and Hubbard arrived. When he saw Pickens' SUV, he threw his hands up as if to say, "finally."

"I was expecting you sooner." He checked his watch. "I've got an appointment in an hour, so you better make this quick." Sonjay looked at Tatum. "What are those dogs for?"

"To search the backyard," said Pickens. "Mr. Tatum will take the dogs back there. Mr. Sonjay, meet Mitch Hubbard. We're going to walk through the house. It shouldn't take us long. Shall we?"

Sonjay frowned. "Whatever. Let's get it over with."

Pickens and Hubbard followed Sonjay to the front door and waited while he unlocked it. Tatum took his dogs around back.

Inside the house, Pickens walked around the living room while Hubbard went to the bedrooms. Hubbard spent time examining the wall where a bed would be and the surrounding baseboard. After Pickens finished in the living room, he joined Hubbard.

Hubbard was on the floor examining the baseboard.

"See anything, Mitch?"

Hubbard pulled the carpet up by the baseboard.

"Maybe. I know it was thirty years ago but look at this." Pickens got down on the floor. "Is that a spot of blood?"

Pickens took a closer look. "Could be tomato juice or soda." He took his pocket knife out, scraped the dot, and placed it in his handkerchief. "I'll send it to Marge. Let her analyze it. You see any other spots?"

"Just that one. I'm sure the walls were painted a number of times, and the carpet isn't the original. If that's blood, we got lucky. Especially if it belongs to one of the victims."

"This isn't the master bedroom, so it's probably the girl's. You finished?"

"Yeah. Let's see what Tatum found."

"Mr. Sonjay, we're done here. You can lock up. Thanks for your help."

Sonjay checked his watch. "Thank goodness. I might make my appointment."

Pickens and Hubbard went out the back door. Sonjay locked the house and left.

"Anything, Bo?" said Pickens.

Tatum's dogs were still sniffing the yard.

"Nothing yet. Just some animal bones. Must have been a pet cemetery."

Pickens shook his head. Hubbard grinned.

Tatum's dogs stopped sniffing and wandered over to him.

"The dogs are done," said Tatum. "You need us for anything else, JD?"

Pickens shook his head. "Nope. We're done, too. Thanks, Bo."

"Anytime."

Tatum left with his dogs. Pickens and Hubbard got in the SUV.

"Know what, Mitch? I hope the sample we took isn't blood."

"Me, too."

"If it is and doesn't belong to one of the victims, then it could be the son's. Which means he's dead or alive somewhere. Or he got cut in the act."

"Or that. I hate this case. Wish we could solve it."

"You're not the only one. Let's go back to the office. I'll drop the sample off with Marge on the way."

"I'm done for the day, JD. I'm going home after we get back to the office. I've had enough murder for one day."

"Same here. I'll see you tomorrow morning."

CHAPTER 24

Thursday morning, when Amy arrived at the sheriff's office, she went looking for Hubbard. He wasn't there, so she walked into Pickens' office.

Pickens looked up when she entered. "Morning."

"Good morning. I was looking for Hubbard."

"Mitch is in Warfield with Sergeant Dunne."

Amy's eyes knitted. Her first thought was that Pickens had Hubbard and Dunne interviewing one of her witnesses.

"They're interviewing someone in the Groves case," said Pickens. "He'll be here in plenty of time for your interview with Hobbs this afternoon."

"I got a text from Hobbs. She can't make it this afternoon. Wants me to go to Warfield to interview her. She has an hour for lunch. Then she has other appointments she can't reschedule. If I want her to come here, it has to be next week."

"Hobbs texted you? She didn't call? I wonder why."

"So do I. I don't like this. What should I do about Hubbard?"

"I'd call him, but he may be in the interview. I'll text him. He can meet you at Hobbs' office. What time?"

"Twelve-thirty."

Pickens sent the text. "Okay. And, Amy, we're a team here. I need you to work with Mitch. He has way more experience than the two of us combined. It's still your case. Accept some help. Isn't that what you tell me?"

Amy half-heartedly shrugged. "You're right. Sorry about yesterday."

"Forget it." His phone chirped. "Mitch said he'll be there. I think Billy wants to talk to you. He may have something for you."

Amy left and joined Billy at his desk.

"Got something for me?"

Billy's eyes gleamed. "You bet I do. Remember I said she divorced in 1999. Hobbs isn't her married name. It's her maiden name. Her married name was Barton. I did a search on Barton. His full name is Kyle Barton. He had his own company, but it went under in 2000 after the divorce. He was the vice-president of sales at an IT company until 2005. Since then, he's worked in a number of sales jobs at different companies. His last employer was Warfield Electronics."

"Last employer? What's that mean?"

"Barton quit Monday."

"How do you know all this?"

"I called that private investigator. The one that helped on the Liz Price murders. He investigated Barton for me."

"You called Bobby Ellison? Does JD know you did?"

Bobby Ellison was a retired police detective who had become a private investigator and had an office in Warfield.

"No, and don't tell him. I asked Ellison for a favor. I thought you needed a break on the Wilson case, so I called him. He was glad to help, especially after I told him it was for you. Don't ask me why."

"Thanks, Billy. We'll keep this a secret, but I'll use it when I interview Hobbs tomorrow."

*　*　*

At the Warfield sheriff's satellite office, Hubbard and Sergeant Dunne were in a meeting with Alexia Norbin. Dunne had met her at the last PTO meeting. When Dunne asked if any of the parents had graduated from Warfield High School in the nineties, Norbin said she had. Dunne asked her if she had a yearbook from then. Norbin did and agreed to bring it to Dunne's office.

When Dunne told Pickens she had a lead, Pickens told her he only wanted a yearbook with Jesse Groves in it.

"Thanks for coming to see us and bringing the yearbook, Mrs. Norbin," said Dunne.

"I'm happy to. But please call me Alexia."

"Okay, Alexia. May we see the yearbook?" Norbin reached into her backpack and pulled out a Raider yearbook from 1988.

"Here it is."

"Wait, that's not the year you graduated."

Norbin smiled. "It's my brother's yearbook. I borrowed it from him. You specifically asked for a yearbook with Jesse Groves in it, Sergeant Dunne. Groves didn't graduate with me. He was in my freshman and sophomore class. He left school in my junior year. The only class picture he stood for was our freshman year. Check it out."

Dunne opened the yearbook and turned to the picture of the future class of 1988. She showed it to Hubbard.

He squinted his eyes. "Which one is Groves?" said Hubbard.

"That's easy. He's standing next to me." She pointed to her picture.

Dunne traced her finger across the row of names that applied to Alexia's picture.

"That says A. Howard. Not you," said Dunne.

"That was my maiden name." She pointed to the boy standing next to her. "That's Jesse Groves."

Hubbard and Dunne bent closer and almost touched their heads.

"Too bad we don't have a larger picture," said Dunne.

"I made you one," said Norbin, "on my iPad." She reached into her backpack and took out an iPad. "I can make you any kind of picture you need. Large or small. I can even age a picture." Hubbard and Dunne looked dazed. "I'm a graphic designer and the part-time art teacher at the middle school. Want me to do it?" Norbin opened the file that contained the larger picture.

"This is great, Alexia," said Dunne. "Want her to age it, Mr. Hubbard?"

"Sure. Can you also print us copies?"

"All I need is the office's printer type and you'll have them in seconds."

Dunne went to the printer, copied down the name and type, then gave it to Norbin.

Norbin created a facial approximation of Jesse Groves as he would look today. She saved it and then sent it to the printer. The printer hummed.

"There you go. Two copies of both pictures. Anything else you'd like me to do?"

"Did you have any interactions with Jesse?" asked Hubbard.

"Except for standing next to him for the class picture, no. Everyone avoided him. He was—kind of creepy, you know? Anything else?"

"Any chance I could enroll the sheriff in your art class?"

Norbin smiled. "He may be too old, but I teach a drawing class at the Senior Center."

"Just kidding. Thanks, Alexia. Can we keep the yearbook?"

"As long as I get it back when you're finished with it. My brother wants it back."

"No problem."

After Norbin left, Hubbard thanked Dunne.

"If you need any more help, feel free to call me," said Dunne.

"Oh, I will. Now I have to meet Sergeant Tucker."

Amy was waiting in her patrol car when Hubbard parked next to her at Warfield Audiology on Main Street.

Hubbard checked to be sure he had a pad and a pen in his pocket in case Amy wanted him to take notes.

"All set when you are," said Hubbard. "Anything you want to tell me before we go in?"

"No. Just follow my lead." Amy hadn't planned on telling Hubbard what she learned about Hobbs and her ex-husband. Even though she told Pickens she was a team player, she didn't feel Hubbard was part of her team. "Let's do this."

After the receptionist announced them, Amy and Hubbard were led to a small conference room. The receptionist said Ms. Hobbs would be right with them and didn't offer coffee or water.

"Not a pleasant greeting," said Hubbard.

"It's not the greeting I care about. It's the interview."

Hubbard touched the base of his neck. Amy's comment and the way she said it confused him.

Amy checked her watch. It was 12:45, and the meeting was scheduled to start at 12:30. Another ten minutes went by before Hobbs entered the room.

"Sorry I'm late," said Hobbs. "I'm afraid I can't give you as much time as you wanted. I have other engagements."

Hubbard sensed Hobbs was purposely late to annoy him and Amy. He'd seen it many times when interviewing suspects. He noticed Amy was calm about it. The sign of a good investigator.

"We'll try and be as brief as possible," said Amy. "How well did you know Anne Wilson?"

"Let's see. I joined Anne's practice in 1989 and was with her until 1995 when she disappeared. So, six years."

"Any ideas where she disappeared to?"

"No. Like her husband, I thought she went on one of her business trips. We're a franchise business, and she often went to meetings or conferences with the franchisor."

Amy decided since she didn't have much time, she'd be direct.

"How well do you know her husband? Did you interact with him in any manner?"

"What's that supposed to mean?"

"Did you associate with him after hours? Did you have any contact with him other than for business? Do you now?"

"I don't approve of your questions, Sergeant Tucker."

"Why did you and your husband divorce?"

"That's none of your business."

Amy's questions and the way she phrased them confused Hubbard. He wondered where she was coming from and where she was going with her questioning.

"Did your husband have any interaction with Mrs. Wilson?"

"Again, none of your business. If you continue this line of questioning, this interview is over, Sergeant Tucker. I agreed to talk to you, but you sound like me or my ex-husband are suspects. Are we?"

"Just asking questions, Ms. Hobbs. How long did it take before you took over Mrs. Wilson's practice?"

Hubbard saw the anger in Hobbs' expression.

"I ran the practice for three years then I offered to buy it from her husband. He was the majority partner. We agreed on a price, and it became mine. I changed the name from Wilson Audiology Associates, to Warfield Audiology. It was all legal."

"Can you give me your ex-husband's address?"

"No, and no more questions."

"Just one more thing," said Amy.

Hubbard saw Hobbs' nostrils flare.

"Would you be willing to give me a sample of your DNA and fingerprints?"

"Absolutely not." Hobbs glanced at her watch. "I gave you all the time I had. So, excuse me. I'm leaving. The receptionist will show you out." Hobbs stood and abruptly left the room.

"Whew. That was harsh," said Hubbard.

"I don't like it when someone shows up late for an appointment and rushes me. And I don't like that bitch. I'm changing my opinion on Wilson. Hobbs is now my prime suspect."

"That's hasty. Maybe you should wait and talk to Hobbs' ex. He could be a suspect."

"They both are as far as I'm concerned. This is my case, Hubbard. I'll decide what to do."

"Just making an observation."

At that moment the receptionist entered the room, and their conversation ended.

"I'll escort you out," said the receptionist.

Once they were back on the street, Hubbard decided to ask Amy her opinion on something to do with the Groves matter.

"Sergeant Tucker, before you leave may I ask you something?"

"What Hubbard?"

"What's the difference between a sociopath and a psychopath?"

Amy was caught off guard by Hubbard's seeking advice on Pickens' case. She mellowed and decided to answer Hubbard.

"While both share similar traits, sociopathy is an antisocial personality disorder and less severe than psychopathy. Psychopathy is a more severe form of sociopathy. Psychopaths lack guilt and remorse. They lack empathy, lack deep emotional attachments, are narcissists, dishonest, manipulative, reckless and risk-taking. Why?"

"Some things I learned about Jesse Groves suggest he may have been a psychopath. Thanks, Sergeant Tucker."

"You're welcome." Amy felt awful that she had excluded Hubbard from the information Billy gave her. And here Hubbard was seeking her opinion. "Say, Mitch, I'm sorry for the way I reacted. Billy discovered somethings about Hobbs and her ex. That's why I came on so hard with her."

"No sweat. Happy to be part of your team. I'm not going back to town. Tell JD I got an errand to run. I'll see him in the morning. Good job today, Amy."

Hubbard left. Amy got in her car and drove back to the sheriff's office feeling ashamed for deceiving Hubbard.

When she returned from Warfield, Amy sought out Pickens. He was in his office and had just finished a call. Pickens looked up when he heard her enter.

"You're back. How did it go?"

Amy sat. "I've changed my mind about Wilson. Hobbs is now my number one suspect."

"You met with for what? An hour? And you concluded that she killed Anne Wilson?" Pickens turned his palms up. "How and why?"

"Her attitude. It was worse than Wilson's, and she refused to answer questions. She declined a DNA and fingerprint sample."

"Why did you ask for them?"

Amy smiled. "The same reason you asked Wilson. You wanted him to think we had evidence that might incriminate him."

Pickens grinned. "You caught me. Good work, Amy. If we only did have evidence to link someone." Pickens raised his index finger. "Hold on. I've got an idea. Something we forgot about."

Amy raised her eyebrows in curiosity.

Pickens picked up his phone and dialed.

"Marge, I have an idea, and I think you can help. Can you tell from Wilson's skull if the blow that killed her was by a right or left-handed person? Okay, I'll wait." He covered the phone.

"She's checking." Pickens waited. "Okay, thanks. I love you, too."

"Well, what did she say?"

"Two possibilities. The blow could have come from a right-handed person if the killer stood in front of Wilson, but Marge believes the killer was left-handed based on the fractures."

"We're looking for someone left-handed. That narrows the suspects. Wilson is right-handed. He used his right hand to drink from the cup of coffee."

"What if he's ambidextrous?"

"Don't say that, JD. We just found a clue. Don't screw it up."

"Just thinking, but for now we'll stick with left-handed. What hand did Hobbs use?"

"Didn't notice. Maybe Mitch did."

"You okay with Mitch now?"

Amy pursed her lips. "Yeah. I kept some things from him, but then I came to my senses and realized he was helping me. So I told him. I'm okay, JD."

Amy then told Pickens what she learned from Billy's search, but not about Billy calling in a favor from Ellison.

"Good detective work. What are you going to do about Barton?"

"Try to find him and talk to him. I'll see if Billy can."

"You could try Bobby Ellison."

Amy bit her lip to conceal her surprise.

"That is if he's in town and not off getting dirt on a spouse. Worth a try."

"You don't mind?" asked Amy.

"Nope. Not if he can help, and we need all the help we can get. The leads aren't dropping from the sky like manna from heaven. So call him."

"Thanks, JD. By the way, Mitch said he had an errand to run and would see you tomorrow."

Pickens smiled. "I know. He texted me. Now, let's update the murder board."

Amy shook her head. Then she and Pickens updated the board. Amy wrote left-handed in the Wilson case and added Barton's name.

Pickens entered his office and picked up the envelope that contained the medical examiner's report on the Groves case. He read it thoroughly. In it, Vadigal posited that the killer stood over the parents and that they were on their backs probably in bed when the killer viciously stabbed them. The striations on the ribs suggested the killer was right-handed. The same thing happened to the daughter except the striations indicated the killer was left-handed. Vadigal's conclusion was that there were two killers.

Damn," said Pickens to himself. "Two killers? Was one Jesse and the other the person Jesse met off campus? If it was, then Jesse was alive, and if Amy's profile was correct, he might do it again. I've got to find him."

Pickens then picked up the envelope that contained the Wilson report. After going through it, he was grateful that Marge hadn't disparaged him for not reading the report before calling her about what hand the killer used. But something in the report caught his attention. It said Anne Wilson was struck twice with a flat object. Pickens wondered if both blows were delivered by the same object and at the same time.

Pickens then went to the murder board and updated the Groves case, adding what he learned from the medical examiner's report.

CHAPTER 25

FRIDAY MORNING, AMY called Bobby Ellison to ask if he was available to find Kyle Barton. Fortunately, he was in town and available. Ellison's office was in Warfield.

"So, can you help me, Ellison?" said Amy.

"I can, but it's going to cost you."

Amy was sure Ellison was smirking. "How much?"

"Dinner with me. My treat."

Amy wanted Ellison's help, but not at the cost of having dinner with him.

"How about coffee?"

"Make that lunch, and I'm all yours."

Lunch was better than dinner, so she acquiesced. "Deal. How long will it take?"

"Meet me at Jackson's Café across from my office at noon today."

"Are you serious? You can find him that quick?"

"Hey, you're talking to the best, make that the only, PI in town. See you at noon, Sergeant Tucker."

After Amy finished the call, she felt like Ellison had played her and might already know where Barton was.

"Damn you, Ellison."

"What did Bobby Ellison do now?" asked Hubbard as he stepped into the bullpen.

"He played me, and now I have to have lunch with him."

"Bobby's known for doing that. But he's a damn good investigator. Ran into him a few times when I was on the job."

"Yeah well, he better be. I asked him to locate Barton."

"Piece of cake for Bobby. Is JD in?"

Amy pointed her thumb over her shoulder. "In his office."

Hubbard nodded and headed for Pickens' office, but stopped when he saw the updated murder board. He then walked into Pickens' office.

"Knock, knock," Hubbard said. "See you were busy yesterday. Where did that info come from?"

Pickens held up the medical examiner's reports.

"From these. We're looking for two killers, not one. I got a bad feeling Jesse is one of them."

"You may be right. I talked to Harley. Asked her if she had ever had contact with Jesse or his parents."

"And?"

"She didn't, but her husband did. Harley said her husband suspected Jesse might have been abused. It was just a feeling he had. After Harley thought about it, she thought maybe Celia was, too. Which means—"

"Jesse might have had a motive. But why his sister?"

"Maybe Jesse didn't kill her. Whoever was with him did."

"Two psychopaths?"

Hubbard exhaled. "Yeah. It would help to know who Jesse's friend was. The woman Sergeant Dunne and I talked to yesterday said she didn't know."

"And Underhill said none of Jessie's classmates knew either. We got zilch, Mitch."

"We could put Jessie in the crime database as a person of interest. And—you could have that reporter write an article about Jesse and include this." Hubbard handed Pickens the aged picture of Jesse that Alexia Norbin made and the one of his class photo. "It can't hurt."

"Where did you get these?"

"That lead Sergeant Dunne turned up it turned out to be one of Jessie's classmates. She's a graphic artist and an art teacher." Hubbard grinned. "By the way, she teaches a class at the Senior Center. I enrolled you."

"Very funny." Pickens shook his head. "Anyway, I like your idea. I'll have Billy take care of the POI, and I'll call the reporter. He's gonna jump for joy."

Amy went to meet Ellison in Warfield at the restaurant. She hadn't expected him to be early. She knew he'd be late. Ellison liked to make a grand entrance and this morning he did.

Ellison strolled into the restaurant looking cocky. His clothes were slightly rumpled as if he slept in them. As a bachelor, Ellison lived his life the way he wanted to. He was in his late sixties, having retired in his fifties.

"Amy. It's great to see you. Looking good as usual." Ellison had an eye for the women and didn't hide it.

"It's about time you got here, Ellison. I agreed to meet you about Barton so let's get it over with."

"But, Amy, we haven't had lunch yet. What's your hurry?"

Amy's eyebrows narrowed. "Are you going to help me or not? I haven't got time for games."

Ellison smiled. "Let's order lunch, and then I'll help you." Ellison waved for the waitress. She walked over and handed both menus. "I'll have a cheeseburger and fries and a cup of black coffee. Amy, what will you have?"

Amy pursed her lips and acquiesced. "I'll have a chef's salad. Honey mustard dressing on the side and black coffee. Satisfied, Ellison? Yes or no? Will you help me?"

Ellison's grin spread from ear to ear. "Of course, I will. If you want to find Barton, all you have to do is go out the door, turn left, and walk fifty yards to Doyle's Tavern. He's there every Friday night for 'Happy Hour.'"

Amy's nostrils flared. "You couldn't tell me that over the phone? How do you know that?"

"Because I go there occasionally on Fridays."

"Is he there now? You told Billy that Barton quit his job."

"Probably. After we eat, I'll go with you. Barton might not want to talk to a woman. He's got issues with them."

"What's his problem?"

"Bad divorce. I know because when Barton has too much to drink, he talks about it."

The waitress brought their lunch and set it on the table with their bill. Ellison took out his wallet, paid the bill, and left a generous tip.

"For you, sweetheart." He winked at her. She smiled back. When she left, he added, "I come here often. I'm her favorite customer."

Amy ate her salad in silence. Most of it. She wanted to go to the bar and talk to Barton.

"I'm ready, Ellison. Let's go."

"Already?"

Amy glared at him.

"Okay. One last bite." Ellison bit into his cheeseburger took a sip of coffee and wiped his mouth. "Let's do this."

Amy exhaled, got up and followed Ellison.

Although it was early afternoon, Doyle's Tavern was dark inside except for the bar area. The barroom was empty, and chairs were on the tables. But for the lone figure at the end of the bar, it was empty, too. The bartender was cleaning glasses. When he saw Amy in uniform, he froze. Ellison pointed to the guy at the bar. The bartender continued cleaning glasses.

Amy thought the man might be Barton.

Ellison walked over and sat on the stool next to the man. Amy sat next to Ellison.

The man gave a disinterested look at both. He was unshaven, his eyes were bloodshot, and he looked like he had fallen on hard times.

"Kyle Barton?" said Ellison.

The man took a sip of his beer. "Yeah, who wants to know?"

"I'm Bobby Ellison, and this is Sergeant Amy Tucker from the sheriff's office."

"So? Did my ex-wife send you? What's she want now? I told her I'd keep my mouth shut."

Ellison turned to Amy and tilted his head in Barton's direction.

"Can we talk somewhere?" Amy said.

"What about?"

"Anne Wilson."

Barton flinched. "What about her?"

"Why don't we go to my office?" said Ellison. "It's across the street. We don't want to talk about it in here."

Barton glanced around the bar room. "Why can't we do it here?"

Amy got off her stool and stood between Barton and Ellison. "We found her remains. That's why."

Barton's arm tensed, and he almost knocked his beer over. That's when Amy noticed he was right-handed.

"When?"

"Christmas week. So, can we talk in private? I've got questions to ask you."

Barton nervously scratched his stubbled chin. "Okay." He tossed three dollars on the bar and followed Amy and Ellison.

There wasn't much to see inside Ellison Investigations. A tiny reception area, a secretary's desk, a small bathroom on one side and a coffee area on the other side with a microwave and small refrigerator. Ellison's office took up the remainder of the space.

Ellison's secretary was surprised to see the three of them. She was about to get up when Ellison said, "Go to lunch, Lu."

"But I already—"

"Go to lunch and take all the time you need." Ellison tilted his head at his guests.

Lu knew that when Ellison said take all the time she needed, it meant he wanted the office to himself for privacy and don't come back for two hours.

"Sure, boss."

After Lu was gone, Amy and Barton followed Ellison into his office.

"Coffee anyone?" said Ellison. Amy shook her head.

"I'll take a cup," said Barton. "Better make it black."

"The way I like it. There should be some left. Lu always makes a fresh pot at lunchtime."

Ellison went to get Barton's coffee.

Amy watched as Barton fidgeted with his watch. He checked the time as if he had an appointment, and he had a bead of sweat on his forehead.

"Got someplace you have to be," asked Amy.

"No. What's taking so long for that coffee?"

"Maybe he had to make a fresh pot." Amy knew that Ellison was delaying so she could talk to Barton alone. "Tell me about your divorce. What caused it?"

Barton scratched his chin. "Do we have to talk about it?"

"Did it have anything to do with Anne Wilson?"

Barton rubbed his shoulder. "I really need that coffee."

"It's coming. Tell me what caused the divorce."

"Have you met Barbara?"

Amy nodded.

"Then you know what a bitch she is."

"Tell me about it."

Barton exhaled. "Okay. Anne and I had an affair. It started several years after her kids were born. I wasn't her first." Amy made a mental note of his comment. "We met on business trips. I planned mine around hers. Barbara found out and threatened to expose Anne's husband and us. She knew about his extramarital affair."

"And she filed for divorce?"

Barton rubbed his chin. "No. Barbara is a vindictive bitch. Anne told me there wasn't enough business for two audiologists, and she had planned to part company with Barbara."

"Let me guess. Barbara blackmailed Anne and forced her to keep Barbara on the payroll."

"Yes. She also threatened Daniel. Barbara coerced him into selling her the business. After Daniel had Anne declared legally dead, I had enough of Barbara and filed for divorce. She used my infidelity and ended up with everything I owned. Believe me, Sergeant, there were many times I thought about killing that bitch."

Just then Ellison entered with Barton's coffee.

"Sorry, it took so long. I had to make a fresh pot. Lu forgot to." Ellison handed Barton the cup.

Amy fanned her face. "It's a little warm in here, Bobby. Could you turn the air conditioner up?"

"No problem." He knew Amy wanted more time alone with Barton.

After Ellison was gone, Amy said, "Did you ever try?"

"You mean try and kill Barbara?"

Amy nodded.

"No. I'm a coward. I wish I had the guts to."

It was obvious to Amy that Barton resented his ex-wife. There was plenty of animosity between Hobbs and Anne and Daniel Wilson. But was it enough to make Hobbs a killer?

"I'm curious, is Barbara left-handed or right-handed?"

"Right-handed. Does that mean anything?"

"Just curious. Can you think of anyone who might have wanted to kill Anne?"

Barton took a sip of coffee and set the cup on Ellison's desk. "No, but I wouldn't put it past Barbara. She threatened to kill me when she found out about Anne and me. I thought she was just angry, but you never know."

"Did anyone else have issues with Anne?"

Barton scratched his chin. "Hmm. You might want to talk to Barbara's assistant. She might know."

"Thanks, I'll do that."

"Anything else?"

Amy shook her head. "No. Thanks for talking to me. You've been very helpful."

"I don't know if I was any help."

"You were."

Ellison stepped into the office. "Cool enough now?"

"Yes, thanks, Bobby. We're done here."

Barton stood, shook hands with Amy and Ellison, and left.

"What's with the left-hand, right-hand business?" asked Ellison.

"The killer was left-handed."

"Oh. Good job, Sergeant Tucker." Ellison checked his watch. "It's a little early, but why don't you hang around and join Lu and me for a drink?"

Amy patted Ellison on the arm. "Sorry, Bobby, I got to get back to the office. Maybe another time. But I will take that cup Barton drank from. Got a bag?" Ellison got her a bag, and Amy put the cup in it. She held the bag up. "Evidence."

"Next time you're in Warfield," Ellison made the phone sign with his hand, "call me."

CHAPTER 26

W HEN AMY RETURNED from Warfield and walked into the sheriff's office, Pickens and Hubbard were huddled around the murder board. She noticed what Pickens had added to it and walked up to the board and wrote *RH* next to Hobbs and Barton's names then drew a line out from the picture of Anne Wilson. She wrote *Another Affair* with a question mark.

"What's that mean?" asked Pickens.

"A comment Barton made. He said he wasn't Wilson's first. And both he and Hobbs use the wrong hand. Any new ideas about Jesse Groves?"

Pickens explained what he and Hubbard had theorized.

"That's interesting," said Amy, "but what if the killer spared Jesse and forced him to watch, then made Jesse help bury the bodies? The killer then took Jesse captive and made him live with the killer."

Pickens eyed Hubbard. "What do you think, Mitch?"

"Interesting theory. But why didn't Jesse escape captivity?"

"*Stockholm syndrome*," said Amy. "Jesse may still be with the killer."

Pickens wrote *captivity and SS* next to Jesse.

"Makes sense," said Pickens. He turned to the Wilson case. "I'm curious, Amy. Why hasn't Wilson's son contacted you?"

She hunched her shoulders. "Don't know. I'll ask his sister."

Pickens checked his watch. "Been a long week, and I've had enough with murder. It's rib night at Leroy's. I'm going to pick up Marge and Sarah and have dinner there."

"And I'm heading for Warfield to have drinks with two lovely ladies," said Hubbard.

"At Doyle's Tavern?" asked Amy.

"Hell no. At home. See you Monday."

After Hubbard left, Pickens left as did Amy and Billy.

*　*　*

Almost a week had passed, and Amy hadn't gotten an appointment to talk to Hobbs' assistant. Amy was told the woman was busy with clients and couldn't make time for Amy. Then on Friday, Amy was told the assistant was on a two-week vacation and couldn't be reached. She thought about visiting Warfield Audiology and barging into the assistant's office and demanding she speak with Amy. But Amy had no probable cause to do it and decided against it. She had no other suspects, not even the name of the other man Anne Wilson had an affair with. The Wilson case was now in limbo.

Pickens and Hubbard weren't making much progress on the Groves case either. The only suspects they had were Jesse Groves and Jessie's unknown friend. The sample they took from the baseboard wasn't blood. It was paint. Like the Wilson case, the Groves case was also at a standstill.

With clues scarce and leads few, tempers started to flare, making matters worse. Pickens used every ounce of patience he could muster to remain calm and in control. Hubbard helped by keeping things in perspective.

In the Wilson case, Hubbard suggested Amy consider that Hobbs' assistant might be avoiding her because the assistant had something to do with Anne Wilson's murder and was avoiding answering questions that might implicate her. Amy considered Hubbard's suggestion and had Billy do a thorough background check on the assistant telling him, to dig deep.

As for the Groves case, Hubbard still had a hard time believing Jesse killed his family. Hubbard clung to the notion that Jesse was an unwilling witness and was a victim of *Stockholm Syndrome*. He suggested Pickens have the reporter write an in-depth article about the case including the gory details and a picture of Jesse as he would look today. Also, he suggested having the reporter get the article published in newspapers throughout the country. Pickens agreed, and contacted the reporter and took care of it.

Another week passed, and still, nothing happened. Pickens considered using Bobby Ellison to locate Jesse Groves. Hubbard agreed, and Pickens called Ellison to invite him to Pickens' office.

Friday morning, Ellison strolled into the sheriff's office looking cocky like a man who had just won the lottery. He waved to Amy and Billy. Both ignored him. Pickens and Hubbard waited in Pickens' office. Ellison availed himself of the office coffee and poured a cup, then joined Pickens and Hubbard.

"How much will it cost me, Ellison, to use your services?" asked Pickens.

"Now, JD, you know I can't charge you much. Did I charge you much last time?" Ellison raised an index finger. "Oh yeah, I didn't charge you anything. This time I have to."

"How much?"

"JD, we're all law enforcement officers. I'll make it easy on you."

"Quit bullshitting, Ellison," said Hubbard. "Answer the man."

Ellison grinned. "Mitch, did I ever charge you much?" Hubbard exhaled. "I didn't, did I? Okay, I'll waive my fee for time, but I gotta charge for expenses." Another grin. "I have to cover them. Fair enough?"

Pickens exhaled. He needed Ellison's services but he had the county commissioners to deal with. He'd tell them Ellison was a necessary paid consultant, and his fee was fair. He was sure they'd agree.

"Fair enough," said Pickens. "Here is a copy of the file. It includes a picture of what Jesse Groves would look like today. We have no idea who Jessie's friend was. As soon as you find something, you call me."

Ellison nodded. "Will do. Hopefully, it won't take me long. Adios amigos." Ellison turned and left.

"What do we do while we wait for Ellison, JD?"

"Good question. How about we review Nolan's file again, get the names of Jessie's classmates that Nolan spoke with, and interview them?"

"If we can find them, but we got nothing to lose."

Pickens and Hubbard went through Nolan's file and Underhill's notes. They made a list of the names and had Billy search for current addresses and phone numbers. As for the females, they had Billy search under possible parent's names and addresses. They also copied down names from the yearbook picture and had Billy search Warfield for any males with the same last names that might still live in Warfield.

Amy had called Jenny Wilson and left a message. Two hours went by and still no call from her. Amy paced the floor waiting for Jenny to return her call. Finally, she called.

"Sorry, it took so long. I was waiting for my brother to get here."

Amy wondered where here was.

"We're in Warfield at my grandmother's house. We'll both be coming to see you, Sergeant Tucker. We have something to talk to you about."

"I'll be here." After the call, Amy sought out Pickens.

"What's up?" he said.

"Wilson's daughter just called. She and her brother are coming in to talk."

"Want me to sit in?"

"Yes."

Forty-five minutes later, Jenny and Jeremy Wilson arrived. Amy ushered them into the conference room. Pickens joined them.

The first thing Pickens noticed was that both twins had facial features that resembled their mother, but neither of them bore any resemblance to their father.

"Thanks for coming in," said Amy. "Miss Wilson, you know Sheriff Pickens." Pickens nodded. "Mr. Wilson meet Sheriff Pickens." Both men nodded.

Pickens' phone chirped. He checked to see who was calling.

"Excuse me. I have to take this." He mouthed ME to Amy and left the room.

"Marge, what's up?"

"The DNA results came in on Jenny Wilson. There's a discrepancy." She explained the discrepancy and what they had learned.

"Are you sure?" Pickens asked.

"YES, I'm sure." Pickens heard the harsh tone and imagined Marge narrowing her eyes like when she got annoyed.

"There's no mistake?" said Pickens.

"NO. And you—"

"I'm not going to tell them. It's not my responsibility, Marge. Okay, I'll think about it."

After the call ended, Pickens grabbed a sheet of paper off a nearby desk, wrote five words on it and folded the paper in half. He then entered the conference room and placed the sheet of paper in front of Amy.

Amy picked it up and read the note. She glanced at Pickens and squinted. He gave her a slight nod. Amy then slid the note to Pickens. He pushed it back.

The twins watched the tennis match with the sheet of paper and raised their brows.

Jeremy Wilson interrupted the match. "Is my father a suspect, Sheriff Pickens?"

"Not yet. We're still exploring options."

"I don't understand what that means, but there is something we would like to share with you."

"Your sister already mentioned she overheard a comment about a divorce."

"It's not that," said Jenny.

Pickens' brows raised. He noticed Amy's did, too. She was also curious.

"We're listening." Pickens wondered if he should tell them what the ME learned or should he have Amy.

"Our father isn't our *biological* father," said Jeremy.

Pickens felt a sense of relief in his stomach. He didn't have to break the news to the twins about their father.

"But he's the *only* father we know," said Jenny.

"In case you're wondering how we know," said Jeremy. "After Jenny told me you took a DNA sample from her, I decided to have one taken from me and compared to our father. I learned he wasn't my biological father. Our biological father died in an automobile accident in 1996."

"So, you can see that our father would never have killed our mother," said Jenny. "Maybe he knew he wasn't our biological father or maybe he didn't. If he did, he married our mother, stayed with her, and raised us."

"There's no way he's a murderer," said Jeremy.

Amy turned to Pickens. He tilted his head.

"Excuse us, while we talk in private," said Pickens.

Pickens and Amy left the room.

"What do you think?"

Pickens scratched his cheek. "I'm glad we didn't have to break the news to them. I don't think Wilson killed his wife."

"I don't either. But I'm more than curious about Hobbs and her assistant."

"What do you want to do?"

"Give the assistant another week. If I don't hear from her, get a BOLO on her and a search warrant for her house. Can you get approval?"

"I'll get it. Let's go back in."

Pickens and Amy sat at the conference table across from the Wilson twins.

"We agree with you."

Both twins breathed a sigh of relief.

"Thank you, Sheriff," said Jeremy. "Now we have to break the news to our grandmother. It's not going to be easy."

"Why don't you have Harley Baxter go with you. Or Donna Hubbard. They both know your grandmother and could help pave the way."

"Thanks, Sergeant Tucker," said Jenny. "We think that's a good idea, especially Harley."

"What about your father?"

"He already knows," said Jeremy. "I told him. I think he knew all along and was protecting us. Do you need anything from me?"

"No, Jeremy, we're fine," answered Pickens.

"Before you go," said Amy. "Do either of you know what hand the woman who was your mother's assistant, and is now Barbara Hobbs' assistant, used?"

The twins looked at each other and pursed their lips. Jeremy slowly shook his head as if in thought. Jenny glanced up and toyed with her necklace.

"Right-handed. No, left-handed. I'm positive," said Jenny. What do you think, Jeremy?"

"I agree. Definitely left-handed. I remember because she once tried to help me with my hand-writing homework, and she had a difficult time because of it. Yes, definitely left-handed. Is that helpful?"

"It is. Thank you both."

All four shook hands and then the twins left.

"Left-handed assistant," said Amy. "A possible suspect."

"One week, then she's all yours. I'll get the warrant. You get her"

Later that evening at home after dinner, Pickens told Marge about the conversation with the Wilson twins, and their revelation about their father.

"So, you were off the hook about telling them," said Marge.

"Yeah, and was I relieved."

"What about Jesse Groves? Anything new on him?"

"No, and it's getting frustrating."

"You'll find him." Marge smiled and nodded toward the bedroom. "Want to play some football?"

Pickens smiled. "I'm hot on your trail."

CHAPTER 27

ANOTHER WEEK WENT by, and still, Amy hadn't heard from Hobbs' assistant. And Pickens hadn't heard anything from Bobby Ellison. The good news was that Jimmy Noseby, the reporter, was able to get his article published in several Florida newspapers. Noseby was working on getting it published in out of state newspapers as well.

Billy was able to locate four men from the list of names taken from the yearbook picture. The four were married and still lived in Warfield. He had their addresses and telephone numbers.

"Good job, Billy. At least we have something to work with. Mitch and I will each take two names and contact them. Hopefully, they'll remember something."

Pickens noticed Amy frowning. He imagined it had something to do with Hobbs' assistant.

"Amy, any luck yet?"

"No. the information Billy learned was useful, but it doesn't help locate her. There was something, though."

"What?"

"Isabella Asado, Hobbs' assistant's, last known address. She has a driver's license, and vehicle registration with 134 Blueberry Lane listed on them."

"You could try that address. Maybe Asado is there. If not, she may be on the run. Give it a try."

"But why would she run?"

Pickens tapped his chin thoughtfully. "Only thing I can think of is Asado was in the country illegally. Maybe both Wilson and Hobbs knew it. Wilson might have confronted Asado about it, and she killed Wilson because she was afraid Wilson would report her."

"Or Wilson overlooked it, but Hobbs didn't," said Amy. "Whatever happened between the three women, I think it led to Wilson's murder. If I could find Asado, maybe she'd tell us. Hobbs wouldn't. Can you get me that warrant?"

"You'll get it, but for where?"

Amy pinched her lips together. "Asado's last address. Maybe her neighbors know something. Anything is better than nothing."

Pickens contacted the county prosecutor, gave her a cock-amamie story about Asado being a person of interest and convinced her to get the warrant, but it was only useful if the premises belonged to Asado.

Amy called Sergeant Dunne, and together with Betty-Jean Carr and Andy Doring, the two criminalists, they went to 134 Blueberry Lane with the warrant in hand. The address was in a duplex neighborhood which was filled with families. Toddlers were playing in the front yards and mothers were watching them.

The sight of two sheriff's cars caused the mothers to grab their children and hurry them inside.

Amy and Dunne got out of their vehicles.

"This doesn't look a neighborhood where a single woman in her fifties would live," said Dunne.

"I agree," said Amy. "Maybe we should knock on the door and ask whoever lives there if they know Asado. We could also try the neighbors."

Amy looked up and down the street. It was deserted. What

houses she could see had the blinds or curtains in the front windows closed.

"This doesn't look like a neighborhood where people answer the door for the authorities," said Amy.

Dunne scanned the street. "You thinking what I'm thinking?"

"Yeah, *sanctuary neighborhood.*"

"What do you want to do?"

"Knock on the door. What choice do we have? We have to abide by the warrant."

Amy and Dunne walked up to the door and knocked. A woman who Amy thought looked to be in her thirties and dressed in workout clothes answered.

"Can I help you?"

"I'm Sergeant Tucker and this Sergeant Dunne. We're from the sheriff's office."

"I can see that, but what do you want with me? I haven't done anything."

"You haven't done anything. We just want some information. Do you know Isabella Asado?"

The woman shook her head. "Never heard of her."

"We have information that lists this as her address."

"I don't care what you have. This is the Cushman residence. My husband and I have lived here over ten years and, like I said, I never heard of Asado or whatever her name was. Now, if you'll excuse me, I have to finish my workout before my kids get home. It's my day off." The woman closed the door.

"That didn't go over well," said Dunne. "Now what?"

"I haven't a clue, and I need to find Asado."

"You could ask Bobby Ellison if he could find her. Bobby's been in Warfield a long time."

Amy sighed. "I hate to do it, but what choice do I have? The warrant was worthless. Thanks, Sergeant Dunne."

"Anytime, Sergeant Tucker."

The two walked back to their vehicles. Dunne left. Amy took another look at the house and the neighborhood and then got into her vehicle and left.

*   *   *

Since Amy was already in Warfield, she decided to stop by Bobby Ellison's office to see if she could wrangle some investigative work from him. When she entered Ellison investigations, Lu, his assistant, was on the telephone. When she saw Amy, she raised an index finger. Ellison's office door was closed, so Amy grabbed the nearest chair, sat, picked up a magazine, and thumbed through it.

After Lu hung up the phone, she smiled at Amy. "Can I help you, Sergeant Tucker?"

"Is Bobby in?"

"No. He's out of town doing some investigative work for Sheriff Pickens. Is there anything I can do?"

Amy stood and noticed a tennis racket behind Lu.

"Is that your tennis racket?"

Lu smiled. "It is. I'm taking lessons, and I got new hearing aids." She bent the top of her ear down. "Now Bobby doesn't have to yell when he wants me. My audiologist, Barbara Hobbs, suggested I start playing tennis."

"Does she play tennis?" asked Amy.

"Yes," replied Lu.

"Is she any good?"

"Oh, she's good. Except she frustrates her competition."

No doubt thought Amy. "How?" she asked

"She doesn't use a backhand. She switches the racket to her left hand."

A light bulb went off in Amy's head. *Hobbs was a switch hitter.*

"I can see how that would be frustrating. Is Bobby taking lessons?"

"No, but I'm working on him. Do you want to leave a message for Bobby?"

Amy waved her palm. "No, I'll call him. Thanks, Lu. Good luck with your lessons." Amy started for the door but stopped and turned. Lu was practicing with her tennis racket. Doing backhands and forehands. "Say, Lu, do you know your audiologists' assistant?"

Lu paused her backhand. "Isabella?" Lu continued practicing.

"LU."

Lu froze.

"What do you know about her?"

"Geez, you scared the hell out of me. What about Isabella?"

"Do you know anything about her?"

Lu did a forehand. "Last I heard she was on extended vacation. Barbara is lost without her."

"You wouldn't by any chance know where Isabella lives would you?"

Lu did a backhand. Amy was losing her patience and felt like hitting Lu over the head with the racket.

"Well, Lu, do you?"

Lu put the racket down. "She once mentioned that she had a daughter and lived with her. Don't ask me her name. I could try to find out, but it will cost you."

"How much?"

Lu licked her upper lip.

Amy thought, *Shit. She's going to hit on me.*

"Lunch with me."

Amy felt relieved. "When?"

"Now. It's a little early, but I'm hungry. I skipped breakfast. After lunch, I'll tell you how I'm going to help you."

"You're worse than Bobby."

"Sweetheart, no one is worse than Bobby."

Lu put the closed sign on the door, and she and Amy crossed the street and entered Jackson's Café. They ordered lunch. After the waitress brought it to the table, Amy couldn't wait any longer.

"Okay, Lu, I'm having lunch with you. Now tell me how you'll help find Asado."

Lu set her fork down and grinned. "If you want to find Isabella, she lives on Blueberry Lane. The same house she always lived in."

Amy's jaw dropped. "No, she doesn't. I just came from there. A young woman lives there."

"That's Isabella's daughter. Isabella lives with her daughter and grandchildren. I know because she once told me." Lu winked. "People tend to tell me things about them." Lu smiled. "Guess I got a face that says you can trust me with anything."

"But the woman said her last name was Cushman, and she said she never heard of Asado."

Lu covered Amy's hand with hers. "Honey, that's Isabella's daughter."

"But she said she never heard of Asado."

"Of course, she did. In that neighborhood, everyone says they never heard of anyone. Especially, to the authorities. You wasted your time going there in uniform." Lu hunched her shoulders. "Hell, it wouldn't have made a difference. No one in that neighborhood talks to strangers."

Amy wondered if that was why the neighbors were quick to get their children inside and front windows had the blinds and curtains closed.

"I had a warrant. I should have executed it."

"Wouldn't have done you any good. You would have had to

beat down the door to get in. Trust me, in that neighborhood everyone watches out for each other. You would have had a lawsuit filed against you and Sheriff Pickens."

Amy didn't want that. Besides, she had to abide by the conditions of the warrant which prohibited her from entering the premises and arresting anyone, especially Asado. The warrant only allowed her to bring Asado in for questioning.

"Somehow I have to speak to Asado. Any ideas?"

"Ask Bobby when he gets back. He knows how to navigate that neighborhood. He's done it before."

Yes, Amy thought, *and he'll want something in return.*

"Anyway, thanks for lunch, Sergeant Tucker. I'm glad I could help you."

"Yeah, thanks." As it turned out, Lu was as bad as Bobby Ellison.

As soon as she returned to the sheriff's office, Amy went right to the murder board and added *SH* next to Hobbs' name. Next, she moved Asado up to the top of the suspect list.

"Impressive, Amy. Did you learn anything from Asado?" said Pickens.

Amy felt her blood boil. "No, we couldn't execute the warrant because of its contingencies. I'll bet my ass she's hiding in her daughter's house."

"Her daughter's house?"

"She lives there with her daughter and grandchildren. I had to get that from Ellison's assistant. And it cost me lunch. Now I have to ask Ellison to track Asado down."

"Why?"

"Because it's a *sanctuary neighborhood* according to Ellison's assistant. Ellison knows how to get around it, but he's out of town investigating the Groves matter."

"What choice do we have?" Pickens glanced at the murder board. "What does *SH* stand for?"

"Hobbs is a *switch hitter*. Ellison's assistant saw Hobbs play tennis and noticed it."

"Hobbs is a *switch hitter*? Interesting. She's back to the top of the list of suspects along with Asado." Pickens rubbed his chin. "Let's go over everything again."

Amy was still fuming about her trip to Warfield, but she was willing to listen.

"Now that you know Hobbs uses both hands that means she could have delivered the blow that killed Wilson. Let's suppose it took two people to bury her. Asado could have helped Hobbs."

"And with the discovery of Wilson's remains and our investigation, Hobbs tells Asado to hide out so we can't talk to her."

"And Asado goes into hiding because she's undocumented and afraid of being arrested and deported."

Amy stroked her chest. "But why did Hobbs murder Wilson?"

Pickens scratched his head. Then he pointed to Wilson's husband. "Because she discovered something Hobbs was doing that was detrimental to the business and confronted Hobbs. Or Hobbs was going to go public about Daniel Wilson's love interest."

"And maybe Wilson's affair with Hobbs' husband."

"Hobbs threatens Asado that she'll report her to the authorities. Asado had no choice but to help. But it doesn't exonerate her. I think you should talk to Daniel Wilson again. He might know if his wife suspected Hobbs of something."

"And never said anything because he was afraid Hobbs would bring him out of the closet."

"Talk to him. And find out who the accountant was for Wilson's audiology business."

Amy was tired and exhausted from the long day, but at least now they had strong motives and some clues. But no credible evidence. It was imperative that she talk to Asado. Maybe she could provide the evidence needed to break the case wide open.

"Now that we have it, what do we do with this information?"

Pickens sat on the edge of a nearby desk. "First, I get a warrant without conditions. Second, we set up surveillance."

"In that neighborhood? No way that will work."

Pickens rubbed the back of his head. "Were there any for sale or rent signs in the neighborhood?"

"Didn't see any, but then I wasn't looking."

"Call Sergeant Dunne and have someone do a drive through. If there are any, we contact the agent and arrange a walk through and set up surveillance. We do it at dinner time. That way no one will notice only one person leave with the Realtor."

"I like it. How did you come up with that idea?"

Pickens grinned. "Easy. I saw it on a crime show the other night. I just remembered that the police in the show did it."

"What if there aren't any for sale or for rent signs?"

"Then we're screwed."

Billy was eavesdropping on the conversation and interrupted.

"You could catch the mailman tomorrow and ask him who lives in the house. Or, I could go online and search for the owner. Amy, you said the woman was expecting her children home from school."

"Yeah, so?" said Amy.

A light bulb went on for Billy. "We go to the school Monday and find out whose listed as contacts."

Billy beamed over his suggestion.

"Find out who owns the house," said Pickens.

Billy spun in his chair, put his fingers on the keyboard, and let them do the walking.

Pickens and Amy watched in awe.

"Got it. Lyle and Frances Cushman. It was deeded to them twelve years ago by Jorge Entenada."

"Good job, Billy. I'd love to see Frances' birth certificate," said Amy.

"I can look that up," replied Billy.

Pickens raised his palms up. "Hold on. Let's not go there yet. First a warrant, then surveillance, and then the school record."

"And if everything fails?"

"Then, Amy, screw a warrant. We go in guns blazing." He grinned when Amy and Billy gasped. "Just kidding. Everything is not going to fail. We'll get lucky. We need luck."

CHAPTER 28

UNFORTUNATELY, WHEN PICKENS called the county prosecutor, she had already left for the weekend and wouldn't be back in town until Monday. With no chance of getting a warrant, Pickens' only option was to wait. He ruled out the mailman for Saturday. But Billy had another idea. Possibly the best idea yet.

Billy suggested that he use his drone Monday morning for surveillance of the house. His suggestion was that when the Cushman children left for school, he'd have the drone take pictures of whoever sees them to the bus, walks them to school, or drives them. If it's not Asado, the drone can then be used to do the same thing after school. And Billy wouldn't have to be on the same street.

"Brilliant idea," said Pickens. "I'm sure Sergeant Dunne would be pleased we don't have to ask her husband to let us look at school records. If we get lucky and capture Asado on camera, we use that to get the warrant without the same condition. And, I can assure you I'll get that warrant."

Billy beamed with pride. Amy high-fived him.

*　*　*

Monday morning, Billy drove to Warfield in his personal vehicle and parked two blocks over from the Cushman residence. He

had already done a drive-by to locate the house. At 7:15, Billy
launched his drone and flew it to Blueberry Lane. He kept it
high enough so as not to arouse suspicion and out of hearing
range but within camera range. After several passes, at 7:40 the
door to the Cushman house opened and out came the children
followed by Asado. They got into a black car, and then Asado
drove to the Warfield Elementary School. The school was about
a mile away and within range of the drone. The drone flew low
enough to capture the license plate number. When Asado
dropped the children at school, Billy had the drone follow
Asado. She went back to the Cushman address, parked, and
entered the house. Ten minutes later, Frances Cushman came
out, got in the car, and drove off. Billy retrieved the drone and
returned to the sheriff's office.

Pickens and Amy were waiting anxiously for Billy.

When Billy walked into the sheriff's office, he had a smile on
his face and was holding a laptop above his head. Pickens and
Amy couldn't resist high-fiving.

"Got her," said Billy. "Even got the color and license plate
of the car she drove to the school. And I got a shot of Frances
Cushman leaving the house after Asado got back and drove off
in the same vehicle."

Amy pumped her fist. Pickens dialed the county prosecutor.
He had to listen to her admonish him for taking surveillance
photos without a warrant. Pickens yes ma'amed over and over
but eventually, the prosecutor reluctantly agreed to an arrest
warrant with the condition that Asado was taken alive. The
clincher was that Pickens told the prosecutor that Asado was
now their number one suspect in the Wilson murder, and he
had evidence to prove it.

"Call Sergeant Dunne and then saddle up, Amy. We're going
to Warfield and get us a suspect. Her hidden days are over."

Amy smiled, then called Dunne.

Pickens and Amy went to the prosecutor's office, got the warrant, and then met Dunne at 134 Blueberry Lane.

"Check the garage, Sergeant Dunne," said Pickens.

Dunne raised up on her toes and peered in the window.

"There's a gray car inside."

"Go around back in case she tries to flee."

Dunne went around to the back of the house with her weapon in hand. Pickens and Amy walked up to the front door and knocked. Both kept their hands on their weapons.

The curtain of a front window peeled back. Asado looked out, then closed the curtain.

"ISABELLA ASADO," shouted Pickens, "we have a warrant for your arrest. We know you're in there. Open the door, or we're coming in."

The door slowly opened and Asado stood in the doorway with her hands up.

"Don't shoot. I'm not armed." Asado looked weary as if she worried they weren't going to take her into custody but shoot her on the spot.

Pickens sensed that Asado believed they were like the authorities in her home country.

"We're not going to shoot you, but we will cuff you. Amy, you get the honor."

Amy grabbed Asado wrists and cuffed them. Then she read Asado her rights as a precautionary measure.

Dunne came from the back of the house and joined them. Asado was placed in Pickens' SUV and taken to the sheriff's office. Dunne went back to her office.

* * *

On the drive from Warfield, Asado was quiet in the back seat, mouthing her prayers and not making eye contact with Pickens and Amy.

At the sheriff's office, Asado was ushered into the conference room for interrogation. Pickens and Amy had agreed that he would play the bad cop, and she would play the good cop.

After letting Asado sweat a little, they entered the conference room.

Asado's head was slumped down. She looked up when Pickens sat across from her.

"Are you going to arrest my daughter and her husband?"

"That depends on whether you answer our questions," said Pickens with a harsh tone.

It didn't faze Asado. "Can I call my daughter and tell her she has to pick up the grandchildren?"

Pickens was surprised that Asado was under arrest and would possibly be charged with murder, but she was more worried about her grandchildren and her daughter than herself. Did that make her a cold-blooded killer?

"Again, that depends on whether you answer our questions," said Pickens.

Asado sat firmly in her chair with her head bent down. "I'll answer your questions if you let me call my daughter."

Since Amy's role was the good cop, she answered, "You can call your daughter. What's her number?"

Asado gave Amy the number, and she dialed it on her phone. When it rang, Amy pressed speaker, and put the phone close to Asado.

The daughter answered and Asado told Cushman she had to get the children. She wasn't feeling well and couldn't drive.

"Okay, Momma, I'll get them. You lie down and rest."

"*Si*, Francesca."

Amy ended the call. Pickens glanced at Amy. Like him, she wondered who Francesca was.

"Do you know why you're under arrest, Ms. Asado?" said Amy.

Asado nodded but kept her head down. "Because I was hiding from you as I was told to."

Amy assumed she meant by Hobbs, so she didn't ask by who.

"Why were you hiding?" said Pickens harshly.

"Because I'm not supposed to answer questions about what I saw."

Pickens looked at Amy. Her eyebrows had hitched like his.

"About what?" asked Amy. "What did you see?"

Asado suddenly reverted to her native language. "*Madre Mia. Por favor, Dios perdoname.*"

Pickens knew a little Spanish and understood, *God, forgive me.*

"For what? Pickens asked.

Asado rocked back and forth. Pickens and Amy worried she might smash her head against the table, but eventually, she stopped rocking.

"What happened to Mrs. Wilson," she said.

At last, they had a witness to the Wilson murder. But they wondered if Asado was complicit in the crime?

"Tell us what you saw," said Amy.

Asado still kept her head down and avoided eye contact. "Will I go to jail?"

"Depends on what you saw and what you did."

Asado raised her cuffed hands, put them together to her mouth as if in prayer, and then rocked.

Amy waited for an answer. The wait seemed like an eternity as Asado mumbled a prayer.

Without looking up, Asado said, "Mrs. Wilson was going on a business trip, but first she came by the office in the afternoon. I heard arguing. I was in the reception area and walked back to see what the argument was about. I heard Mrs. Wilson say, 'This isn't over. We'll finish it when I get back.' Suddenly I heard a thud. When I got to the door to Miss Hobbs' office, she said Mrs. Wilson had an accident and hit her head. I asked if I should call 911. She said *no*. Mrs. Wilson was dead, and if I called 911, the authorities would investigate."

"Why didn't you call 911 anyway?" asked Pickens.

"I wanted to, but Miss Hobbs said she knew I was undocumented and would report me to the authorities if I didn't keep my mouth shut."

"Hobbs threatened you and then what happened?" asked Amy.

Asado hesitated. "She made me help her bury Mrs. Wilson in a field. Afterward, she told me if I ever said anything, she would make sure I was deported and lose my daughter. I went home and never said anything to anybody. I had no choice."

Pickens stood and slammed his palms on the table. Asado's head jerked back as did Amy's.

"I'm sick of your bullshit, Isabella. You had a choice. You could have called 911. Mrs. Wilson might not have been dead." Asado shuddered. "You deprived her children of their mother. She's all yours, Amy." But Pickens had a daughter, and he had to wonder if he would have done the same thing? He stormed out of the conference room.

"I'm sorry, Ms. Asado. You did have a choice, but you chose not to make the right one." Amy had waited a long time to say it. "You're under arrest for being an accomplice to murder after the fact of Anne Wilson. I've already read you your rights, but I'll do so again. You have the right—"

When Amy finished reading Asado her rights, she escorted Asado into a holding cell and uncuffed her.

"I'll call your daughter and tell her you've been arrested. She can get you a lawyer. You'll need one."

Asado sat with her face in her hands and sobbed.

Amy shook her head, turned, and walked away. She should have, but Amy couldn't find it in her heart to feel sorry for

Asado. To have aided in the brutal crime of murder and cover it up for over twenty years was despicable to Amy.

Pickens had called Marge and told her about the arrest of Asado. He told Marge that he couldn't agree with her and show mercy for Asado because the woman was doing what she thought best for her daughter. They agreed to disagree.

After Asado was safely locked up in a cell, Amy went to talk to Pickens. He stood by the murder board pondering their next move. Amy walked up beside him.

"One down, one to go," said Amy. "Did you notice how she never looked at us? Just kept her head down to avoid eye contact. She's hiding something."

"I agree. Sorry about my outburst, but she deserved it."

Amy put her hand on his shoulder. He was not only her boss, but they were friends.

"She did. What's our next move?"

"Get a warrant and arrest Hobbs. But first I have to call Mitch. By now word has gotten around about Asado's arrest. Once Hobbs hears it, she's liable to run. I'll have Mitch keep eyes on her."

"Do we have enough to secure a warrant?"

"We'll find out."

CHAPTER 29

PICKENS DECIDED THE case was too important to make a phone call to the prosecutor's office, so instead, he made a personal visit.

When Pickens returned from the prosecutor's office, Amy was waiting for him.

"Wilson is in the conference room with an attorney," Amy said. "The attorney represents Asado."

"That was quick, but why is Wilson here?"

"He said he'd explain it to you. How did it go with the prosecutor?"

Pickens frowned and shook his head. "Not good. I'll explain it to you after we talk with Wilson and Asado's attorney."

Amy didn't push the issue. She could tell by his frown that Pickens wasn't pleased. She followed Pickens into the conference room.

Wilson and the attorney stood.

"Dr. Wilson, it's good to see you again. But why?"

"Sheriff Pickens, meet Howard Larson. He will be representing Isabella. Her daughter called me and told me that Isabella had been arrested, so I called Howard."

"Why did Mrs. Cushman call you?"

"Because she knew I would help. When Isabella called her daughter Francesca, it was a signal that she was in trouble and to call me. Isabella and her daughter had it planned that way, and I knew their plan. My wife and I set it up that way to protect Isabella."

"Then you knew she was undocumented."

The attorney interrupted. "Let me answer that Daniel. Sheriff, when the Wilsons hired Isabella, they knew she was undocumented but hired her anyway. They had just started their businesses and money was tight. Both practices shared the same space until Anne purchased the audiology franchise. She moved the audiology practice when office space became available to its current location. Anne needed someone to assist her. Not a specialist. She trained Isabella and helped her with her pregnancy. And now, I've been asked to represent Isabella in her fight to stay in this country."

"It's more than that," said Pickens. "Isabella Asado was arrested for the murder of Anne Wilson."

"You can't be serious?" said Wilson.

"But we thought this was about her legal status," said the attorney.

"Isabella confessed to her part in the murder of your wife, Dr. Wilson. She's in jail, at least until her arraignment." Pickens directed his next comment to the attorney. "Will you be representing her, Mr. Larson?"

The attorney turned to Wilson. "Daniel, I'm not a criminal defense lawyer. I practice immigration law. I'm sorry, but you'll need someone else. I can recommend someone."

"Can we at least talk to Isabella, Sheriff?" asked Wilson.

Pickens considered Wilson's request. "If Mr. Larson wants to represent Isabella temporarily, I can allow him to talk to her. You can join him if she permits it."

"She will," said Wilson. "Richard, will you represent Isabella until I can get her a criminal defense lawyer?"

"Since I'm here, I might as well."

"Amy, bring Asado here. But cuff her."

"Is that necessary, Sheriff?" asked the attorney.

"Yes," said Pickens.

With that, Pickens and Amy left the room. Amy went to get Asado. Pickens walked over to the murder board.

Amy escorted Asado to the conference room and then waited outside. When the attorney said they were through, Amy accompanied Asado back to her cell.

As they were leaving, Wilson said, "Thank you, Sheriff."

"Hold on, Mr. Wilson. I have a question." Wilson eyed Pickens with curiosity. "Do you know if your wife and Hobbs had any legal or financial issues?"

Wilson frowned as if in thought. "I'm not sure, why?"

"Something Isabella said. Does your wife's accountant represent Hobbs?"

"No. He was both our accountants. He's retired now. Why?"

"Again, something Isabella said. Would you ask him to call me?"

"Will it help Isabella?"

"Maybe."

"I'll have him call you, but only if it has to do with Anne's business and not mine."

Pickens put a palm up. "I'm not interested in your business, but I'd like to know about your wife's."

"Fine. You'll hear from him."

Wilson and Larson left.

Amy returned from putting Asado back in her cell and stood beside Pickens who was looking at the murder board.

"That was interesting," said Amy. "Especially about the signal. You going to tell me about the warrant?"

Pickens exhaled. "There's not going to be a warrant."

"Why not? We've got Asado's testimony."

"Doesn't mean anything according to the prosecutor.

According to her, a good defense lawyer would challenge it as hearsay. Asado didn't know what the argument was about and didn't see Hobbs murder Wilson. Therefore, we don't have a motive, don't have a weapon, and don't know if a crime actually took place. The prosecutor argued that it might have been an accident."

"What about them burying Wilson?"

"Best case, *negligent homicide*." Pickens took a deep breath. "As for Asado's testimony, the prosecutor claims that possibly Asado killed Wilson and blamed Hobbs to obtain a plea deal that would save her from deportation."

"What about a search warrant for Hobbs' office?"

"I'll ask you the same thing she asked me. Do you really think that the office wasn't painted and carpeted at least once in twenty years?" Amy shook her head. "That was my answer."

"What about the fact that Hobbs was ambidextrous?"

"The prosecutor had an answer for that. She wrote something on a piece of paper, balled it up in her right hand, and threw it at me."

Amy looked confused. "What was on the note?"

Pickens grinned. "So am I."

"So, now what?"

"We need hard evidence that it was Hobbs that killed Wilson. Like a weapon and a motive. That's why I asked to talk to Anne Wilson's accountant. If he still has the books, we can have a forensic accountant go over them. There might be something in them that leads to motive."

"Or maybe not. We're looking for a needle in a haystack."

"A tiny needle at best if we're lucky. Hopefully, Hobbs will make a mistake, and with Mitch watching, we'll nab her."

Pickens and Amy thought they had gotten lucky with Asado, but now it appeared their luck had run out. And now, the case was wearing on their nerves.

"Sucks, doesn't it?"

"Yeah, and we got shit on the Groves case."

The next day, Bernard Sanders, the accountant for Anne Wilson's audiology business contacted Pickens. Unfortunately, he no longer had the books for the business.

Amy waited for Pickens to enlighten her on the call from the accountant.

"Does he have the books?" Amy asked.

Pickens nostrils flared. "No. They were destroyed in a fire shortly after the accountant retired. Without those books we have no way of coming up with a motive. And without a motive, we can't get a warrant."

"And, without a warrant, it appears that Hobbs committed *the perfect murder.*"

"And Asado will be deported."

CHAPTER 30

Thursday morning the atmosphere in the sheriff's office was somber. Amy slumped over her desk. Billy was on his computer. Pickens was hidden in his office.

When Mitch Hubbard strolled into the office, he felt like he had walked into a wake. He went right to the murder board. After checking for updates, he startled everyone.

"What's with the doom and gloom? You all look like you just lost your best friend."

Amy sat upright. Billy swiveled in his chair. Pickens came out of his office.

"Mitch," said Pickens. "What the hell are you doing here?"

Hubbard grinned. "And, hello to you too. Other than to go out to lunch or play tennis, Hobbs hasn't gone anywhere except home and the office. She either made me, is one smart cookie, or is innocent." Hubbard pointed to the board. "So, what's new with the case?"

"There is no case."

Hubbard eyed him curiously. "What do you mean? I thought you arrested Asado."

"We did. She's in a cell until her arraignment Monday. She'll probably be released."

"Why?"

Pickens told Hubbard about his conversation with the county prosecutor.

"With no warrants, we can't build a case on Hobbs. Asado's confession most likely will be tossed, leaving us with nothing on Hobbs. Unless you got a brilliant idea, we got shit."

Hubbard sat on the corner of a nearby desk, drummed his fingers on his right knee, and studied the murder board.

Pickens and Amy waited impatiently.

"Well, Mitch, you got any ideas?" said Pickens.

Hubbard walked up to the board, grabbed a marker, and turned around.

"Okay, let's start from the beginning again. Asado claims Hobbs killed Wilson and that Asado helped her dispose of the body. Or Asado killed Wilson, disposed of the body, and is blaming Hobbs. In either case, how did they get the body out to that field and bury it? I say *they* because we know what Asado and Hobbs look like. Do we really believe either of them could dig a grave and bury a body in it without help?"

Hubbard waited while Pickens and Amy considered his question.

"A man could," said Billy.

Hubbard pointed the marker at Billy. "Excellent idea. But hold that thought."

Billy raised his chin and beamed with pride. Hubbard cleared a space on the Wilson side of the board and wrote *22T*.

"What the hell does that mean?" asked Pickens.

Hubbard laughed. "Two to tango. That's what it means. It had to be two that dug the grave and buried the body. So, whoever killed Wilson had help."

"We already know that," said Pickens.

"Yes, but how did they get the body into that field? You've all seen it. Do you think they used a car?"

"I've hunted that field and fished in the lake," said Pickens. "No sane person would drive into that field in a car, especially if they did it at night."

"But the killer or killers weren't sane," said Amy.

"I know, but they would have had to drive an SUV or a truck. A car would never get in and out of that field."

"Ah ha," said Hubbard, "now we're getting somewhere. What kind of vehicle did Asado and Hobbs drive in 1995? And let's not forget Anne Wilson. What kind of vehicle did she drive because they might have used her vehicle."

"Asado won't talk to us without her lawyer," said Pickens. "But I don't see her owning an SUV or truck. She had a kid and probably couldn't afford anything but a used car."

"Or a used truck," said Amy. "But I agree. Asado probably didn't own an SUV or truck."

"Amy, can you contact Hobbs' ex-husband and ask him what she drove?"

"I don't have a contact number for him, but I know someone who could contact him. Hold on." Amy took out her phone and dialed. "Lu, I need a favor." Amy walked away so she could talk without being disturbed. When she ended her call, she joined the men.

"Was that Ellison's assistant?" asked Hubbard.

"Yes. Lu's going to walk down the street to the bar where Hobbs hangs out. If he's there, she'll ask him what his wife drove in 1995."

"We're getting somewhere," said Hubbard.

Amy's phone chimed. "That was fast."

"Is it Lu?" asked Hubbard.

"Nope. It's Wilson's daughter." Amy answered the call and stepped away. She then ended the call and returned.

Pickens and Hubbard waited to hear what Wilson's daughter said.

"The daughter heard that we arrested Asado and were charging her with killing Wilson. Asado's daughter called her."

"And?" said Pickens.

"She doesn't believe Asado killed her mother." Amy held up four fingers representing the quote sign. "Her words, 'Isabella would never kill my mother or help anyone do it. And, she wouldn't keep it a secret.' Are you ready for this? She said she would have told my father.'"

"Interesting," said Pickens. "What's she going to do about it?"

"She wants to talk to Asado. She'll be in Warfield tonight and will be here in the morning. I said I'd be here and let her talk to Asado. After she talks to Asado, she's going to talk to her grandmother. She doesn't believe her grandmother would think Asado killed Wilson." Amy paused. "Oh, I managed to ask her what her mother drove in 1995. She said a Camry. She remembered because they used to joke that it didn't have power windows like her father's."

"Now we know the killers didn't use Wilson's vehicle," said Hubbard. "We need to know—"

Amy's phone chimed. "It's Lu." Amy listened than thanked Lu. "Hobbs drove a used Volvo like he did. So, they didn't use Hobbs' vehicle or her husband's."

"Somebody owned an SUV or truck," said Pickens. "Or Asado is lying and neither she or Hobbs killed Wilson." Pickens took a deep breath. "Which means we got squat."

Pickens' phone chirped. He checked who was calling. "It's the son. It looks like the family is circling the wagons." Pickens answered the call and stepped away. When he finished talking, he returned.

"What did he have to say?" asked Amy.

Pickens tilted his head. "The same thing as his sister. She called him after you spoke to her. He confirmed that his mother drove a Camry." Pickens walked up to the murder board and pointed. "His father also drove a Toyota sedan. But—" He pointed at the board again for emphasis. "Uncle Larry owned a pickup."

"And that suggests?" said Hubbard.

"That I was right all along," said Amy. "Wilson killed his wife."

"But why did Asado lie?" asked Hubbard.

Pickens sat on the corner of a nearby desk and scratched his chin. "Remember what Asado said when we asked why she was hiding."

"Because she was told to," said Amy.

"She never said by who."

"I just assumed she meant Hobbs."

"I did, too," said Pickens. "Shit. We let David Wilson in to see Asado. Who knows what he might've said to her. What threats he might've used."

"And he told Asado to hide and had her lie about Hobbs," said Amy.

"Suppose Hobbs wasn't there, and it was Wilson she heard arguing with his wife," said Pickens. "He kills her, threatens Asado, and has Uncle Larry help him dispose of the body."

"Which was why I told Billy to hold his thought that a man could dig the grave and bury the body," said Hubbard. "You've been looking at the wrong suspect."

"Now what?" asked Amy.

"We tell Wilson's daughter that we suspect her father and ask her to get Asado to admit that it wasn't Hobbs that killed her mother."

"You think she'll go for it? I mean, hearing that her father brutally murdered her mother."

Pickens hunched his shoulders. "What choice do we have? Without Asado's admission, Wilson might get away with *the perfect murder.*"

"Aren't you guys glad I came in today?" said Hubbard. "You might solve the case. Somebody owes me lunch."

"If we solve this case," said Pickens. "I'll buy you lunch and dinner. And, Mitch, you can lay off Hobbs. I've got someone else I want you to keep eyes on."

"Wilson or Meade?"

"Neither. There's an accountant I want you to watch." Pickens told Hubbard about Sanders, the books, and the fire.

"You don't believe there was a fire?"

"No, I don't. It just seems to convenient."

*   *   *

Friday morning, Pickens and Amy were in his office. Pickens had Chief Nolan's case file from 1995 on Anne Wilson's disappearance. He planned to go through it. Pickens had also scheduled a meeting with Noseby, the reporter, regarding the Groves case.

Amy was discussing her meeting with Jenny Wilson at ten o'clock. They went over the theory about the murder, and Pickens offered a few suggestions.

"I hope I can pull this off," said Amy. "I've never had to convince a daughter that her father killed her mother."

Pickens took a deep breath to calm himself. Now was not the time for Amy to question her skills. He needed her at her best.

"If anyone can do it," said Pickens. "you can. Think of it as convincing a client to come face to face with their demons. You've done it before."

"Yes, but I'll be creating the daughter's demon in her father."

"She has to know sometime. It's imperative you get her to convince Asado to recant her confession and tell what really happened. We know the approximate date Wilson went missing based on Chief Nolan's missing person file, but it would strengthen our case if we had the time, the day, and the date. I'll take the time and date."

Amy breathed deeply. "I'll do my best. What are you going to talk to Nosey about?"

Pickens' desk phone rang. "Hold on." He picked up the receiver and answered. "Okay, send him in." He put the receiver in the cradle. "Speaking of the devil, he's here."

"I'll leave you two alone. Fill me in later."

Noseby tapped on the door jam. Amy smiled at him and walked past him.

"Nice to see you, Sergeant Tucker." Amy waved over a shoulder. "Morning, Sheriff Pickens. You wanted to see me?"

Pickens laced his fingers on his stomach and rocked back in his chair.

"Sit down, Nosey."

Noseby raised both palms. "Sheriff, it's—"

"Sit, Nosey." Noseby sat. "I haven't had any calls on the Groves matter. Update me on your newspaper article."

Noseby smiled. "You know the article was published in every Florida newspaper, which is good. I got calls yesterday from several out of state newspapers that said they would print it. One said the horrific nature of the crime seemed similar to one in their state." Noseby's eyes lit up. "That's good isn't it?"

Pickens' interest piqued. "Which state?"

Noseby scratched his forehead. "I think it was Ohio."

"You think or was it Ohio?"

Noseby shook an index finger. "Ohio, yes it was Ohio. Maybe you'll get a call."

Pickens wasn't sure he would but hoping was better than nothing. "We'll see. Try to get it in more out of state newspapers. It's important."

"I'll do my best, Sheriff. You know I will. And again, thanks for the scoop. I might become famous."

Pickens pursed his lips and shook his head. "Yeah, sure. Now get the hell out of here."

Noseby knew when he was being dismissed. He stood and left.

At 9:50, Jenny Wilson arrived and Amy led her to the conference room. Amy offered her coffee, but she declined. She sat opposite Amy.

"Thank you for agreeing to let me talk to Isabella," said Jenny. "Will I be talking to her in this room?"

Amy measured her words carefully. She didn't want Jenny to panic.

"Not yet."

Jenny looked confused.

"I want to talk with you first. It's important we do before you talk to Isabella."

Amy then told Jenny about their theory of how the murder took place and that a woman couldn't have committed it. Nor could the body be taken into the field by car. It had to be done using a truck. Jenny shifted in her seat. Amy suspected the mention of a truck hit a nerve.

"Jenny, we believe the argument was between your mother and father over a divorce." Again, Jenny shifted in her seat. "It's our premise that your father was against it, but your mother insisted on the divorce. The argument got heated, and your father struck the blow that killed your mother." Jenny's hand flew to her chest. "We don't believe Isabella had any part in burying your mother."

Jenny looked poleaxed. "I'm sorry, Sergeant Tucker, I don't want to talk to Isabella. I need to talk to my grandmother. I'll get back to you." Wilson stood and left the conference room.

Amy sat perplexed. Was Jenny going to let Asado hang out

to dry and keep her father out of jail? Was Jenny going to lie to her grandmother? Amy got up and left the conference room.

"That was quick," said Pickens. "How did it go?"

"It didn't." Pickens' jaw dropped. "She wants to talk to her grandmother. I don't know what she plans to do. She said she'd get back to me, but I'm doubtful."

Pickens' face tightened. He was frustrated. "Another setback. I was hoping we'd be able to get an arrest warrant for Daniel Wilson. Now, what do we do?"

"Be patient? Maybe I'm wrong."

Pickens rubbed the back of his head. "I can't be patient. I've got to do something." He raised his palms up as though he was about to catch the kickoff. "We're missing something. I need to go through Nolan's file again. Maybe it's in there."

Pickens' phone chirped. "It's Mitch." He answered. "What's up, Mitch?"

"Nothing. Sanders went to lunch across from Ellison's office. I saw Wilson go there, too. I was lucky to find a parking space in front of Ellison's office."

Suddenly, it hit Pickens. "Mitch, where does Hobbs park her car?"

"In the rear of the building. Same place as Asado did."

"Do you know where Wilson parks?"

"Yeah, behind his building. Why?"

"Go have lunch and then come here. I need you."

"I'll be there as soon as I can."

Pickens ended the call.

"What was that about?" asked Amy.

"I got a hunch. Come into my office. I need you to help me go through Nolan's file."

Pickens dumped the contents of Nolan's file on his desk.

"What am I looking for," asked Amy.

"Any mention of Wilson's Camry. There should be something."

Both went through everything that was in the file including Nolan and Underhill's notes. Unfortunately, Pickens was disappointed.

"There should be something. Nolan and Underhill made copious notes. I don't understand it."

"There's nothing. Why don't you call Underhill?"

Pickens pointed an index finger at Amy. "Good idea." He searched the records for Underhill's phone number and found the business card that Underhill gave him and was thrown in with the file. Pickens dialed. Underhill answered.

"Thad, it's JD Pickens. I need your help."

"Hey, JD, what do you need? Was there something missing in the file?"

"Yeah. There wasn't any mention of Anne Wilson's car. Any idea what happened to it?"

Pickens imagined Underhill scratching the top of his head.

"Let's see. I remember. We asked what make of car she drove. The husband said a Camry. It wasn't parked behind her office when we checked. The husband said she either drove it to wherever she was going or parked it in the Tampa or Orlando airport."

"Did you verify it?"

"Come to think of it, we didn't. Chief Nolan felt that since the husband said his wife had left for a business trip, there wasn't any need. Geez, JD, you think we should have?"

Pickens didn't want to annoy Underhill by saying he and Nolan were incompetent, so he fibbed.

"I don't know. I was just curious. Thanks, Underhill."

Pickens ended the call before Underhill could ask more questions about the car.

"What did he say?" asked Amy.

"They had no clue as to what happened to the Camry, but I got an idea. Let's talk with Billy."

They left the contents of the file on Pickens' desk and went to Billy's desk.

"Billy."

Billy swiveled in his chair and looked surprised. "Yeah, Sheriff."

"You still have that drone video of Tatum's field?"

"It's on my laptop."

"Open it. I want to look at it."

Billy opened his laptop, found the file, and opened it.

"Anything, in particular, you're looking for?" asked Billy.

"Yeah. Something we weren't looking for before. Show me the area of Tatum's property where he said he doesn't go because of the mud."

Billy hit *play*, and the video started.

"Can you make it any bigger?" asked Pickens.

"Hold on. I'll put it on a flash drive then bring it up on the monitor." He inserted a flash drive, copied the file, and then opened it on his computer. The video appeared much larger on the large monitor.

Pickens, Amy, and Billy carefully watched the video.

"If you tell me what you're looking for, Sheriff, I can zero in using my laptop."

"I'm looking for a car."

Using the video on his laptop, Billy was able to bring the scene closer into view, and he slowed the video.

"That could be the top of a car," Billy said. "But it could just be bushes."

When the spot where Billy saw the top of what looked like a car appeared on the large monitor, he paused the video.

"Still can't tell for certain," said Pickens. "Billy, where do you keep your drone?"

"At home. Why?"

Pickens breathed a heavy sigh. "Because I want to get a look at that spot. We're going out to Tatum's property. We'll stop by your house and pick up your drone. First, I have to make two calls. Hubbard first."

Pickens dialed Hubbard's number. When Hubbard answered, Pickens said, "Mitch, forget about coming here. Meet me at Tatum's property. I'll explain when I get there."

Next, Pickens dialed Bo Tatum. When Tatum answered, Pickens skipped the pleasantries.

"Bo, where are you?"

"I'm at the lodge. I had a hunting party this morning. Why?"

"Is the gate locked?"

"The lock is on the chain, but it's not fastened."

"Good. Stay there. I'll meet you at the lodge. Can you get a hold of your friend with the backhoe?"

"Sure, he's with me. What's this about, JD? Not more bodies?"

"I'll tell you when I get there and keep your friend there. I need his services."

Before Tatum could ask more questions, Pickens ended the call.

"Let's go, Billy. Amy you stay here in case Wilson's daughter calls."

Amy tilted her head toward the front entrance. Pickens looked and saw Wilson's daughter entering.

"Looks like I got a visitor," said Amy.

"Remember," said Pickens, "you can do this. Let's go, Billy."

Pickens and Billy walked past Wilson's daughter. Pickens nodded. She nodded back.

Amy met Jenny and greeted her. "Thanks for coming back. I appreciate it."

"I came back to help Isabella. May I talk to her now?"

Amy bit her lip. She was uneasy about getting Asado to recant and tell Jenny about her father but knew she had to.

"Yes, but first I would like to talk with you. Let's go into the conference room."

Jenny followed Amy into the conference room and sat across the table from Amy.

"Jenny, before I get Isabella, let me repeat what I told you last time. It's important you understand it. We don't want Isabella to take the blame for something she didn't do."

"You don't have to repeat it, Sergeant Tucker. I understand what you're trying to do. May I talk to Isabella? Please."

Amy felt frustrated. She thought Jenny and her grandmother had decided to throw Asado under the bus for a crime she didn't commit.

"I'll get her."

Amy left the conference room and went to get Asado. She returned shortly with Asado cuffed.

"Does she have to be handcuffed?" said Jenny.

"Yes," said Amy, and she left the room.

Amy paced the floor waiting for Jenny and Asado to finish their conversation. It felt like an hour had passed before Jenny opened the door.

"We're ready, Sergeant."

Amy entered the conference room and sat across from Jenny and Asado.

"I've talked to Isabella, and she is willing to tell what really happened." Jenny put her hand on Asado's arm. "Go ahead, Isabella. Tell Sergeant Tucker what you told me."

Asado kept her head down and avoided eye contact with Amy.

"Miss Hobbs didn't kill Mrs. Wilson. She was out of town on a trip. She left Thursday." Asado lowered her voice. Amy could barely hear her.

"I'm sorry, Isabella, but could you speak louder?"

"It's okay, Isabella. Just tell the Sergeant what happened," said Jenny.

"It was Mr. Wilson. He was arguing with Mrs. Wilson. When I went back to close the door in case a customer came in, Mr. Wilson told me Mrs. Wilson had an accident, but she was okay. He said I should go home and not worry about what happened to Mrs. Wilson. I wanted to call 911, but he told me to go home, and if I ever mentioned he was there, he'd have me deported." Asado looked up and into Jenny's eyes. "I'm sorry, Jenny, I shouldn't have listened to your father. Maybe if I called 911, your momma might be alive."

Jenny rubbed Asado's arm. "It's okay, Isabella, you did what was best for you and Frances." Jenny turned to Amy. "Is that what you wanted to hear, Sergeant?"

Amy needed more information. "Why did you say Miss Hobbs killed Mrs. Wilson?"

Isabella looked at Jenny. She nodded her head, and Isabella answered. "Mr. Wilson told me to. After you spoke to my daughter, I called him. He said to hide, and if you found me, he would help me. He said if you ask about what happened to Mrs. Wilson, I should blame Miss Hobbs. Mr. Wilson told me what to say, and he said he would protect me."

"Thank you. Isabella, do you remember when the argument took place?"

For the first time, Asado made eye contact with Amy. "It was a Friday in November. I remember that it was right after Halloween. We had a lot of candy left over."

"Thank you, Isabella. You've been very helpful."

"What's going to happen to me?"

"Your arraignment is Monday, but if you tell the prosecutor and the judge what you just told me, I'm sure you'll be let out on bail."

"My brother and I will pay her bail. Will she be—"

"I can't answer that, but I'll see what I can do."

Asado reached across with her cuffed hands. "Thank you, Sergeant Tucker."

"There's something else." Amy mentioned Jenny's father and the attorney who'd be representing Asado.

Jenny took a business card out of her blouse pocket and handed it to Amy. "This is Isabella's attorney. He couldn't make here in time, but he will be here later this afternoon to talk to Isabella. He agreed to let you talk to Isabella as long as I was present, and he will also represent Isabella Monday at the arraignment."

Jenny patted Isabella's hand and smiled. Then they stood and Jenny hugged her.

When Jenny turned and thanked Amy, she noticed Jenny's eyes were moist. And Jenny didn't look like someone who had faced their demons and conquered them. She looked like someone who had given up faith in everyone and everything that mattered.

Amy said goodbye and thanked Jenny, then led Asado back to her cell.

CHAPTER 31

AFTER PICKENS HAD stopped at Billy's house so he could get his drone, he drove to Tatum's property. The gate was open, so Pickens drove up to the lodge. Hubbard had already arrived and parked next to Tatum's hunting rig. An extended cab pickup truck that was high off the ground because of its raised chassis and the large tires covered with mud was on the opposite side of Tatum's truck. Pickens parked next to it.

Pickens and Billy got out of the SUV and went into the lodge. Hubbard, Tatum, and his friend were sitting around a table enjoying beers. Tatum's dog Rocker was lying at Tatum's feet.

"Hey, JD," said Tatum, "what took you so long? You want a beer?"

"No." Pickens pointed to Tatum's friend. "Are you the backhoe operator?"

The man stood. "Yup. Name's Wayne Dixon." Like Tatum, Dixon wore knee high boots with his trousers tucked inside them and a camo jacket. His face was red from being in the sun and covered with stubble. "I remember you, Sheriff. You were there when I dug those bones up. Bo says you might need me for something."

"That your truck outside?"

"Yep."

"Does the winch work?"

"Yep. You need me to tow something?"

"There might be a car out in the field. If there is, can you pull it out?"

Dixon lifted his baseball cap and scratched his head. "You want to pull that old clunker that's stuck out there in the mud?"

Pickens' eyelids hiked. "You know there's a car out there? You've seen it?"

Dixon nodded. "Yes, sir. Both Bo and me saw it. It was there when I pulled him out of the mud. Damn fool shouldn't have been out there."

"Hey, I was checking my property," said Tatum.

"So, Dixon, can you pull it out and get it onto the road?"

"I can pull it out of the mud, but not to the road. You'll need a tow truck. I ain't taken any chance on destroying my truck. Smitty's Garage in Warfield has one. You want me to call him?"

"No. I'll call McCann's Salvage. They handle all our impounds. I'll have them tow it there." Pickens made the call.

"Fair enough. By the time I get it out, they should be here. We'll need Bo's rig to follow me. He may have to get me out if my truck gets stuck." Dixon waved Tatum off. "Ah, he won't need to, but if you all are going out there, it's best you went in Bo's rig. When do you want to do it?"

"Now," said Pickens. "And if you have to touch the car, make sure you wear gloves. I don't want your prints on it.

"Soon as I finish this beer we can go."

"You sure you can find it? My deputy has a drone. He can locate the car for you."

"A drone huh? Ain't never seen one of them." Dixon rubbed his chin. "Might be better if he did, but he'll have to ride in the truck bed."

"No problem," said Billy.

Suddenly, there was a *toot* sound. The men stepped away

from Dixon. Tatum's dog scooted away. "Sorry," said Dixon. "It happens when I drink too much beer. That's why it's best your deputy ride in the bed."

"Hold on," said Pickens. "I have to make a call first." He took his phone from his shirt pocket, dialed, then stepped away. "It's JD." Pickens had called the prosecutor and told her about the vehicle in the field, why it was important to tow it out, and did he need a warrant to do it. "Yes, I'm sure. I don't? Thanks. Will you be available over the weekend?" Pickens frowned. "I didn't mean for that, and yes, I'm still married and love Marge. Goodbye."

"One of your old girlfriends, JD?" asked Tatum. Pickens waved him off. "JD had a lot of girlfriends in high school and after he became a deputy."

"That's right," said Dixon. "Remember that doctor he dated?"

"Hey," said Pickens, "that doctor is my wife."

Hubbard laughed. Tatum and Dixon did too.

"Let's go before I put a-hurtin' on someone."

Billy was the first to leave the lodge so he could escape Pickens' annoyance. The rest of the men followed. Hubbard, Tatum, and Dixon were smiling.

Billy got his drone from Pickens' SUV and climbed aboard Dixon's truck. Pickens and Hubbard got in Tatum's rig. Rocker jumped in and sat in the passenger seat.

Pickens and Hubbard sat comfortably behind Tatum. Billy, unfortunately, huddled in the back of Dixon's truck, attempting to avoid the cold since the temperature had dropped into the low sixties but felt colder from the open-air breeze as the truck crossed the field.

Dixon grabbed the tin can on the dash board, took out a wad of chewing tobacco, and stuffed it in his mouth. He then backed away from the lodge and drove to the spot where previously he had entered the field when he excavated the Groves' remains.

Dixon stopped so Billy could fire up the drone. Then he entered the field with Billy's drone as his eyes in the sky. Tatum followed his tail.

When the drone spotted the car, Billy pounded on the top of the cab. Dixon stopped.

Billy yelled, "We're almost there. I'll bring it to us and then turn it around and fly it low, so you can see it through your windshield. Honk the horn when you think we're close enough."

Dixon stuck his left arm out and waved his hand. Following the drone, Dixon moved forward until the rear of the car was within view some fifty yards away. He honked the horn when he felt they were close enough. Tatum stopped. Dixon called Tatum on his cell phone.

"What's up, Wayne?" said Tatum.

"Get over here and get in beside me. I'll need your help. I'll send the drone kid to your rig."

"JD, can you drive the rig?" said Tatum.

"Sure. Why?"

"I gotta help Wayne. He'll send Billy here."

"No," said Pickens. "Billy stays put. I want him to film everything."

"Suit yourself." Tatum then spoke to Dixon. "Wayne, the kid stays with you. JD wants him to film everything." After Dixon agreed, Tatum ended the call.

Pickens got out of the rig and got back in and sat in the driver's seat. Tatum walked over to Dixon's truck and climbed in. Billy readied his drone, stood, and leaned on the top of the truck cab.

Dixon slowly moved forward until he was within twenty feet of the car. He tucked his pants into his boots and then he and Tatum got out.

"Get that shovel from the bed," said Dixon. Tatum got it. "You work the winch. Ease the cable out. I'll take it to the car and hook it up."

"What are you gonna do with the shovel?" said Tatum.

"Beat the ground and the bushes to chase any snakes."

Tatum worked the winch as Dixon cautiously approached the car, beating the ground with the shovel as he did. After hooking the cable to the car, Dixon tried the driver's side door. He could barely open it because the car was low in the mud and brush prevented him from getting it open. He stomped on the ground and beat the shovel on it until he was able to get the door open enough to reach in and shift the transmission into neutral.

Dixon spat tobacco juice then said, "Okay, Bo, haul it out."

Tatum started the winch and slowly tugged the car out from where it was bogged down and close enough to the truck so Wayne would be able to pull it to dryer ground. Dixon sloshed his way through the muddy ground until he reached his truck and then put it in reverse and backed away slowly until he had it on what he believed was dry enough ground that the tow truck would have no problem towing the car. Tatum unhooked the car and reeled in the cable. Both men then removed their high boots and got in Dixon's truck. Dixon made a U-turn and pulled alongside Tatum's truck. Pickens got in the backseat, and Tatum got behind the wheel. Billy took a chance and got in the passenger seat next to Dixon.

When McCann's tow truck arrived, the driver made a U-turn then backed up to the car, hooked it, and pulled the car up onto the flatbed. The driver honked his horn then drove out of the field. Tatum and Dixon followed.

Billy had filmed the entire scene using the drone.

McCann's tow truck turned right when it reached Grange

Road. Tatum and Dixon turned left and drove to the lodge. The men all got out of the trucks. Dixon turned his head and spat tobacco juice.

"Thanks, Dixon. You too, Bo," said Pickens. "We're heading out now." Tatum and Dixon each gave Pickens a thumbs-up. "Mitch, I'll see you back at the office. Billy, you're with me."

Hubbard waved and went to his car. Pickens and Billy got in the SUV.

"I have to make a call first," said Pickens. He reached for his phone and dialed. "Marge, it's JD. McCann's just towed a Camry to the yard. Can you send someone there and have them dust it for prints and any other evidence? You'll send Andy? Thanks. Yes, the Camry is evidence. I'll fill you in later. I gotta go." Pickens ended the call then called McCann's and told the owner that a crime scene van would be there to go over the Camry and to keep the car in impound covered with a tarp. After that call, Pickens headed back to the office.

Hubbard was waiting for Pickens and Billy to arrive. After Billy put the drone in the trunk of his car, he joined Pickens, and they entered the office.

"By that smile on your face," said Amy. "I bet you got lucky."

"We got more than lucky. After the criminalist goes over the Camry, I'll bet he finds Wilson's prints all over it."

"Then we can arrest him?"

"You bet your ass we will, as soon as the prosecutor gives me a warrant." Pickens grinned and shook his head. "I bet Wilson had a hard time getting from the car to Meade's truck. He was lucky he didn't get bogged down like the car." Pickens smiled. "He would have still been out there. Mitch, you get the honor of updating the murder board."

Hubbard walked up to the board. Next to the word *Camry*, he wrote *1995*—the year Anne Wilson went missing. Pickens, Amy, and Billy watched.

Stacie, the receptionist/emergency operator, walked up and tapped Amy on the shoulder.

"Amy," said Stacie. "There's a Keith Jackson to see you. He said it's about Isabella Asado."

Pickens gave Amy a curious stare.

Amy reached into her shirt pocket and took out the card Jenny Wilson gave her.

"He's Asado's attorney," said Amy. "Jenny hired him."

CHAPTER 32

AMY INTRODUCED HERSELF to Keith Jackson, the attorney. After checking his credentials, she put him in the conference room, then went and got Asado. After Amy took the handcuffs off Asado, she left them alone.

"Isabella's attorney wanted to talk to her without interference," said Amy. "He'll call me when he's ready to talk. He's from a prestigious firm in Jacksonville. Jenny and her brother must be able to afford him."

"Maybe the grandparents are helping," said Pickens. "But why?"

"Maybe they're all rallying around Asado and don't care what happens to Wilson." Amy tilted her head. "I'd bet the grandmother doesn't. She's finally getting the justice she wanted for her daughter."

"That's providing we get enough evidence from the car that proves Wilson left it in the field." Pickens pointed at the board. "One thing is certain. A woman didn't drive it there. If you had seen Dixon after he opened the Camry's door and changed the gear to neutral, you would have agreed. Dixon was knee deep in mud and brush and had to trudge his way to the rear end and hook it to the winch." Pickens shook his head. "No way a woman would drive a car into a place like that and trudge her way through that mud."

"We'll prove it was Wilson," said Hubbard.

While they waited for Asado and her attorney to finish talking, they also waited to hear from the ME's office about the forensics found in the Camry.

Hubbard turned the murder board around and erased the chalkboard. He wrote <u>What We Know</u> at the top and listed Asado's stories. Then he pointed out the inconsistencies in both starting with Asado didn't see the blow that killed Wilson and all she heard was loud talking which might not have been an argument. If there was an argument, Asado didn't know what it was about. The only thing plausible in her story where Hobbs killed Wilson was that Asado helped bury the body. And Asado didn't know if Anne Wilson was alive or dead when her husband sent Asado home.

"Basically, Asado's statements are worth zilch," said Hubbard.

"What's that mean?" asked Amy.

"It means both may not be worth the paper they were written on." Pickens looked at Amy. Both stiffened. "You didn't get them in writing? Did you record them?" Pickens bit his lip. Amy shook her head. Hubbard turned his palms up. "Neither one? Tell me you're kidding."

"Wilson's daughter was present when Asado accused her father. Doesn't that count?"

Hubbard exhaled. "No." He glanced toward the conference room. "I wouldn't be surprised if Asado's attorney tells you that you've got squat on his client, and he'll make you look foolish at the arraignment."

Pickens raised his hands. "Hold on, Mitch, let's not jump to conclusions. Let's wait and hear what the attorney says." Pickens pointed at the chalkboard. "In the meantime, continue with what we know."

Hubbard stressed that Asado's only statement that was

useful was the one in which Asado admitted she helped bury Anne Wilson's body.

"Which means—" Hubbard started to say.

"Which means we got shit," said Pickens.

Hubbard waved him off. "Not necessarily." Hubbard wrote *2 people to bury Wilson*, and *killer drove truck, not car.*

"I agree," said Pickens. "And it could be that the Camry was put there by someone other than a woman. Hopefully, forensics will establish who did."

"And it doesn't matter what scenario Asado sticks with," said Amy. "She can put Wilson in the office. If forensics prove Daniel Wilson drove the Camry, then we've got him at the burial site. He had to have someone help him so that he could get away from the burial site."

"All we have to prove is that *Uncle Larry* was that someone," said Pickens. Hubbard wrote their comments on the board. "Billy, any chance you could get us telephone records from 1995?"

Billy hunched his shoulders. "That's a stretch, but I'll try. No promises."

"Just try. What I'm looking for is a call from Anne Wilson's office to Meade."

"What about Hobbs?" said Amy.

Pickens wrinkled his forehead. "What about her?"

"Maybe she knows what the Wilsons might have argued about. And maybe she saw the phone records. It's worth a try."

"If she'll talk to us." Pickens pointed an index finger. "But there's someone else who might have the phone records."

"The accountant," said Hubbard.

"Right," said Pickens. "Once we put Wilson having been in the Camry, we'll bring him in and pressure him."

Hubbard had listened to the exchange between Pickens and Amy with mild interest, but the mention of the accountant and phone records gave him an idea. He reached for his phone, stepped away, and made a call.

Meanwhile, Amy was wondering what the attorney and Asado were discussing since they'd been in the conference room for over an hour. She worried that the attorney might convince Asado to recant her statement about Wilson. Just as she was about to mention it to Pickens, the conference room door opened and the attorney stepped out.

"We're ready, Sheriff," said the attorney. "I'm finished talking with my client."

Amy looked confused and wondered why he spoke to Pickens and not her.

"I wonder why he wants to talk to you," Amy said softly so the attorney couldn't hear.

"Let's find out."

Pickens and Amy entered the conference room and sat across from the attorney and Asado. On the table in front of the attorney was a yellow legal pad. Pickens noticed there was writing on it. The attorney flipped the pages to a blank page and put his pen on it.

Before Pickens could ask a question, the attorney launched into his spiel.

"After talking with my client, I discovered you don't have any signed statements from her." Pickens sat back, tightened his jaw, crossed his arms, and stared at the attorney. Amy expected Pickens to object, but she knew by the steel in his eyes that it meant he had contempt for the attorney and resigned himself to listen, although, it was against his nature. "If you recorded anything, you didn't advise my client that you were, and it's inadmissible. You have no evidence that my client did anything. If you do, you have to tell me about it. Also, you knew counsel represented my client, and yet you talked to her without counsel present."

Amy guessed that Jenny Wilson must have told Jackson about Wilson and his attorney, Howard Larson. She was about to mention Jenny Wilson's presence, but Pickens nudged her with his foot, and she kept silent.

The attorney continued. "Therefore, you falsely arrested my client and held her against her will. Your actions caused undue stress and harm to my client. If you persist on arraigning her in court Monday, I'll not only embarrass you, but will file a lawsuit against you, the prosecutor, and the county. Trust me. You don't want that, and you know I will win." The attorney leaned back, crossed his arms, and glared at Pickens. Proving he wasn't intimidated by Pickens. "I want my client released today and the arraignment canceled. And I want her record cleared."

"Anything else?" said Pickens.

"Yes. If you insist on holding Ms. Asado because of her immigration status, I'll challenge that because you have no grounds to do so." Daring Pickens, the attorney added, "It's your move, Sheriff."

"Can I ask your client a question?"

"Depends on the question, but I'll listen."

"Does your client know if Barbara Hobbs used the same accountant as Anne Wilson did?"

The attorney turned to Asado. She whispered in his ear. "My client has no knowledge of that."

"Does she know if Lawrence Meade drove a truck at the time of Anne Wilson's murder?"

"That's two questions, Sheriff. You said a question."

Pickens uncrossed his arms and straightened in his chair. "It's a simple yes or no question. Does she, or doesn't she?"

The attorney put his ear to Asado so she could whisper in it. "The answer is yes, but that's all she knows. Are we done?"

Pickens stood. "Last question. Who is Jorge Entenada?

The attorney shook his head but lent an ear to Asado. "My client can answer that."

"He's the man that rented the house to me," said Asado. "When I first moved into the house. Mrs. Wilson arranged it for me when I was pregnant with my daughter. When my daughter married, he sold the house to her and her husband, and they let me live with them to help with the children."

"That answer your question, Sheriff?"

"Yes. You're free to go Ms. Asado. Sergeant Tucker will get your personal belongings and have you sign the release papers." Before leaving, Pickens addressed the attorney. "One last thing. As far as anyone is concerned, you pushed the arraignment up to today and got your client released. Anyone asks, you answer, 'No comment.'

"Why would I do that?"

"To give me time to catch Anne Wilson's killer, that's why."

"No comment," said the attorney.

Pickens left the room. Amy stood and watched Asado hug her attorney. Then she led Asado and her attorney to booking, retrieved Asado's personal belongings—which were just the clothing Asado wore when arrested. Asado went to the ladies' room and changed clothes. Then she left with her attorney.

Amy approached Pickens. "Now what do we do?"

"Mitch, I hate to ask you, but would you keep eyes on Sanders over the weekend? If he has a storage locker and goes there, I want you to be there when he does. You call me, and I'll get a subpoena for the locker and a subpoena for questioning him. I want to know what's in the locker."

Hubbard smiled. "No problem with the surveillance. Donna may not like it, but she'll get over it. If it's a storage locker you're looking for, there are only two storage facilities in Warfield." Hubbard checked the time. It was four-thirty. "I'll stop by each on my way home and ask if Sanders rents a locker. I know the owners of both storage facilities. They'll tell me."

"Thanks, Mitch."

Hubbard waved Pickens off and left.

"Why did you ask about Jorge Entenada?" asked Amy.

"Just a hunch." Pickens then wrote something on a piece of paper, folded it, and handed it to Billy.

Billy read the note and gave Pickens a thumbs-up.

"If we don't get a call from the ME about the forensics from the Camry, we might as well call it a day and go home. I'm sure we'll know by Monday."

"What are you going to do about the arraignment Monday?" asked Amy.

"Shit. I'd better call the prosecutor and tell her to cancel it." Pickens took out his phone and made the call. Needless to say, she wasn't pleased and she said the judge wouldn't be either. Pickens would have been well off if he left it at that, but he had to ask a question.

"You want me to spend my weekend waiting for you to call?" the prosecutor said harshly. "And you want the judge to wait also? Because you might want a subpoena or a warrant? Are you out of your mind?"

"Something like that. But if it all goes as I expect, I'll have the evidence I need, and be able to arrest Anne Wilson's killer." He listened as she cursed him, but in the end, she agreed. Pickens ended the call.

"I take it she wasn't happy?" said Amy.

"She'll get over it." Pickens smiled. "I'll send her a dozen roses."

Pickens was about to give up on the ME calling about the *forensics* from the Camry when his phone rang. He checked the ID. It wasn't the ME, it was Bobby Ellison. Pickens hadn't

heard from Ellison in over a week and thought maybe Ellison
had gone on vacation instead of tracking down Jesse Groves.

"Where the hell you been, Ellison? You better have good
news for me."

"Hey, I've been busy," said Ellison, "tracking Groves. It's not
easy. The guys a ghost, but I think I found something."

Ellison told Pickens that in his travels he happened upon
some newspaper articles about killings that resembled the
Groves murder. He spoke to the reporters and learned that the
authorities had no clue as to who the killers were, and there
was no forensics to help identify them. Ellison said he talked to
several detectives that handled the cases, and they verified that
they had nothing to go on.

"Like you, JD, they got squat. But I learned more. The killings
I checked on happened in several cities and states." Ellison's
comment made Pickens's skin tighten, and his flesh felt like it
had crawled. "If the killers are Jesse Groves and his friend, Jesse
grew up to be a serial killer."

Pickens' chest heaved. "The son of a bitch started with his
family." Pickens tried not to let his hatred for Jesse Groves get
the best of him, but it boiled over. "I don't want to capture him.
I want him dead."

"Hold on, partner, I didn't sign up for that. You're angry,
but you gotta do what's right. They'll make a mistake, and some
law enforcement officer will find and capture them."

Pickens took a deep breath and managed to subside his
anger. "You're right. Thanks, Bobby. You coming home or are
you gonna keep looking?"

"Not much more I can do, so I'm coming home. Lu misses
me." Ellison ended the call.

Amy waited to hear what Ellison had said. Pickens gave her
the short version and said Ellison was done looking for Groves.

"Maybe Nosey's article will turn up a lead," said Amy. "But

if they're on a cross-country spree, there is nothing we can do except wait and hope it ends soon."

"Hope and wait. I don't have patience for that. It's been what—almost three months since we discovered both sets of remains, and we haven't arrested anyone except Asado. And that was a waste of time." Pickens checked the time. "Why the hell hasn't the ME called? They've had enough time to go over the Camry."

"We want them to be thorough, so try to be patient."

Pickens glared at Amy. She ignored him.

"I think we should take another run at Hobbs."

Pickens looked confused. "Why, what for?"

"She might know what the Wilsons argued about and if the accountant is hiding something."

Pickens considered it might be a possibility. "I don't think she'll talk to you. She knows you were checking on her. I'll call her, and I'll offer to go to Warfield to talk to her. It's worth a try."

"Maybe Lu would go with you. Lu and Hobbs are somewhat friendly. Lu is a client of Hobbs."

"Why not, it's worth a try." Pickens phone chirped. "It's the ME finally."

"Be calm, JD. You don't want to make her mad."

Pickens took a deep breath and exhaled. "Marge, how has your day been?" Amy smiled. "Mine's been okay." Pickens tone changed. "Yes, I've been on edge waiting for your call. How did you expect me to be? Okay, I'm sorry. But, Marge, please give me some good news. I need it." He listened then smiled. "Son of a—. That's what I thought, and it's just what I need. Damn I love you, and your forensics team. What? Yes, I'll tell you all about it when I see you tonight. But I might have to work this weekend. I know we were going to visit your parents, but this case is important, and I've waited too long to make an arrest." Pickens grinned. "Yes, I'll make it up to you. Thanks."

A sudden thought came to Pickens. "Marge, before you hang up, I have a question. You once told me Wilson's killer was left-handed, but a right-handed person could have killed her if standing in front of her. Is that possible? Uh huh. Yes. Okay, thanks."

Pickens held his arms up signaling a touchdown. "Daniel Wilson's prints were on the steering wheel, the turn signal, the inside door handle, and the gear shift—which means he was the last person to drive the Camry. We got the son-of-a-bitch." He and Amy high fived.

"What did she say about a right-handed killer?" asked Amy.

"She said it's possible, but she would need the murder weapon to be sure. That may be a problem, but I'm still calling the prosecutor. Then I'll call Hobbs."

He dialed the prosecutor and waited while her office phone rang. He listened as the prosecutor's assistant explained that she had left for the day and would be at an evening affair and wasn't to be disturbed for anything.

"Shit. She's unavailable. I'll try her at home tomorrow," said Pickens.

"Maybe you should wait until we have more than Wilson had been at the burial site and the office the day of the murder. The weapon and a motive would seal the deal for the prosecutor."

Pickens exhaled. "You're right. No sense in getting turned down twice. Let's see if Hobbs will talk to me." He dialed Hobbs office and was lucky to catch her before she left for the weekend. "No, Miss Hobbs, you're not a suspect. I just want to ask you a few questions. I'll come to your office on Monday if you prefer." He held up crossed fingers to Amy. "One o'clock is fine. I only need an hour, not more. No, Sergeant Tucker won't be with me. Thank you, Miss Hobbs."

"I heard you," said Amy. "She doesn't like me."

"If you heard what she said about you, you'd know she can't stand you. Doesn't matter. She'll talk to me." Pickens checked the time. "Let's go home. Billy, anything on that project I gave you?"

"Not much yet, but I'm working on it. I can't work late. I have a date, but I'll come in early tomorrow and work on it."

"Thanks. Enjoy your date tonight. I'll see you in the morning."

Pickens left, and Amy saddled up to Billy. "What project did he give you?"

Billy quickly opened another file so Amy couldn't see what he was working on for Pickens. "It's nothing, and I'm sorry, but it's confidential. Goodnight, Amy."

Amy glared at Billy. "Yeah, goodnight to you," she said and left.

CHAPTER 33

SATURDAY MORNING, BILLY was in bright and early before Pickens and Amy. He wanted to get a quick start on the project for Pickens and wanted to impress him. The night before, he had collected quite a bit of data, but still had more work to do.

At nine o'clock when Pickens and Amy strolled through the entrance, Billy shot his hands and arms in the air and shouted, "Touchdown." Then, he pumped his fist. "You the man, Billy."

Amy wasn't impressed by Billy's antics. She was still annoyed about yesterday when Billy said what he was working on for Pickens was confidential. But Pickens was impressed and pumped his fist. He knew Billy had come through for him and got what he needed.

"All done, Sheriff," said Billy. "What do I do now?"

"Make me a copy and save what you have. I'll take it with me Monday. Thanks, Billy."

"You're welcome." Billy glanced at Amy. She had her arms crossed and didn't look pleased.

Amy followed Pickens into his office and closed the door behind her.

"Are you going to clue me in on your project or keep me in the dark?"

"Not yet, Amy. Not until I'm sure I've got something. It's a hunch, but if it pans out, you'll be happy. Trust me."

Amy sat and crossed her arms. "I trust you, but I don't like when you exclude me. Whatever it is, I at least deserve to know."

Pickens was torn between being Amy's superior and her friend. They had known each other for years and he didn't like keeping her in the dark, but this time he needed to because he was on a fishing expedition.

"You're right, but not this time. It's important, Amy."

Amy stood. "If we weren't friends, I'd drop my badge on your desk and walk the hell out of here for good." She opened the door and left.

Pickens was about to go after her, but his phone chirped. It was Hubbard calling.

"What's up, Mitch?"

"You don't sound too happy. Did something go wrong?"

"Sort of," Pickens replied, but he wasn't about to share the argument with Amy. "You have something for me?"

"I hear you," said Hubbard. "I located Sanders' storage locker. The facility has security cameras. The owner and manager let me look at the recordings for the past week. Guess who visited his locker last week?"

"Son of a bitch. Did he remove anything?"

"No. I'm parked nearby where he can't see me if he comes back. I called Sergeant Dunne on my way home yesterday and asked if she could provide me backup. She said to call her, and she'd be my backup. You have an excellent team, JD."

Pickens smiled. "Don't I know it. You gonna sit there twenty-four?"

"Donna wouldn't let me, but I got the day shift. Sergeant Dunne will have someone relieve me. I don't think we'll need anyone past nine-o'clock. If he's coming back, he'll come during the day."

Pickens didn't hear another word from Hubbard. He thought he was cut off. "Mitch, you still there?"

"Yeah, I'm here. The son of a bitch just arrived. What do you want me to do?"

Pickens rubbed the back of his head contemplating a course of action. "Call Sergeant Dunne and have her back you up. If he removes anything, have her stop him. I'll get a warrant, and I'll get it e-mailed to Sergeant Dunne if I have to strangle somebody."

Pickens and Hubbard ended the call. Hubbard called Dunne. Pickens called the prosecutor at her home and got her.

"Now what, JD?" she said. "It had better be important."

"It is. I need a search warrant, and I need it now. And I need it e-mailed or texted to Sergeant Dunne's phone. I'll text you both. Don't say it's impossible. I really need you to do this, please."

"Dammit, JD. What do you think I am, a miracle worker?"

"Yes. Come on, Connie, do it for me for old time's sake." Connie Dupree, the prosecutor, had been one of Pickens girlfriends when he lived in Tallahassee and attended law school.

"Screw you and old time's sake. You dumped me. There is no old time's sake, but I'll do it for you. Why? I don't know. I'll call Judge Tomlin and ask him. You owe me, JD, and you'll owe Judge Tomlin, too."

Pickens grinned. "I don't care who I'll owe. If you get me the warrant, my next call might be for an arrest warrant and another search warrant. Thanks, Connie. I'll send you roses again." He wasn't sure she heard his last comment because she had ended the call. Pickens texted the prosecutor Dunne's e-mail and text number. Next, he called Sergeant Dunne and told her to expect an e-mail or a text message with a search warrant.

It was a monumental task that Pickens had asked of the prosecutor and the judge. Getting a search warrant e-mailed or texted wasn't an everyday occurrence. He hadn't bothered to ask if it had ever happened or if it was possible. Pickens just assumed it was. He called Hubbard.

"Mitch, is he still there?"

"Yeah. Sergeant Dunne just pulled up in her patrol car with lights flashing. She's out and waving something."

"It must be the warrant. I expected she'd have a text or e-mail warrant."

"An e-mail or text warrant? Are you shitting me? I never heard of such a thing."

"Me, too, but I begged the prosecutor to do it."

"You must have done a good job. Your prosecutor is a miracle worker. Is she good-looking, too?"

"I plead the fifth on that one, but I agree on the miracle worker. So is a certain judge. Go get the son of a bitch, Mitch."

Sanders was about to enter the storage locker when Dunne arrived waving the warrant and came up behind him. Hubbard was right behind Dunne.

"Hold on," shouted Dunne. "I have a search and seizure warrant for the contents of that locker." Dunne handed the accountant the warrant.

Sanders froze and stepped away. He looked frightened and as though he would pee his pants.

Dunne grinned. Hubbard did too.

"Now what?" asked Sanders. "Do I need an attorney?"

"Depends on what we find in the boxes," said Hubbard.

"And I suggest you don't leave town," said Dunne. "We'll be watching you."

"I won't. I'm calling my attorney."

"Go ahead," said Dunne. "We're going to search the locker."

"What are you looking for?"

"We'll know when we find it. If we find what we want, you'll need a good attorney."

Sanders rubbed both hands on the back of his head then made a call.

Dunne and Hubbard entered the storage locker and began their search. After they found what they were looking for, Dunne called Pickens.

"The accountant called his attorney, Sheriff," Dunne said as soon as Pickens answered.

"Let him," said Pickens. "I'm on my way. You get what we needed?"

"Fifteen boxes. They'll be at the station. The accountant doesn't know we took them."

Pickens thanked Dunne then walked out of his office and approached Billy. "You got that stuff ready for me, Billy?"

"The last few pages are printing. There are ten pages."

"Get them for me. I'm going to Warfield to meet Sergeant Dunne and Hubbard." He looked at Amy. She was staring at the chalkboard. "AMY." She turned abruptly when he shouted her name. "When I get back, I'll have fifteen boxes of records from the accountant. If they're the records from Anne Wilson's audiology business, I'll need help going through them. Will you be here?"

"Where did you think I'd be," she snapped. "I'll be here. It's still my case, isn't it?"

Pickens ignored her anger. "It is."

"Then why aren't you taking me to Warfield with you?"

Amy had stumped him. "Grab your hat and let's go."

*   *   *

On the drive to Warfield, the temperature in the SUV was frosty, and you could hear a feather land. When they arrived at the satellite station, Amy got out and slammed the door shut. Pickens ignored her and followed her into the station.

Sergeant Dunne greeted Pickens and Amy. Amy was cordial, but Dunne could tell she wasn't in a good mood.

"Sergeant Dunne, may I see the warrant?" Pickens was curious what an e-mailed warrant looked like.

Dunne handed Pickens the warrant. He was surprised that it wasn't an e-mail; or text warrant, but an actual paper warrant. The judge had faxed the warrant to Dunne. It was a simple statement authorizing the search and seizure of the contents of the storage locker and signed by Judge Tomlin. When the prosecutor told the judge about the heinous nature of the case and why the contents of the locker were necessary, he signed the warrant.

"Amazing," said Pickens.

"Are those the boxes with the files?" asked Amy.

"Yes," said Dunne. "Fifteen of them. They're all marked 'Wilson Audiology' with dates spanning sixteen years. I sealed them with yellow tape, and I sealed the storage locker entrance, too."

"Do we go through them here or at your office, JD?" said Hubbard.

"At my office," said Pickens. "Where's Sanders?"

"He left in a hurry after he made a call," said Dunne. "I presume it was to his attorney."

"Or he might have called Daniel Wilson," said Amy.

"That's a possibility," said Pickens. "If he did, Wilson will be worried we might find something incriminating in those boxes."

"Sanders was scared shitless," said Hubbard. "He'll want Wilson to protect him."

"I agree," said Pickens. "What do you think, Amy?"

"The same," replied Amy. "Can't wait to see what's in those boxes and what they might have had to do with Wilson's murder." The exchange between her and Pickens had caused Amy's anger at Pickens to subside.

"Do you want me to take the boxes to your office, JD, or load them into your SUV?" said Hubbard.

"Fifteen boxes might not fit in the SUV. I can take some and get the rest Monday. I have an appointment with Hobbs."

"Why don't you let me take them in my truck," said Hubbard. "I'll drop them off then go home. It's no problem."

"If you don't mind. I have to make a stop at Ellison's office, first. Good work, Sergeant Dunne. Thanks, Mitch." Dunne saluted Pickens. Hubbard did, too.

"You okay with me stopping at Ellison's office, Amy?"

"No problem. You're going to give Bobby that folder, aren't you?"

Pickens nodded and drove to Bobby Ellison's office. He parked in front, grabbed the folder, and went into Ellison's office. Pickens knew Ellison would be there because he texted him to be sure.

"Hello, Sheriff," said Lu. "Bobby's expecting you. "BOBBY!" she shouted. "The sheriff is here."

Ellison opened his office door and stepped out. "I hear you. Damn, Lu, I didn't miss your shouting while I was away. Hey, JD, you got that info for me?"

"Yes." Pickens handed Ellison the folder. "You have mine?"

"Lu, give JD that file from my travels and the bill for expenses. Don't worry, JD, they're more than reasonable." Lu handed Pickens the file and the expense report.

"I'm not worried about your bill, Bobby, but I'd appreciate it if you could handle this matter as quickly as possible."

"That important, huh?"

"Much more. Thanks, Bobby."

"I'll start right away. You take care, JD.

Pickens said goodbye to Lu and left.

"Is Bobby going to help you?" asked Amy.

"Yes. I promise if Bobby gets what I need, I'll tell you about it. For now, I don't want to because I don't want you to get your hopes up high, or mine."

Amy noticed Pickens had a different file than when he entered Ellison's office. "What's in that file?" she asked.

"It's Bobby's work on the Groves' case. You're welcome to look at it. I'll wait until Monday."

Amy picked up the file and went through it. When she finished, she said, "Interesting. Bobby was thorough."

When they returned to the sheriff's office, Pickens made a call. He called in a favor and was able to contact a forensic accountant and set up an appointment for Monday morning for her to go through the boxes of files. Amy would be available to answer questions and make notes.

"Hopefully, the forensic accountant will find something," said Pickens.

"We need something," said Amy. "And we need a break in the case."

"We do. I'll see you Monday."

When Pickens pulled into his driveway, he was surprised to see Marge's car. He thought she had gone to visit her mother. He got out of the SUV and entered the house. Sarah and Bailey immediately greeted him. Sarah hugged him. Bailey stood on his hind legs and put his front paws on Pickens' thighs.

"Where's Momma?" Pickens asked.

"I'm right here," answered Marge as she came from the kitchen, walked up to him and kissed him.

"I thought you were going to visit your mother?"

"I changed my mind and went to the office. I wanted to take another look at Wilson." Pickens raised his eyebrows. Marge waved a hand. "I left Sarah and Bailey at your parents' house.

Sarah, you and Bailey go play. Mommy wants to talk to daddy."
Sarah and Bailey went out onto the back porch. "Join me in the
kitchen and grab a beer."

Pickens followed her, got a beer from the fridge, and sat at
the counter.

"What made you take another look at Wilson?"

"I was curious about the fracture on the skull. I know I said
a left-handed person did it, but a second look showed it was
possible a right-handed person did it. Whoever struck the blow
could have been standing in front of Wilson or she had turned
just as the blow hit her." Marge thrust her chest out. "My
conclusion could be challenged in court, but I'd stand by it."

Pickens wrapped her in a bear hug. "Damn, Marge, that's
what I needed to hear, and I'd stand with you." He released
her from his hug. "It means with your conclusion and the
forensic evidence from the Camry, Wilson might have killed
his wife. We might have a motive Monday after the forensic
accountant goes through Anne Wilson's files. Now, if only we
had a weapon."

"It would certainly help your case. A defense attorney would
argue your evidence is circumstantial."

"Maybe so, but I'll find more." Pickens smiled. "We playing
football tonight?"

"I plead the fifth." She laughed. "Okay, you're on, quarterback."

Later that night, Pickens held Marge in his arms, felt the
warmth of her body against his, and passionately kissed her.
He caressed every curve and crevice and relished her moans
as he did. She did the same to him. Then he took her hard, and
as he did, his thoughts were about her and not about murder.
He loved her and would do anything to protect her even if it
meant he had to lay down his life for her. She felt the same way
toward him. As he gave his all to her, his body lost control,

and he reached the cusp of delirium. There were no thoughts of anything but her and the pleasure he experienced. Both wished it would last forever, but as always, it didn't. They clung to each other until their heartbeats and breathing subsided. They stayed in each other's arms until sleep overwhelmed them.

*   *   *

Pickens heard the loud chirping sound from his phone and a nudge from Marge that woke him from a deep sleep. He grabbed the phone, noticed the time was five-thirty, and it was Sunday morning. The caller was Sergeant Dunne. Dunne had never called before dawn, and never on a Sunday Morning. Sunday's were Dunne's day off.

Dunne told Pickens that there was a fire at the storage facility, and she was at the scene. According to the fire inspector, someone had torched the locker where Wilson's files were. Since the owner of the facility was there, she asked for the security tapes and had them in her possession. She 'd give the tapes to Pickens Monday so he could review them.

Pickens knew someone didn't want him to see those files.

"Sorry about that, Marge," Pickens said but had said it to a pillow. Marge had gotten up and went to make coffee. Pickens got out of bed, dressed, and went to the kitchen. Marge had a cup ready and waited for him. He explained the call to her. She understood the demands of being a sheriff, and the demands of the cases Pickens was working.

It wasn't long before Sarah and Bailey woke and joined Pickens and Marge for breakfast. The rest of the day, Pickens relaxed with his family and did his best to forget about homicide.

CHAPTER 34

Monday morning, Pickens waited with Amy for the forensic accountant to arrive before making the trip to Warfield and Hobbs' office. At ten-thirty the forensic accountant arrived. She didn't look like the person they expected. Iris Janson didn't wear glasses, didn't have a potbelly, didn't wear a suit, and wasn't a man. She was an attractive forty-nine-year-old woman who dressed like she was twenty-four. Short skirt, tight-fitting, and the same for her blouse. The male deputies turned their heads when they saw her. If Pickens weren't a happily married man, he would have whistled. Amy made a slight whistling sound for him.

"That's your forensic accountant?" said Amy. "She looks like a model."

"I wasn't told what she looked like, just that she'd be here today. Want to trade places? You take Hobbs. I'll help go through the files."

"No way. By that smile on your puss, you wouldn't get anything done."

Janson strolled up to Pickens and Amy and introduced herself. She shook hands with Amy then Pickens.

"Can I have my hand back, Sheriff?"

"Sorry. I didn't expect—"

"An attractive woman?" said Janson smiling. "I get that all

the time, but I can assure you I'm good at what I do. Where are the files?"

"Sergeant Tucker will show you. She'll be working with you. I have another appointment."

Amy pointed to the conference room.

"I hope you find something," said Pickens"

"If there is anything to find, I'll find it. Lead the way, Sergeant Tucker."

"Call me Amy, please."

"I will if you call me Iris."

"Let's go, Iris. Good luck, JD."

Pickens left. Amy and Janson went into the conference room.

On the ride to Warfield, Pickens had considered canceling the meeting with Hobbs because the latest events and evidence had stacked up against Wilson as his wife's killer. But there was a lingering question in the back of Pickens mind, and maybe Hobbs would provide the answer.

As Pickens parked in front of Warfield Audiology, he noticed it was at the end of a row of commercial businesses. There was a driveway that led to the rear of the building. David Wilson's ENT practice was within walking distance. It made it possible that Meade could have driven around back, and he and Wilson could have put his wife's body in Meade's truck and then drove her car to the field, left it, and then helped Meade bury her.

Pickens expected the inside of Warfield Audiology would be extravagant, but it wasn't. The reception area was sparse, just a desk, two chairs, and a magazine table.

Unlike the last time when Hobbs met with Amy and arrived well past the appointment time, Hobbs was on time and didn't keep him waiting, and she was cordial.

He guessed Hobbs' office would be lavish, but it was spartan.

Her office was at best twelve by twelve, and her desk and audiology equipment took up most of it.

"Thanks for meeting with me," said Pickens.

Hobbs frowned.

"This won't take long. As I explained when I called you, you are not a suspect. But you could help by answering a few questions."

"Ask me whatever you want, Sheriff."

"Was this always your office?"

"No. It was Anne's. I settled into it once I felt Anne wouldn't return. I had it painted and carpeted along with the rest of the office space."

That answered Pickens' question about whether there might still be trace evidence of the crime.

"It's my understanding that you were out of town the first weekend in November 1995. Is that correct?"

Hobbs pinched the bridge of her nose and thought—thought about that weekend with her husband. "Yes. My husband and I used the weekend to rekindle our marriage. He had an affair with Anne. It was a one-time thing, but if you asked him, he'd say it was ongoing. Anne told me about it." Pickens looked surprised. "I forgave her. I wasn't the best wife then, and if you know anything about Daniel, you'd understand why Anne strayed."

"Were you surprised when you returned Monday that she wasn't in the office?"

"No. Anne was invited to a conference by the franchisor and wasn't due back until Friday. I was surprised when she didn't come in the following Monday."

"Did you believe Wilson when he told the police that she might have run off with a lover?"

Hobbs hesitated. "No. Anne had someone that she met when she went to conferences. She told me about him but never said his name. She mentioned that she was thinking about divorcing Daniel. Anne might have contacted a lawyer, but if she did, I don't know who the lawyer was."

Pickens was concerned about the lover, but since he wasn't from Warfield, Pickens didn't consider him a suspect. However, knowing if there was a divorce lawyer and if Anne Wilson had already initiated divorce proceedings would add to a motive for her husband. Pickens also didn't want to dredge up old memories—which might anger her—so he didn't ask about Hobbs' divorce.

"Did the police question you?"

Hobbs exhaled sharply. "Question me? If you want to call it that. They hardly asked me any questions. I didn't tell them about Anne's lover because of her children. The police bought Daniel's lie and never really investigated Anne's disappearance. You've asked me more questions than they did."

"After you bought the franchise, did you use the same accountant as Anne did?"

Hobbs sat back with her eyes knitted. "I feel like you're interrogating me. I thought I wasn't a suspect."

"You're not. I'm just curious."

"Once I owned the franchise, I fired the accountant. I didn't trust him. Anne didn't either. She told me she felt he was hiding something and was going to question Daniel about it. Unfortunately, she never got a chance to tell me what it was."

Pickens had the answer to the lingering question. Hobbs had provided it, and the proof would be in the accountant's files. He glanced at the trophy shelf on the wall behind Hobbs.

"Are those your trophies?"

Hobbs smiled. "Yes, except for the one with two players on it. That one Anne kept in her office. We won it in a doubles competition. It's the only trophy Anne ever won. Daniel wanted to throw it away, but I kept it and put it with mine."

Pickens wondered if the trophy's shape and weight were enough to make it the murder weapon. It would have made for a handy bludgeon if the murder had been unplanned.

"May I see it?" Hobbs stood and reached for the trophy. "Wait, let me get it. It might be evidence since we believe Anne might have been murdered here in her office."

Pickens watched Hobbs' face for a reaction.

"Go ahead," she said.

Pickens used his handkerchief and grabbed the trophy. He studied it carefully, especially the date on it—1995. Next, Pickens held the trophy in his hand attempting to determine its weight, and if it was heavy enough to kill Anne Wilson. He couldn't be sure, so he'd let the ME say if it was.

"May I take it with me?"

"If you think it would help, take it. But I'd like it back."

"No problem. Do you have a bag I can put it in?"

Hobbs got up and left the office. She returned with a bag and handed it to Pickens. He stuck his hand inside the bag and pulled it inside out so he wouldn't touch the trophy like someone picks up dog poo.

Before leaving, Hobbs asked if Isabella was still in custody as she hoped Isabella would return and help in the office.

Pickens said no comment and left to meet with Sergeant Dunne. First, he called Hubbard and asked Hubbard to meet him at the satellite office.

Once Hubbard arrived, Pickens, Dunne, and Hubbard reviewed the security tapes. The tapes provided the answer to who torched the storage facility. They had expected it would be the accountant, but it wasn't. It was Lawrence Meade. The accountant must have given Meade the key to the locker so he could open the door and toss a Molotov cocktail into it.

"That's all the proof I need," said Pickens, "that Meade had a part in Anne Wilson's murder. And the files will provide a motive for why he and Daniel Wilson murdered Wilson's wife. The forensic accountant should have the proof sometime today. Thanks, Sergeant Dunne for working yesterday."

Dunne saluted Pickens. "Should I arrest Meade for arson?"

"Not yet. Let Meade think he got away with it. We'll use it later when we sweat the accountant about his role in the cover-up. Thanks, Mitch, for your help. I'll take the tapes with me."

"You're welcome," said Hubbard. "How about we go to lunch, my treat?"

Pickens hadn't eaten since breakfast, and a free lunch was just what he needed to celebrate. Dunne joined Pickens and Hubbard for lunch.

After lunch, Pickens made the trip back to the office, and it felt like the bus ride in high school after winning an away game. The only thing missing was his high school teammates. He not only had the makings of a motive but possibly the murder weapon.

Before going to the office, Pickens stopped at the ME's office to drop off the trophy. He hoped it might prove to be the murder weapon and possibly it had forensic evidence on it.

Next, Pickens headed for the office to find out what the forensic accountant had discovered.

Pickens had hoped Amy and the forensic accountant would be waiting to greet him when he walked into the office, but they weren't. But Billy and Bobby Ellison were.

"Got something for you, JD," said Ellison. "Billy's been helping me, and you're going to like what we have."

Pickens had hoped his news from Warfield would be the highlight, but if Ellison had something on Jesse Groves or Jorge Entenada, he'd be more than thrilled.

"Groves or Entenada?" said Pickens.

"Entenada. We found him, and I talked to him. Are you

ready? He's Asado's father, and he asked that we don't tell her."
Ellison pointed his index fingers in the air. "Wait for it. He has
a birth certificate that says Asado was born in the good old
USA. She not illegal, she's a citizen, and she's never known it."

"Are you shitting me, Ellison?"

"He's not, Sheriff," said Billy. "We're waiting for a fax with
the certificate and his statement."

"And I'm not charging you for this, JD. Lu said I couldn't.
But I want a big thank you."

"Thank you? Hell, I'll hug you." Pickens walked over and put
an arm around Ellison. "I've got a shit load of evidence against
Wilson, and now I can use Asado's testimony that he was the
last person to see his wife." Pickens smiled. "I'm gonna nail the
bastard."

"Anything else you want me to do?" asked Ellison.

"Yeah, keep your eyes on Wilson and Meade. I'll have
Hubbard, and Sergeant Dunne also do it. And they'll watch the
accountant."

After the fax came in, Billy gave it to Pickens and Ellison
left for Warfield. Amy and the forensic accountant came out of
the conference room. Both looked like they spent an all-nighter
studying for exams.

"Any luck?" asked Pickens.

"We found a few things in the books that don't add up," said
Amy, "but we'll be here all night."

"If you get me a hotel room," said the forensic accountant,
"I'll finish tomorrow. Whoever the accountant was, he was
good, but he made some mistakes and left a trail. I'll wrap it up
tomorrow and give you my report."

"Get her a hotel room, Amy, and charge it to my office."

"Iris can stay at my house," said Amy. "It's better than a hotel
with all the comforts of home. Plus, you'll have my company."

The forensic accountant smiled. "Can't ask for better

company with all the comforts of home." She raised her palms. "I'm all yours for the night."

"Now that that's settled," said Pickens. "Wait till you hear my good news."

Pickens told Amy about his visit with Hobbs, the trophy, the security tapes, and Asado's father.

"Damn, that's great," said Amy, "I want to be the one to tell Asado she's legal and can testify. I'll call her attorney first thing in the morning. Iris and I are going to dinner."

Pickens went into his office, called Sergeant Dunne and Hubbard, and gave them their instructions. Feeling good, he decided to go home early and have dinner with his family.

After dinner, Pickens told Marge about his day and the evidence that was stacking up against Wilson and Meade, and the news about Asado.

"You were busy," said Marge. "We did a fingerprint analysis on the trophy. Unfortunately, too many people had touched the trophy over the years. Our equipment wasn't designed to detect trace evidence, so I sent the trophy to Vadigal's lab for microscopic forensic analysis. I asked for a quick turnaround. If there's any trace evidence from the murder, they'll find it and can perform super glue fuming to detect any latent fingerprints. But don't get your hopes up high; it's possible they won't find anything useful."

"Thanks, it's worth a try." Pickens rubbed his palms over his eyes. "I don't know about you, but I'm tired. You ready for bed?"

"Ready when you are."

Pickens turned the lights out and joined Marge in the bedroom for a good night's sleep.

*   *   *

Pickens felt the heavy pressure on his chest and opened his eyes. What he saw was the face of *evil*. He tried to get up but couldn't. Both his arms and legs were restrained. He looked at Marge. She was also restrained. He heard Sarah scream and saw Bailey on the floor in a pool of blood. Then Marge screamed as they watched a man slice Sarah's throat. Both Pickens and Marge struggled to get free, but it was hopeless. The man who had killed Sarah approached Marge and started viciously stabbing her in the chest. Another man stood over Pickens and smiled.

Pickens yelled, "I'll catch you, Jesse, you son of a bitch, and I swear I'll kill you." Those were his last words as the knife penetrated Pickens' chest several times, and his life ended.

CHAPTER 35

THE NEXT THING Pickens felt was the hard slap on his cheek. Then he heard a harsh voice.

"Wake up, JD, you're scaring Sarah." Another slap. "Wake up, dammit." And another slap.

Pickens opened his eyes. He didn't see the face of *evil*. He saw his wife's lovely face. He reached for her, expected he wouldn't be able to, but he could.

"It's about time, JD," said Marge. "You had a nightmare." Pickens sat up. He was drenched in sweat. "You need to take a break from the Groves case. It's starting to affect you."

"How bad was it?"

"Worse than the last time you had a nightmare."

Pickens saw Sarah and Bailey standing in the doorway and felt a sense of relief that both were alive.

"Sorry, sweetheart, I didn't mean to scare you."

"It's okay, Daddy. Bailey said you were dreaming about the *evil* that was in that field."

"Sarah," said Marge, "go get dressed. I'll make breakfast after daddy gets up." Sarah and Bailey left. "You okay now, JD?"

Pickens exhaled sharply. "Yeah. What time is it?"

"Six-thirty. We're all up, so we might as well have breakfast. I'll get dressed. You take a shower then come have breakfast."

Marge dressed and went to the kitchen. Pickens got out of

bed, showered, dressed, and then went to the kitchen. Marge had a cup of coffee for him.

Pickens sat at the table with his coffee and marveled at being in the presence of his family, all wonderfully alive and smiling. Jesse Groves hadn't killed him and his family, but Pickens still vowed he would catch Jesse and kill him.

"Marge, why don't I take Sarah to school, then drop you off at your office. I'll take Bailey to work with me."

Marge's brow wrinkled as she wondered why Pickens made the unusual offer. "It's not necessary. I can take Sarah, and I don't need a ride."

"I know, but I want to."

"Do you really think it's necessary?"

Pickens feigned a smile. "Humor me and let me do it for my peace of mind."

Marge wondered if it had something to do with his nightmare. "Okay, but you have to pick up Sarah before five o'clock."

"No problem. One more thing. Would you call me after lunch? I'd like to hear your voice."

Marge squinted her eyes. "Are you okay, JD?"

"Yeah. I just want to know you're okay."

"I'll call you, and I'll even tell you I love you." Pickens smiled.

After he dropped Marge and Sarah off, Pickens drove to his office with Bailey beside him.

Amy and the forensic accountant were in the conference room diligently going through Anne Wilson's business records.

With Bailey at his side, Pickens went right to his office and closed the door. He sat back with his feet up on the desk and smiled. He was alive, his family was alive, and his team was hard at work solving the Wilson and Groves murders. Soon, he'd get Daniel Wilson in custody and convicted for his wife's murder. Thanks to Ellison, he was closer to finding Jesse Groves.

Pickens picked up his copy of Entenada's statement

about how Isabella had become a citizen. Entenada's wife was pregnant, and they wanted the baby to be born in the United States, so they crossed the border, found a doctor that delivered the baby, and when mother and child were well enough, Entenada and his family crossed the border back into their own country. When Isabella was two, Entenada's wife became ill, so he brought them back into the United States with another family. His wife died, and Entanada left his daughter with the Asado family but kept tabs on the child. Entenada met the Wilsons and offered to rent a house he owned to Isabella, then sold it to his granddaughter and her husband after they married. Entenada stayed in the shadows until Ellison contacted him.

Pickens was distracted when his phone chirped. It was a long-distance call from a reporter in Columbus, Ohio. She was working a cold case that she had reported on two years ago. When she saw Noseby's article, it reminded her of the one she reported on. It was of a family brutally stabbed to death in their home. The Columbus police had investigated but found no evidence or clues as to the perpetrator. The reporter had hoped Pickens would help with the solution to the murder, but Pickens could only give her what he had—which was little.

Before the day would end, Pickens would receive several other calls from reporters and law enforcement in several states. The ones from law enforcement also described the same horrible scenes and vicious nature of their crimes. None had clues to the identity of the perpetrators. At least now, having talked with Pickens, they had a person of interest in Jesse Groves.

After lunch, Pickens called Marge, and as she promised, she told him she loved him.

At three-thirty, Amy knocked on the door and opened it.

She was smiling. "We're finished. Iris is typing her report. Good news, JD, we got a motive."

"Great, I was hoping we would. Is there enough to sweat the accountant and get him to testify against Wilson and Meade?"

"Iris wants to talk to you in the conference room."

"Let's go."

In the conference room, the forensic accountant had two copies of her report on the table for Pickens and Amy. She also had the particulars of the evidence laid out in an orderly fashion so Pickens would understand what she found.

"Essentially," said Janson, "Wilson was skimming from his wife's account by paying one of his employees. The accountant handled the payroll for both businesses. That's how it started. Then there were transfers into the ENT business. If the wife had managed her account, it wouldn't have happened. But she didn't. She left it to the accountant."

"It that enough of a motive, JD?" asked Amy.

"It's enough for me."

"I found something else," said Janson. "A few of the boxes contained Anne Wilson's records." She held up three documents. "A bank statement, an invoice, and a cashed check for five-hundred dollars payable to an attorney and signed by Anne Wilson." Janson handed them to Pickens.

Pickens perused the invoice. "Why would Anne Wilson pay an attorney in Tampa? Unless she's a divorce attorney and Wilson had started divorce proceedings."

"Another motive," said Amy.

"Yeah. We got Wilson, and we'll get Meade and the accountant. Thanks, Ms. Janson."

"It's Iris, and it's all in my report. Now, if Amy will put up with me for another night, I won't have to make the trip back to Tampa until tomorrow morning."

"I wouldn't have it any other way," said Amy. "You're spending the night with me."

Pickens' brow hiked, and he grinned.

With the evidence he now had, Pickens contacted the prosecutor, requested a warrant for the accountant, and got it. He had enough to arrest Wilson and Meade but wanted the accountant to roll on them first. Then he'd go after Wilson and Meade.

Pickens had Amy and Billy remove the boxes from the conference room. He left the office in time to pick up Sarah before five o'clock and then picked up Marge and took them out to dinner including Bailey.

* * *

Wednesday morning, after the forensic accountant had left for Tampa, Pickens and Amy traveled to Warfield to arrest the accountant. With the warrant in hand, they went to the accountant's home, arrested him, brought him back to Creek City, and left him alone to sweat in the conference room.

After an hour passed, Pickens and Amy entered the room and presented the accountant with the evidence from the forensic analysis and the security video. It didn't take long before the accountant broke down and confessed to his part in the skimming cover-up and that he had called Wilson that day when Dunne showed up at the storage locker with the warrant. He signed a detailed statement linking Wilson and Meade to everything and that he had told Wilson about the invoice to the attorney. Amy had already contacted the attorney and learned that Anne Wilson had hired her to start divorce proceedings, but when Anne didn't return her calls in November 1995, the attorney dropped the matter. The accountant was put in a holding cell until his arraignment.

Armed with the accountant's statement and the other evidence, Pickens obtained arrest warrants for Wilson and Meade.

Late that afternoon, Amy went with Pickens to Warfield. Sergeant Dunne and a deputy met them at Wilson and Meade's office. The receptionist protested that they couldn't barge in, but Pickens held up the warrants, and the four walked past her and went right to Wilson and Meade's offices. Pickens and Amy to Wilson's, and Dunne and the deputy to Meade's. Both doctors were with patients.

"What's the meaning of this?" said Wilson. "You can't just barge in. Can't you see I have a patient?"

Pickens gave Amy the honor. "Daniel Wilson, you are under arrest for the murder of Anne Wilson. You have the right to—" Wilson's patient excused herself and left the office in a panic. Amy continued reading Wilson his rights then handcuffed him.

In Meade's office, Sergeant Dunne did the same thing. His patient excused himself and bolted for the door. After reading Meade his rights, Dunne handcuffed him.

Wilson and Meade were escorted out of their offices, past an astonished receptionist, and placed in custody. Wilson in Pickens' SUV, Meade in Dunne's patrol car. They were both taken to the sheriff's office in Creek City. Both men protested during the entire ride.

Pickens glanced at Amy. She grinned as did Pickens.

At the sheriff's office, Wilson was taken to a holding cell. Meade was put in the conference room to be interrogated by Pickens and Amy.

First order of business was to play the security tape. Meade watched without comment.

"Meade, the tape proves you committed arson, and you'll spend time in prison for it," said Pickens. "But we can prove

Daniel Wilson killed his wife, and we'll show that you aided in burying her. That makes you culpable. I'm sure a jury will convict you."

"I want an attorney," said Meade.

"Suit yourself," replied Pickens. "I can't wait to watch you in court, especially when the prosecutor airs you and Wilson's dirty laundry. Let's go, Sergeant Tucker. Have him taken to the county jail. His attorney can talk to him there."

"On your feet Lawrence Meade."

Meade stood. Amy escorted him out of the conference room and turned him over to Dunne.

"Take him to the county jail and book him," said Amy.

"My pleasure," said Dunne. "What about Wilson?"

"Depends on what he has to say, but the sheriff and I will take him to the jail and book him."

Dunne and her deputy left with Meade. Amy then got Wilson and brought him to the conference room.

"It's over Daniel," said Amy. "We have enough evidence to prove you were the last person to see your wife alive and we have proof you buried her. We have evidence of motive and the murder weapon." The last wasn't true as they hadn't yet received the trophy from Vadigal's lab and the results, but Amy used it anyway. "You're going to prison for a long time, and I doubt your children will visit you after the jury hears about you and Meade and how you mercilessly took their mother from them and led them to believe she deserted them."

Up until then, Wilson had sat there smug and belligerent, but Amy's last comment must have gotten to him. His demeanor suddenly changed.

"Is that what you want your legacy to be?" continued Amy. "Because it will and if they ever have children, you'll never be mentioned as family."

Pickens was enjoying Amy's interrogation method, especially using Wilson's children as a means to get to him.

"Not only that," said Pickens, "when the trial starts, you can bet there will be a media circus. Right now, my deputies are searching your home, Meade's home, and your office for more evidence. They'll find something." Pickens stood. "We'll take you to the jail now, and you can call an attorney from there."

Wilson was suddenly worried and had a pained gaze. "Wait. I want to make a deal, but I want an attorney first. Let me make a call."

Pickens looked at Amy. She nodded.

"Uncuff him, Sergeant Tucker. Let him make his call."

Amy uncuffed Wilson, handed him her phone, and she and Pickens left Wilson alone to make his call.

"That was quick," said Amy. "I thought he'd be tougher than Meade."

"So did I, but his pride got to him. He's a son of a bitch, but he cares about the twins and doesn't want the public to know about his relationship with Meade."

"What kind of deal do you think he'll want?"

"One that doesn't involve a trial. Maybe Meade would plead, too."

Amy checked her watch. "What's taking him so long?"

"Maybe he couldn't find an attorney to take his case." Wilson pounded on the door. "Let's go." Pickens and Amy entered the room and sat. "Do you have an attorney?"

Wilson slid Amy's phone to her. "Yeah, but he can't get here until tomorrow."

"In that case,' said Pickens, "we'll take you to the county jail and book you, or we can do it here, and you can spend the night in one of our holding cells. It's your choice."

"I'll spend the night here."

Wilson stood, Amy cuffed him, booked him, and then took him to a holding cell.

"Sleep tight tonight," Amy said and walked away. She found Pickens standing in front of the murder board. "One down, one to go."

"Yes, thanks to forensic science. And we'll solve the Groves case. A good day's work, Amy. Lets' go home. Tomorrow's another day."

"I'll second that."

Later that night at home in their bedroom, Pickens and Marge were preparing for a needed night of lovemaking. With the Wilson case coming to a close it was time to return to something normal. Both lay naked on the bed.

Pickens was stroking her arm. He told her about Wilson wanting a deal and Meade requesting an attorney.

"I reread your report," said Pickens. "Something is bothering me. In it, you mentioned that Wilson was struck with more than one blow. Was it possible the first blow didn't kill her?"

"It's possible, but if something else delivered the second one. That means—"

"Wilson might have been alive when they removed her body from her office and was killed sometime between then and when they buried her."

"Maybe one of them hit her with a shovel."

"It's a long shot, but I'll have a deputy search the garages for a shovel. Maybe it will still have evidence on it."

"Maybe. But, JD, can we forget about the case and make love? I'm so damn horny." Marge reached for his head and pulled it to her chest. "If you don't do something, I may have to take matters into my hands."

Pickens grabbed a breast and suckled it. Then he did it to the other breast. Next, he kissed her passionately and straddled her as she spread her legs and welcomed him.

Heat and desire consumed them as they made love. Love that lasted until both were emotionally and physically exhausted.

CHAPTER 36

I N THE MORNING, when Pickens arrived at the office, Amy was waiting for him. He had hoped Wilson's attorney would be in the conference room.

"Meade got an attorney," said Amy. "They want to talk to us."

Pickens considered telling Amy about the shovel but decided not to.

"They can wait until we talk with Wilson and his attorney. Is he here yet?"

Amy tilted her head in the direction of the entrance. "Looks like he just arrived, and he's not alone."

Pickens turned and saw two people walking toward him. One was Marilyn Nudley, the county prosecutor, the other was a man dressed in an expensive suit, polished shoes, and slicked back hair. Pickens presumed he was Wilson's attorney. The two attorneys were smiling at each other.

"Ain't they chummy," said Pickens.

The prosecutor strolled up to Pickens. "Sheriff Pickens, this is Carlos Arroya, Daniel Wilson's attorney."

Arroya extended a hand.

"Would you please get Mr. Wilson and put him and Mr. Arroya where they can talk in private?"

"Amy, get Wilson and bring him to the conference room.

Mr. Arroya, if you follow me, I'll show you where it is." Arroya followed Pickens.

"Can we talk in your office, Sheriff?" said Nudley.

Pickens extended his palm and led her to his office. He entered and closed the door.

"What's with you and Arroya?"

"Get your mind out of the gutter, JD. Carlos and I go way back. We both spent two years in Miami in the DA's office. I didn't know he was Wilson's attorney until I met him out front. He's good at what he does and is hard-headed like you. Now, tell me what to expect."

Pickens told her about yesterdays' interrogation of Wilson and his request to make a deal and about Meade wanting an attorney.

Nudley played with the locket dangling from her neck. "Some of the evidence will be argued to be circumstantial, which doesn't help our case. What's more important to you? Wilson behind bars, or a lengthy trial that might end in a hung jury?"

Pickens scratched his chin contemplating a response. "I don't believe Wilson wants a trial, and I'd be satisfied with him locked up for however long you can get him."

"Carlos will try to get Wilson to go to trial. But if his client insists on a plea, Carlos will ask for a minimum sentence. I'll do my best to put Wilson behind bars for as long as possible."

"If he rolls on Meade, I'll take whatever you get. First, I need to ask him a few questions."

Amy knocked on the door and opened it. "They're ready," she said.

"Okay, JD. Let's see what Carlos wants."

Pickens, Amy, and Nudley entered the conference room and sat across from Arroya and Wilson. Wilson was unshaven, his eyes bloodshot, and he looked like a man that had given up hope. A night in a cell had taken a toll on him. Arroya had a legal pad and a pen on the table in front of him. Nudley took a legal pad from her briefcase and set it on the table.

"Against my advice," said Arroya, "my client insists on plea bargaining. If we can make a reasonable deal, he'll confess. What's the best you can offer, Marilyn?"

Nudley glanced at Pickens. He tilted his head. "That depends on his confession. Let's hear what he has to say, and then I'll propose an offer."

Arroya turned to Wilson. "Go ahead Daniel, but if I say stop, you stop."

Wilson took a deep breath and exhaled. "Anne called me to her office the Friday afternoon she was scheduled to go away. She confronted me about the irregularities in the business account and said when she got back from her trip, she was filing for divorce. She was tired of living a lie with a queer." Wilson's voice cracked. "That made me so angry I grabbed the trophy off her desk and hit her with it. I didn't mean to kill her." Wilson hesitated.

"Keep going, Daniel," said Arroya. "You're doing fine."

Wilson continued. "I told Isabella to go home and not to mention I was there. Then I called Larry, and he came to the back entrance. We put Anne in his truck and drove to that field. Larry knew there was an access road. I followed him in Anne's Camry, left it in the grass and then we buried Anne's body. It was my idea to suggest Anne ran away. I didn't want the twins to know I killed their mother."

"I have a question," said Pickens. "Who hit your wife with the shovel?"

Wilson's face turned white, and his hands balled into fists. "Larry did. He wanted to be sure Anne was dead."

"Anything else, Sheriff?" asked Arroya.

"Whose idea was it to frame Isabella and Hobbs?"

"Larry's, as was the arson," answered Wilson.

"You heard enough, JD?" asked Nudley. Pickens nodded.

"What's the verdict, Marilyn?"

"Twenty years to life with the possibility of parole."

"Come on, Marilyn, you can do better than that. It's a decades old case. My client will be almost eighty when he gets out. That's if he lives that long."

"Twenty and no life," said Nudley.

Arroya leaned in and whispered in Wilson's ear. Wilson nodded yes.

"Fifteen with the possibility of parole," said Arroya.

Nudley whispered in Pickens' ear. He nodded okay.

"Twenty and no parole. That's the best I can offer."

Again, Arroya whispered in Wilson's ear. "We'll take it."

"Write it all down and don't leave anything out including Meade's part. And, your client testifies against Meade."

"Done." Arroya slid the pad and pen to Wilson. After Wilson signed his statement, Nudley wrote up the deal and signed it.

"I'll get it to a judge, Carlos. There won't be a bail hearing. Your client stays in jail until he is sentenced to serve his time in prison. Is that understood?"

Arroya shrugged. "I expected it from you, Marilyn. We won't petition for bail."

Amy handcuffed Wilson and had a deputy take him to the county jail.

After Arroya had left, Nudley said, "Satisfied, JD? Wilson will be in his late seventies when he gets out of prison."

"I am. Wilson's in-laws might not be, but Amy will convince the twins we did our best."

"I'd bet they don't go to his sentencing hearing," said Amy. "Are you going to the jail to talk with Meade's attorney or do we bring him here?"

"What do you think, JD?" asked Nudley.

"The jail. And you put him away for life. Wilson struck the first blow, but I bet Meade knew Anne wasn't dead and made sure of it."

"I'll do my best."

Amy didn't mind being left behind. Listening to Wilson's testimony had a dramatic effect on her, and she didn't want to hear Meade's. Before leaving, Pickens asked her to contact Ellison or Hubbard whichever one knew of resources to find and capture Jesse Groves.

At the jail, Meade waited in an interrogation room with his attorney. Pickens and Nudley arrived and joined them. Nudley didn't know Meade's attorney. Pickens felt he wasn't as sharp as Arroya and didn't dress in an expensive suit, but that meant nothing. Meade's attorney had a legal pad and a pen in front of him.

Nudley put a legal pad in front of her. "Is your client ready to make a statement?"

"No," said the attorney. "He has nothing to say and will take his chances with a jury unless you want to plea bargain. And don't suggest life. He's not guilty of murder. Only arson." Meade sat confident and arrogant.

"Not according to Daniel Wilson. According to him, your client bashed his wife's head with a shovel, orchestrated a cover-up, the framing of Isabella Asado and Barbara Hobbs. If I could get the death penalty, I'd go for it. Your client is looking at life." She glared at Meade. "We have the shovel, and the evidence will prove you struck the blow that killed her. Believe me; I have enough evidence to get a conviction."

Meade's demeanor changed. He no longer looked confident, and his arrogance disappeared.

"I don't believe Daniel said I had anything to do with his wife's murder," said Meade.

"Quiet, Larry, let me do the talking," said the attorney.

"I have his statement and a copy of it in my briefcase. Both signed by him," said Nudley. "I'd be glad to let your attorney read it. Of course, he'll get a copy anyway as part of the court proceedings."

"May I read it?" said the attorney.

Nudley reached in her briefcase, took out the copy of Wilson's statement, and slid it across the table to the attorney. After he read it, he showed it to Meade and whispered in his ear. Meade shook his head, but the attorney whispered something else.

Meade exhaled and said, "Okay."

"What are you offering?" asked the attorney.

Pickens held back a smile. He was satisfied with Nudley's performance.

"Twenty to life, and I'll allow parole in twenty."

"Not gonna happen. You have to do better than that. Fifteen and no life."

Nudley leaned in and whispered in Pickens' ear. He whispered back.

"Twenty and no life and no parole. That's the best I can offer. If your client refuses, I'll see you at trial."

Meade and the attorney whispered back and forth. Finally, Meade seemed like he had given up.

"Okay, but I want it in writing."

"No problem, after your client makes a written statement."

The attorney slid the pen and legal pad to Meade. He started writing. Nudley did the same. When Meade finished, the attorney let Nudley read it. After she read it, she gave it to Pickens. When he finished reading, he whispered in Nudley's ear.

"We'd like to hear your client read it," said Nudley.

"Seriously?"

"Seriously," said Nudley.

"Give me the damn statement," said Meade. "I'll read it if it will satisfy them." The attorney gave Meade the statement and he read it out loud. "Satisfied?" he said when he finished.

"Yes, thank you," said Nudley. Then she gave the attorney the plea arrangement. "Thanks for meeting with us. We'll see you at the sentencing." Nudley put Meade's statement and the legal pad in her briefcase, then she stood, and she and Pickens left.

Out in the hallway, Pickens said, "Good work, Marilyn. I didn't expect Meade to cave. I'd hug you, but I don't want you to get the wrong idea."

"You should hug and kiss me anyway, but not until we're in your SUV." She smiled as did Pickens. Once they were in the SUV, Pickens leaned over hugged Nudley and kissed her on the cheek.

When Pickens and Nudley returned to the sheriff's office, he thanked her and said goodbye. Next, he called Asado's attorney, gave him the news about her legal status, and requested a written statement from her about the day Wilson murdered his wife and what she knew. The attorney agreed and said he would have her prepare one and he'd deliver it to Pickens.

Amy told Pickens she contacted both Ellison and Hubbard, and they were reaching out to their sources for help capturing Jesse Groves. She also told Pickens that she spoke to Jenny Wilson and told her about her father's confession. Jenny was satisfied that he'd pay for killing her mother, but in a way felt sorry for him and Amy figured one day she might.

It was fortunate the prosecutor obtained confessions and didn't need the murder weapons as evidence. The trophy produced a myriad of fingerprints including Wilson's but no trace evidence that it had struck Anne Wilson. Two shovels found in Meade's garage had his prints on them, but the only evidence linking them to the crime was specs of dirt that matched the soil samples from Wilson's gravesite.

* * *

It had been a long four months since the discovery of the remains of Anne Wilson and the Groves, but with Wilson and Meade behind bars, the sheriff's office was back to normal. There was nothing Pickens could do about Jesse Groves except hope some authority would find him. Noseby received an exclusive about the Wilson matter and was given another opportunity to do a follow-up on the Groves case.

Bo Tatum's quail hunting business had recovered and was prospering.

The Wilson twins legally changed their last name and adopted their biological father's.

Sergeant Dunne was enjoying time with her family.

Billy and his drone buddies continued meeting.

Amy took a two-week vacation and visited Iris Janson in Tampa.

Spring football practice started, and Pickens was back on the sideline coaching.

Marge was asked to do a lecture on forensic science but declined. She wanted more family time with Pickens and Sarah.

Murder in this small county had taken a vacation.

EPILOGUE

July 21, 2018
Rockford Illinois

Luca Adalito, a fifty-eight-year-old grandfather, was out walking his dog on Delphi Street in the late evening. When he passed by the small rental house in the middle of the block, he heard what sounded like a gunshot that came from inside the house. It frightened both him and the dog, even though it was a common thing in the neighborhood three blocks over. Gun violence and murder in Rockford were high on the list of crimes, like in Chicago, the state of Illinois, and the nation. But for some reason, Luca didn't think this time it was another routine occurrence. He knew that two men lived in the house and often went out at night. Luca reached for his phone and dialed 911.

Within minutes, a police car and an ambulance arrived at the scene. Luca told the police officer what he had heard. Officer Brandon Didier told him to remain on the sidewalk and radioed for backup.

When backup arrived, the two officers approached the house. Officer Didier knocked on the door while Officer Anthony Bozeman went around back. Didier looked in the window and saw what looked like a man slumped in a chair and blood on his clothing. He called out to Bozeman, and together they forced the door open and entered with guns drawn.

The right arm of the man on the chair dangled toward the floor. On the floor, was a pistol. In his other hand, he clutched a photograph. On the table next to the man was a newspaper. Didier signaled for Bozeman to search the house then called for the EMTs to enter but not to touch the body, just be prepared in case there was another victim.

From inside a bedroom, Bozeman shouted, "Didier, you better come have a look."

Officer Didier told the EMTs to wait then went to join Bozeman.

"Another body," said Bozeman. "Damn, this one was stabbed multiple times and whoever did it, left the knife on the floor. Call it in."

Didier radioed the station house and was told to wait outside the house the detectives were on their way.

Twenty minutes later a black unmarked police car pulled up to the curb. Two detectives got out and walked up to Didier and Bozeman.

Detectives Manny Fusco and Deidra Stapinski were twenty-year veterans. Both were off-duty but were called in to investigate the murder.

"This better be good," said Fusco. "I was watching the Cubs' game."

"You and your baseball," said Stapinski.

"Hey, you watch classic movies, I watch baseball."

"You'd be better off skipping it and the beer. And watch your weight."

"There's nothing wrong with my weight." Stapinski rolled her eyes.

Stapinski was slim and athletic with short hair that had

hints of gray, whereas Fusco sported a paunch and wore a hat
to cover his bald pate.

An officer greeted them.

Fusco squinted and read his name tag. "What do we have,
Officer Didier?"

"Two bodies. Both males. One gunshot, one stabbed.
Gunshot's in the living room, the other's in the bedroom."

Stapinski glanced at Adalito. "What's he doing here?"

"He's the 911 caller," said Didier. "Want me to get his
statement or do you want to?"

"He see anything?"

"Heard a gunshot and called 911. That's it."

"Okay, take his statement and send him home. One of you
tape the scene. Let's go, Manny."

The two detectives entered the house.

"You take the bedroom, Manny, I'll check the gunshot
victim."

Fusco went to the bedroom while Stapinski studied the
gunshot victim.

"Come see this one, Deidra," shouted Fusco.

Stapinski went to the bedroom.

"Ain't seen anything like this in a while," said Fusco. "If
he was stabbed and the other guy witnessed it, why wasn't he
stabbed, too?"

Stapinski thought about the other victim. "Because the other
guy was the perp. For some reason, he shot himself," she said.

"Murder-suicide? But why?"

Stapinski shrugged. "Beats me. Let's check the other
bedroom."

Fusco followed Stapinski as she went to the second bedroom.

"Jesus Christ," said Stapinski as soon as she stepped into the
bedroom.

What they saw were pictures of bloody victims tacked to the walls. There were dozens of them. Upon a closer look, they saw written on each picture a city and a date. Some had pictures of one of the men in them.

"Son of a bitch," said Fusco. "Those two were serial killers." He surveyed the wall. "Looks like one's missing.?"

"Maybe. Let's get a crime scene unit in here. But first I want to take some pictures. You take some, too. That way we won't have to wait until CSU finishes with them."

Fusco started taking pictures. When he came to the last of them, he paused.

"Shit," he said, "look at these three. They look familiar to you?"

Stepinski took a closer look. "Yeah, they do. Those are the cases we're working. We found our serial killers."

"That geographical profiler was right on the money when she said the killers lived in the area. And judging by the writing on the pictures, they were busy in a lot of other cities and states. We'll close a lot of cases for a lot of detectives. Where do we start first?"

"With ours, then we'll start calling around. I took a photo of the gunshot victim. You know what, Manny? There was a newspaper on the table next to him. I can't say for certain, but there was an article with a drawing that looked like the gunshot victim. Let's take it with us. I'll take a picture of this guy. Then the CSIs can run their photos and DNA. Maybe something will pop."

After the crime scene investigators finished with the scene, Stepinski and Fusco went back to the station house.

Stapinski entered the photos of the two men into the database. Nothing popped on the stabbing victim, but she found a sketch that looked similar to the gunshot victim and the picture in the newspaper article. Both the sketch and the article said the man was a *person of interest* in a 1987 homicide. There was a BOLO out on the gunshot victim, and the name listed was Jesse Groves. The contact person was Sheriff JD Pickens in Creek City, Florida.

"Got something, Manny. Have a look."

Fusco joined her. "That looks like our guy. Let's call the sheriff and let him know we have his man."

Stapinski checked her watch. "It's kind of late, and there's an hour difference. He may be sleeping." She tilted her head. "You want to wake him, be my guest."

Detective Fusco scratched his unshaven face. "If it were me, I'd want to be awakened. I'm gonna call him."

Stapinski stuck her palm out. "Be my guest, Manny."

Fusco picked up the phone and dialed Florida.

*   *   *

In Florida, Sheriff Pickens rolled over when he heard his phone chirping. He glanced at the clock on the nightstand. It said 2:45.

"Dammit, who the hell's calling at this hour?"

"Who cares. Answer it so I can go back to sleep," said Marge.

Pickens picked up the phone. "It's a 773-area code."

"So, answer it."

Pickens answered the call. "Sheriff JD Pickens. Whoever you are, this better be important, or I'll report your number to the attorney general of Florida."

In Rockford, Detective Fusco covered the receiver. "He's gonna report me to the Florida AG's office."

Stapinski glared at him. "Quit fooling around, Manny. You woke the guy. Tell him why you're calling."

Fusco grinned. "Sheriff Pickens, I'm Detective Manny Fusco of the Rockford, Illinois PD. I'm sorry I woke you."

"You woke me all right," said Pickens. "Now tell me why, Detective Fusco."

"My partner and I worked a murder-suicide earlier tonight of two men. We found some disturbing pictures. One of them had *Florida 1987* written on it."

Pickens bolted upright. "What about it?"

"It was one of many. The two turned out to be serial killers. The picture was of two adults and a child. All three covered in blood."

"I'm listening, detective."

"Some of the pictures had one of our victims in them. A different man in each case. When we ran the photo of one of them, it matched a person of interest you posted, and in a newspaper article."

"Was his name Jesse Groves?"

"No, but it sure looks like your guy. We found licenses from several states. It appears the men were on a killing spree for a lot of years and in a lot of states. We're waiting on DNA results on both."

"When you get them, let me know. That picture was of the brutal murder of a family. Jesse Groves was the sixteen-year-old son of the victims, and no one knows what happened to him. If that guy's DNA matches our victims, then you found Jesse, and he murdered his family."

"Son of a bitch," said Fusco.

"Yeah," said Pickens.

"If he is your guy, I know it's not much, but at least his family got justice for what he did to them."

"It's not much. What will you do with the body when you're finished with it?"

"We can ship it to you if you want it?"

Pickens exhaled. "I'll let you know after we know if he is Jesse. Thanks, Detective Fusco. Wait, was he the suicide or the murder?"

"Suicide. Now, I got a lot of other calls to make. There are a lot of other law enforcement officers waiting to solve their murder cases."

"What was that about?" asked Marge, when Pickens put down the phone.

"We may have found Jesse Groves in Rockford, Illinois. The police out there think he was a serial killer and committed suicide. What should I do with the body if it's Jesse?"

"Jesse doesn't deserve to be buried with his family. Let Rockford have him."

ACKNOWLEDGEMENTS

THIS BOOK WAS a work of fiction, and any resemblance to actual events, places, or people was purely coincidental. The science of forensics was one that required a lot of research. I read books based on fictional events and a myriad of articles dealing with the subject. I also had to learn a little about the sentencing for murder. Rather than get too detailed, I chose to go with plea bargaining to move the story along. It was no easy task writing this book, and like the characters, I was exhausted when I finished it.

The internet provided a trove of information on the subject matter of the nature of the crimes. The characters were limited in their abilities, and I provided them with as much outside help as possible. I learned a lot, but I'm not a professional law enforcement officer and am still a novice at crime solving. That's a job best left for the professional. I'll keep making up the stories.

My thanks again to Heather Whitaker for her editing and helping me be a better writer. She's a taskmaster, but a welcome one.

My thanks also to Elizabeth Babski for the cover design.

For more on my books and me, visit my website at www. georgeencizo.com.